Altha Macomb
a very very good Book
Red 10/97
af 6/2002

25 —
set/3

SHILOH'S CHOICE

SHILOH'S CHOICE

LEE RODDY

WORD PUBLISHING

DALLAS LONDON VANCOUVER MELBOURNE

PUBLISHED BY WORD PUBLISHING

DALLAS, TEXAS

Copyright © 1996 by Lee Roddy. All rights reserved.
No part of this book may be reproduced, stored in a retrieval
system, or transmitted in any form or any means—electronic,
mechanical, photocopy, recording, or any other—except
for brief quotations in printed reviews, without the
prior permission of the author.

Published in association with the literary agency of Alive
Communications, Inc., 1465 Kelly Johnson Blvd, Suite 320,
Colorado Springs, Colorado 80920

Book design by Mark McGarry
Set in Garamond

LIBRARY OF CONGRESS CATALOGING-IN-PUBLICATION DATA
Roddy, Lee, 1921–
Shiloh's Choice / Lee Roddy.
p.   cm. — (Giants on the hill)
ISBN 0–8499–3833–3
I. Title. II. Series: Roddy, Lee, 1921– Giants on the hill.
PS3568.O344S48   1996   813'.54—dc20
96–36274   CIP

678012349 QKP 987654321
PRINTED IN THE UNITED STATES OF AMERICA

*To the honored memory of Emma Enos,
the high school teacher who taught me
to love history as people,
not as names and dates*

SHILOH'S CHOICE

∽ PROLOGUE ∽

THE SHADOWY figure remained motionless, mindful that the full moon might momentarily break through the high San Francisco fog. He held a sack in his left hand. With his right, he pulled his long coat tight against the night chill. He peered at the brick mansion.

It was too dark to make out the horse and buggy waiting in front, but he had seen it earlier. He raised his eyes and silently swore at the faint light shining in the upstairs bedroom window. Well, he had waited this long; he could wait a little longer.

He let his thoughts drift. On his earlier visit here he had seen several red, white, and blue flags with thirty-three stars stirring in the spring wind. The thirty-fourth star would be added on July Fourth for Kansas, which had voted in January to enter the Union as a free state.

On Market Street, an impromptu band had struck up a military tune, bringing shouts from men clustered on the street corners.

He could not make out their words, but he knew the arguments. Ever since Lincoln had called for volunteers to enlist for ninety days of military service, passions had been high and tempers short, regardless of whether a man stood for the Union or the new Confederacy.

Two men had gotten into a noisy fistfight, and others had quickly joined in. Reflecting on that, the solitary figure waiting in the dark of the exclusive neighborhood on Rincon Hill smiled. *There's nothing like a war to bring out unbridled feelings. And to hide the truth.*

Shifting his attention back to the mansion, the silent

onlooker nodded in approval. The upstairs light had gone out. Moments later, the moon shone briefly through the fog. A woman hurried from the front door, entered the buggy, and drove off.

Hesitating a few minutes to make sure the woman didn't return and to let the fog again obscure the moon, the viewer then stealthily approached the residence.

When the moon briefly reappeared, he pressed himself against the side of the front porch. Above the steps, he glimpsed a blue flag with a lone palmetto tree in the center and a crescent moon in the top left corner.

The flag had been created after South Carolina declared itself an independent commonwealth and seceded from the United States in December. A rarity in the city by the bay, this Palmetto flag flew in defiant opposition to the predominant Stars and Stripes.

The Palmetto represented rebellion. It was typical of the mansion's owner to fly that flag, suggesting his membership in the secret Knights of the Golden Circle.

Moving with silent purpose, the interloper hugged the rough brick wall until he came to a window. He set his sack on the ground and quietly forced the window open. Taking up his sack, he noiselessly crawled through and climbed the ornate stairs to the second floor. He entered the open bedroom door and drifted, silent as a shadow, toward the high canopy bed.

When the moon again momentarily broke through the fog, he froze. Then the room plunged back into darkness. Seconds later, a heavy revolver fired, filling the room with explosive brilliance and deafening sound.

As the noise faded, the man reached into his sack and pulled out a dead black-and-white bird. He placed the limp animal on the chest of the still figure in the bed.

As silently as he had come, the invader retraced his steps. He stopped briefly before the Palmetto flag and saluted smartly.

It was done, and someone else would be blamed for the crime.

⟡ CHAPTER I ⟡

T HE FIERCE storm had hurled itself across the Pacific, crashed against the Farallon Islands outside the Golden Gate, and battered San Francisco's sandy hills. Now, on the first day of 1861, the needling winds diminished, gasping in ever-weakening efforts to renew their fading strength.

In homes and saloons, as the moaning storm subsided among the eves, talk drifted from the weather's bluster to passionate speculation on secession. That had become a distinct possibility since mid-November, when the Pony Express had brought the stirring news of Lincoln's election.

Shiloh Patton tried to force such thoughts away as she stood in her two-story brick house in the exclusive South Park of Rincon Hill. She knew she should feel content in spite of the depressing news and weather. She gazed pensively through the rain-streaked window. Dusk softened the damage to the muddy street and downed branches.

Shiloh had everything a married woman of thirty-one could want. She and her husband were financially secure. They had four healthy children. Yet recently she had sensed a threat.

An invisible presence followed wherever she went. She gauged its growing menace by her husband's demeanor. He seemed withdrawn and quieter than usual.

She had first noticed a slight change in Clay after news arrived of Lincoln's victory. Since then, he had anxiously awaited the arrival of each mail delivery. Riders ignored weather to regularly spur across two thousand miles of wilderness to deliver mail and the latest news from the rest of the nation to isolated Sacramento. From there, the mail came downstream by steamer to San Francisco. The mail was due today.

"I hope the mail makes it today," Shiloh mused aloud, "and I hope it brings good news."

"What did you say?" Clay called from across the room. A blast of cold air greeted him as he opened the rear door to put the bare Christmas tree outside. The children had enjoyed its cheerful presence during the long storm, so they had delayed stripping it of its candles and popcorn strings.

Shiloh replied evasively, "I was looking at the storm damage."

She heard Clay cross the carpeted floor toward her and started to turn toward him. But he came up behind her and slipped his arms around her waist.

"Storms always pass," he reminded her.

She resisted speaking her thoughts: *Yes, but look at the damage they leave behind.* Instead, she leaned against him, enjoying the safety and comfort of his arms.

The wall reflectors on the kerosene lamps made highlights flicker in her red-gold hair when she turned to look into Clay's brown eyes. She reached gently to touch his dark, wavy hair. Just recently she'd begun to notice the hint of gray at the temples.

She studied him intently for a moment. "Are you all right?"

"Sure. Why?"

"You've been unusually quiet for several days."

"New Year's Day is a good one for being quiet. It's a time to look back and a time to think ahead." He kissed Shiloh gently and turned away. "I'll finish putting the Christmas things in the closet before supper."

Shiloh watched as his long legs carried him down the hall. He obviously wasn't ready to talk about what was on his mind, but she wished he would.

She stepped to the bottom of the stairs. "Girls," she called, "Lizzie's still at her sister's house, so we'll have to make our own dinner. I'll need your help. Philip, please run next door and tell your brother it's time to come home."

Nine-year-old Philip stuck his head over the top railing. "Ah, Mama, I'll drown out there. Why don't we just wait for Ajay to come home on his own?"

"I've never heard you complain about drowning when you want to play in the mud," his mother reminded him with a smile. "So be on your way. Girls, you coming?"

"Yes, Mama," Julia answered, sliding by her reluctant brother. Julia, although not quite seven, already had a mothering attitude. Most of this was lavished on her two-year-old sister, Emily, who trailed Julia down the stairs. Julia had her mother's red-gold hair and an independent, strong-willed nature that sometimes worried her parents.

"Philip, I mean now," Shiloh said firmly to the boy still dawdling at the top of the stairs. Clay had clearly stamped him with his long legs, dark hair, and reserved disposition. Mumbling to himself, Philip started down the stairs.

Shiloh turned to the girls. "I want to speak to your father a minute, so you two start setting the table. Then you can help me cook."

When Julia and Emily had left the room and the front door closed behind Philip, Shiloh walked down the long hallway just as Clay closed the closet door.

"All put away for another year," he announced, coming to meet her.

She stopped, blocking his way. She hesitated, but she had to know. "I have a feeling there's something on your mind."

"As a matter of fact, I've been thinking about Aldar." Clay looked down at her and continued somberly. "I've thought a lot about him lately—about him and his vision. Everything we have is because of his dreams and plans."

Clay pulled Shiloh to him again and held her tight. He added, "It's hard to believe that it will be twelve years this spring."

Crisp memories rushed into Shiloh's mind. At nineteen, as Aldar Laird's naive bride, she had traveled three thousand miles from her Pennsylvania home to San Francisco. Within a week of their landing, she had found him brutally murdered.

Pregnant and widowed in a lawless tent and shack city, she had only her childhood companion, Mara, who had accompanied them from the east. Shiloh had just met Clay Patton, Aldar's closest friend, but otherwise, she had not known anyone. She would have fled back east in panic if it hadn't been for Mara and Clay.

Now San Francisco was a real city. Gas lights illuminated planked streets that were formerly so deep with mud that they were jokingly referred to as "not even jackassable."

Aldar was long dead, but his vision lived on. Following his plans, Shiloh and Clay had started a small transportation system that had grown to a large stage line, spreading over California like spider webs and finally extending across the wilderness to the Missouri River.

A year ago, Clay had sensed that railroads would soon become reality. He had convinced Shiloh they should sell the stage line before it became an obsolete form of transportation. They had also sold the mine that had supported the stage line and enjoyed profit from both sales.

"Twelve years," Shiloh repeated, then forcibly shoved her memories away. "You're sure you're not worried about something else?"

Clay shook his head. "Not exactly, just . . ." He left his words dangling in the air.

She waited a moment before prompting, "What?"

He took a slow, thoughtful breath. "Sometimes I feel a little guilty. We've accomplished Aldar's dreams except for the house on Fern Hill. We have so much to make our lives complete, but he never had any of this." He dropped his voice, "Above all, I have you and our children."

"Mara really scolded me when I expressed similar feelings."

Shiloh smiled. "You know how she says just what she thinks. She said Aldar was lucky there was someone like you to rear his child and create a family for us and make a success of his business."

Clay shook his head. "He was my closest friend. I certainly hope I've done what he would have wanted." Feeling uncomfortable at the direction the conversation had taken, Clay abruptly switched topics. "Is it true that Mara has a new man in her life?"

Shiloh walked thoughtfully to the foot of the stairs. "So I heard. An attorney named Lyman Wallace."

She and Mara had been as close as sisters since they were little girls, but Shiloh wished Mara would settle down. She periodically changed lovers as casually as she changed clothes. They were always successful white men who discretely installed the strikingly beautiful mulatto into their homes as "housekeeper" or "cook."

Shiloh turned back toward Clay, but he was facing the window, looking out into the dusk. She felt shut out of some private, troubled thoughts that he didn't want to share with her. Shiloh yearned for Mara's keen discernment. Then she might discover what really troubled Clay.

"Aldar isn't all that's on your mind," Shiloh said. "You're worried about the political situation, aren't you?"

"I think about it."

Shiloh waited, but he didn't elaborate. She added, "Every time I go out, all people talk about is what will happen now that Lincoln's been elected. Will there be secession or not?"

Clay shrugged but didn't reply.

"I read in the paper that about two-thirds of San Francisco's men favor the Union over secession. But in the San Joaquin Valley and around Los Angeles, most people are against Lincoln and for secession."

"Yes, I read that. I'm concerned because men I've known for years are already taking sides—Unionists against possible secessionists—and tempers are starting to rise."

She nodded. She and Clay had never allowed their backgrounds to cause problems between them. He was a native Texan, and she had grown up in the Pennsylvania home of strong abolitionists. Like the foster father who had reared her, Shiloh had powerful feelings against slavery.

Clay staunchly kept his political opinions to himself. Even his closest business associates and friends didn't know how he felt about the current volatile issue of states' rights.

Shiloh asked with some trepidation, "What's going to happen when Lincoln takes office in March?"

He shrugged. "I guess we'll have to wait and see."

"Will it make that much difference?"

"It could make a world of difference."

His tone had hardened ever so slightly, but Shiloh sensed that something unwelcome had slipped between them.

She said, "I'd better go help the girls start supper."

Later, when the family had gathered around the long dining table, Clay bowed his head and asked the blessing.

Shiloh usually closed her eyes during prayer, but this evening she kept them open. She looked with love and pride on each of the bent heads. She had married Clay about a year after Aldar's death, soon after his son's birth. Clay was as much a father to Ajay as he was to their three younger children. She felt blessed by her family.

After the prayer, Shiloh started to pass the first plate when the back door opened. She and Clay looked at each other in surprise as they heard heavy footsteps.

Turning to look, Shiloh said, "It's Lizzie. I thought she wasn't coming back until tomorrow."

A stout Negro woman with an ample bosom and dark hair heavily streaked with gray entered. "That sister of mine," she said indignantly. "She ain't got no more sense than God gave a goose."

Lizzie jerked off her cape. "It was just supposed to be me 'n her, havin' a nice supper together. But you know what? She

8

invited some ol' widower without tellin' me. Huh! I don't need her to help me find no man! I been alone for quite a spell, but if I wants to git married agin, I kin do it muhself."

Shiloh suppressed a smile. "I'm sure you can."

"Happy New Year, Lizzie," Clay said. "Pull up a chair."

She didn't seem to notice the invitation as she pushed her problems behind her and smiled warmly at the children. "Well, it's done stopped rainin' and it's real nice outside. Why don't you two growed-ups go out an' enjoy you'sefs after supper? Leave me and the chillen to have fun alone."

Shiloh remarked, "It's customary to celebrate on New Year's Eve, but I expect this evening will be rather quiet."

"I don' know. They's a lot of shoutin' an' singin' an' beatin' drums an' lightin' bonfires downtown, 'specially along Market Street. Can't remember when I seen so many excited folks."

Clay asked quickly, his voice somber, "What's going on?"

"Don' rightly know. When that many white folks git to hollerin' and carryin' on, I git outta the way. 'Specially when they's firin' guns."

Shiloh looked anxiously across at her husband. "Do you think the Pony Express has come?"

He looked thoughtful. "It's possible. It is due today."

"Maybe there's some kind of big news," Shiloh guessed.

"You may be right," Clay said. "Let's finish eating then go find out."

A short time later, they left the children with Lizzie and hurried out the front door. Clearing skies brought colder temperatures and the first stars visible in several nights.

As Clay took the reins and backed the horse away from the hitching post, Shiloh looked toward the top of Rincon Hill, San Francisco's lowest peak. Wealthy and influential men had built homes on a grand scale there.

Among their powerful neighbors were longtime U.S. Senator William Gwin, banker William Tecumseh Sherman, newly arrived General Albert Sidney Johnston, and Lyman Wallace.

Mara's latest friend was one of the city's most powerful and prominent attorneys.

In the early darkness, one of the Pattons' neighbors hailed them as he got out of his carriage. "Clay, wait a minute."

Light from the coach's oil-burning lamps bounced off their polished reflectors. They splintered Jess Wagner's stocky shadow as he quickly tied his horse to the metal post and hurried toward Shiloh and Clay.

"Did you hear the news?" Wagner asked while still several feet away.

"What news?" Clay replied.

"I just got home," Wagner said, "I was going to tell my wife first, then you . . ."

"Tell us what?" Shiloh exclaimed, her fears rising.

Wagner explained. "I was down on Market Street when the Pony Express mail arrived late this afternoon. South Carolina has withdrawn from the Union!"

"Oh, no!" Shiloh whispered, her eyes widening in alarm. "When?"

"December twentieth."

Shiloh shook her head in dismay. "In spite of the threats the states' rights people made when Lincoln was elected, I hoped this wouldn't happen. What a terrible way to start the new year!"

Clay gave her hand a comforting squeeze as he asked, "Jess, are you sure?"

"Positive! I didn't expect all the excitement it caused. You'd think it would make everybody sober and quiet, but everyone's all fired up. Minutes after the news arrived, people began pouring into the streets, bringing out flags and shouting and singing like it was a holiday. And I saw a couple of fistfights. Everybody's emotions are sky-high."

Shiloh felt a sickening anxiety creep over her. She looked up at Clay. "What's going to happen now?" Her voice sounded low and weak; she had already guessed the answer.

"Depends on several things, I suppose," he answered solemnly. "Like how many other states follow South Carolina and what Lincoln does when he takes office in the spring."

Wagner exclaimed, "It means war between the states. Neighbor turning against neighbor and worse! That's what's going to happen!"

"I hope not," Clay replied, tugging at Shiloh's hand. "Let's ride downtown and see for ourselves."

"Take my carriage," Wagner suggested.

"I'm obliged," Clay replied as he retied his horse and hurried Shiloh toward the vehicle.

She fell silent, her thoughts shattering like shards of glass. Shiloh hated the idea that events occurring thousands of miles away were about to spill into San Francisco and threaten her world.

≈≤ CHAPTER 2 ≥≈

SHORTLY AFTER DARK, Mara moved gracefully across the carpeted floor of her quarters in Lyman Wallace's mansion. She knew that his eyes followed the soft swish of her dressing gown. Mara didn't look thirty-one. Her lovely figure caused many men to seek her attention, but she responded only to the rich and powerful.

An hour earlier, Lyman had slipped up the back stairs to her private entrance. Now he sat on the edge of a horsehair-stuffed chair in her spacious second-floor living room. A hint of gray showed in the wavy dark hair that covered the tops of his ears.

"Turn the light up," he said, pulling on his shoes. "I want to take another good look at you before I leave."

As the room brightened, Mara slowly faced him. She smiled at the look on his face. Because she had a white father and a

Negro mother, Mara reasoned she was exactly half white and half black. But the world considered her black. The unfairness of this social decision drove her to achieve everything a beautiful white woman could have.

While she could not be a white man's wife in California's prejudiced social climate, she could enjoy everything else. That included power over certain white men, who gave her the city's finest tangible luxuries. She also held the power of fear over the community's small Negro population where it was secretly whispered that she was a *houngan* with mystical voodoo powers.

That had helped her set up a network of maids, cooks, housekeepers, grooms, bellmen, and other workers; white people seemed to forget they had eyes and ears. What they knew, Mara knew, and she used her knowledge to her advantage.

"Don't you ever get enough?" she teased in a low tone.

Lyman stood. "How could I?" he asked huskily. "Your high cheekbones, beautiful face, perfect body, incomparable creamy tan skin . . ."

"And I'm the best cook in San Francisco," she interrupted with a teasing smile. "Now, you had better get downstairs before Malvina gets home."

He dismissed any concern about his wife with a shrug. "I'm not worried about her."

Mara smiled knowingly. "Oh? So why did you come to my door this afternoon, then leave?"

His heavy eyebrows lifted in surprise. "What're you talking about?"

"I heard you hit that squeaky step."

He shook his head. "I never put a foot on that step this afternoon."

Mara's smooth brow puckered a bit. "It wasn't you? Could she . . . ?"

"No," he interrupted. "Malvina sat in the parlor with me until her friends picked her up. You must have imagined hearing someone outside."

He took a couple of quick steps and ran his hands through her shiny dark hair. He pulled her close, again aware that her eyes were more black than brown. They had a mysterious intensity he had never seen in another woman.

Mara gently pushed him away. "I'll be here when you can return, Lyman."

Reluctantly, he released her and started for the door, then stopped and turned to face her. A long straight nose dominated his clean-shaven face. His grim mouth characteristically set, he asked suspiciously, "Who was that big black buck I saw leaving the kitchen around noon?"

"Samuel. He's a friend from years back."

"How good a friend?" The question had a bite to it.

"Just a friend."

Lyman studied her face. "He's a fine-looking specimen of a black man. Maybe he was the one you heard outside your door."

"He wouldn't dare."

Lyman looked dubious. "Some men would risk a lot for you."

Mara laughed softly. "Not Samuel." She knew that Samuel desired her, but he was also afraid.

"You mean he's a runaway and you might turn him in for the reward?"

In spite of the penalty under the Fugitive Slave Act, Mara would never turn in an escaped slave. "He ran away from Louisiana back in the forties. He made his way to Boston and shipped here on a whaler."

To allay Lyman's suspicions, she gave details with her typical candor. "Samuel jumped ship when they docked here for supplies. The whole crew ran off to the gold fields in '49. Later, Samuel came back here."

"I saw the way he looked at you." Lyman cocked his head slightly, a hint of suspicion in the movement. "You're telling me you've been friends these ten, eleven years and nothing else?"

LEE RODDY

"Oh, it's not his choice," Mara assured Wallace with a satisfied smile.

"Glad to hear that. Anyway, he probably hasn't got a dollar to his name. I do; remember that. Also remember that I don't share with anyone. Understand?"

She nodded and suppressed a smile, knowing how wrong Lyman was about Samuel's finances. Over the years, he had entrusted a part of his meager earnings to her, saving toward the day he could buy his freedom.

Mara had secretly buried Samuel's money under a fence post on the property she had bought from Shiloh. Mara had other unlikely depositors as well, all men and women of color. Each was saving for a specific purpose, knowing that upon request, Mara would return his or her funds.

She had three very strict rules for her depositors: She only accepted gold, she required two days' notice for a withdrawal, and no white person could know. No one had ever betrayed her, out of respect for her suspected *houngan* powers.

Samuel had told Mara that morning that with his last week's earnings and what she held for him, he finally had enough to buy his freedom. She had assured him she would have the rest of his money tomorrow.

As Lyman started toward the door, Mara said casually, "Oh, when you come again, I hope you'll have good news about that property." The lawyer handled her investments with people who did not like to deal with someone of color.

Lyman stopped and frowned. "Are you going to keep harping on that?"

"That lot is the key to the whole block." Her tone had hardened. "I've got to have it."

"I told you that Locke refuses to sell."

"He's refused to sell other property and I've still ended up with what I want."

Lyman shook his head in mock exasperation, "You're a hard woman, Mara."

14

"And you're a powerful man." Her voice softened. "Find a way to get Locke to sell."

Shaking his head, Lyman cautioned, "I wouldn't push him too far. I know men who have regretted doing that."

"I'll take my chances."

"All right. I'll see what I can do." Lyman opened the door to the outside stairs. They were ostensibly enclosed against the weather; they also offered privacy for Lyman's surreptitious coming and going. "I think the rain has stopped . . . " he began, then broke off and cocked his head. "Listen!"

Mara padded on bare feet to the door, listening to shouts and scattered gunshots in the distance.

"What is it?"

"I don't know. Seems to be coming from around Market Street. But it's spread out, so it's not a fight. I'd better go check."

After he had gone, Mara stood in the open doorway, wondering about the unusual sounds. Then she shrugged and closed the door. It didn't concern her.

⚜

Clay and Shiloh remained silent as the carriage rolled toward Market Street. Excited shouting, sporadic gunfire, and the rhythmic sound of a drum made Clay anxious to know what was going on.

Shiloh tried to keep her fears at bay, and she concentrated on watching Clay's strong hands. He separated the reins between his fingers, a subconscious holdover from past years. As a "whip," or jehu, he had handled a six-horse hitch of California mustangs.

When they owned the stagecoach line, he had never asked another driver to go where he had not gone first. He had pioneered new routes all over the state. Those included frighteningly remote and curving mountain roads. Some were barely more than narrow shelves carved from a granite mountain's face above deep canyons. The passenger-laden Concord coach traveled such roads at fearful speeds.

But Shiloh was so confident in Clay's driving that she and little Ajay had joined him on one of those wild rides. With a shudder, Shiloh remembered the threat of catching an iron-shod wheel and plunging to destruction in the chasms far below.

Shiloh reminded herself that those had also been good years. She and Clay had challenged seemingly impossible odds and won. Their staging days were behind them, but a new and more frightful challenge rose ahead.

As they neared Market Street, men raced along the boardwalks and the edges of the street, unmindful of the horse and carriage traffic. Gas streetlamps and bonfires cast eerie black shadows of the surging crowds. Several carriages ahead of Clay and Shiloh turned onto side streets to avoid the mob on foot.

"Look at them, Clay," Shiloh whispered in wonder. "They act as if they're going to a party."

"Looks like a celebration, all right, but why they're behaving this way over a state seceding is beyond me. Can't they see what's starting?"

Shiloh wasn't quite sure she understood, but before she could ask, Clay pulled back on the lines. A fistfight had broken out on the sidewalk and spilled into the street ahead.

"I won't risk taking you any closer," he said as spectators surrounded the two combatants. He carefully guided the horse toward a side street.

Shiloh felt mesmerized by the unusual scene. Beyond the fighting men, hundreds of others had gathered, packed close together as they moved along toward Market. Everyone seemed to be shouting; the massed voices became a roar like the sea crashing off of the Golden Gate.

Several people waved the Stars and Stripes. The new commonwealth of South Carolina did not yet have a symbol, but a burly workman snatched a flag from the man next to

him and trampled it to show that the seceded state had supporters with strong feelings.

In the distance, Shiloh saw a brass band forming, encouraged by the drummer's vigorous thumping on a big bass drum.

As Clay cautiously headed toward the corner, a sound from
a second-story window drew Shiloh's attention. A man fired a
pistol at the night sky. "Huzzah for Ol' Abe and the Union!" he
cried.

When he stopped to reload, a bareheaded man on the street
yelled up through cupped hands, "Down with Lincoln! Hur-
rah for the South . . ."

His words were interrupted by a Union supporter who
struck hard, smashing his fist into the cupped hands. "You
secesh traitor!" he yelled, following up his first blow with hard-
driving fists to the secessionist's face.

Shiloh lost sight of the two men when a ring of excited
spectators closed around them. The fight quickly spread until
a couple of dozen men were flailing away at each other.

The sudden brutal eruption of raw emotion unnerved
Shiloh. She turned her head away. "They're going mad!" she
exclaimed. "They're acting like animals!"

"Nothing justifies violence like a war," Clay replied grimly,
loosening the reins to encourage the horse to a faster pace away
from the crowd. "And nothing makes the blood run hotter
than when a man thinks he's right."

Moments later, they were passing the all-brick New World
Hotel when a man standing in front yelled. "Clay! Hold up!"

Shiloh stifled an exclamation as Clay pulled up and a stout
man in his late forties waddled toward the carriage. Shiloh had
never seen Denby Gladwin without a dead stub of cigar in
his mouth.

"Clay," she cautioned under her breath, "don't get into a
long discussion with him."

"He was a good client when we had the stage line," Clay
reminded her. "It never hurts to be nice to people."

Gladwin approached the carriage to shake hands with Clay then raised calculating gray eyes to Shiloh. "'Evening, Mrs. Patton," he said politely. "I trust you and the children are well?"

"Quite well, thank you."

"I need to speak to your husband a moment," Gladwin said. "Will you excuse us?"

Shiloh nodded stiffly but didn't reply.

Clay handed the reins to her. "You'll be safe here. I'll only be a minute." He stepped down and followed Gladwin through the hotel's ornate front door. The New World was one of three hotels Gladwin owned.

Shiloh had never liked the man. She felt some guilt about her unfavorable opinion because Gladwin had always been good to her. But Shiloh found his bulging middle and hairy black forearms as well as his wild ambition offensive.

Long ago, he had tried to persuade Aldar to get involved in a scheme to make California a separate nation. At the time, Congress had not yet voted on California's statehood. The nation then stood with fifteen free and fifteen slave-holding states. Admitting California as a free state would tip the balance.

Gladwin had seen that as the perfect time to decline statehood and create an independent nation. Even though California had become a state, Gladwin had never really let go of his dream.

Inside his plush office, Gladwin motioned for Clay to take one of the leather chairs opposite the mahogany desk. When Clay had settled his long frame, Gladwin removed the stub of cigar from the corner of his mouth and waved it expansively.

"Guess you heard the news," he began. Gladwin leaned across the desk and lowered his voice to a confidential level. "It means war between the states, you know."

"I figured," Clay admitted noncommittally. He had also guessed why Gladwin had invited him into the office.

Gladwin's next words confirmed his thoughts. "You know I

never gave up the idea of making California into the Empire of the Pacific."

Clay nodded but said nothing.

"I never gave up," Gladwin continued, still leaning forward, his voice low, "not even after statehood. You know why?"

Clay had an inkling, but he merely shrugged.

"Because any fool could see that this war was coming," Gladwin explained. "It took a dozen years, but now it's about to start. That gives us the perfect opportunity to break away from the rest of the states and set up Pacifica."

Gladwin studied Clay for some reaction, but when he saw none, he popped his cigar stub back into his mouth and spoke around it. "When the shooting starts back east, it'll be the perfect time for California to become independent. Both sides are going to want our gold and things like your quicksilver."

"I sold the quicksilver mine. Remember?"

Gladwin waved the interruption aside. "California has everything that both sides will need, and as a separate country, we can sell to both the North and the South. We'll all be rich beyond our wildest dreams." His voice rose in excitement, then he paused to study Clay's face.

"You know I don't support your ideas, so why are you telling me this?" Clay asked.

Gladwin rose without answering and hurried to the office door. He opened it quickly, peered out, and then shut it and returned to his desk. "As a Texan, you must favor South Carolina in its action."

"I don't discuss my political views." Clay's tone held a hint of agitation.

"Well, I can't see you supporting the Union, even if your wife does favor abolition."

"My wife is not a subject for this discussion." Clay's tone was cool. He stirred as though about to stand.

"Wait!" Gladwin forced a smile. "No offense." He jabbed with the cigar stump. "Tell you what, Clay. So you don't have to get involved outwardly, how about just making a cash donation to the cause?"

Clay frowned at the man's brashness. "I've got to be going," he said, rising.

"Just a little something," Gladwin urged, jumping up and hurrying around the desk. "Twenty-five, fifty thousand, or whatever you want. And when California's a separate nation, I'll pay you back, two to one. Fair enough?"

Clay's jaw muscles twitched before he replied with forced calm, "Good-bye, Gladwin."

As Clay's long legs carried him toward the door, Gladwin's notorious short temper exploded. "You'll regret this, Clay!"

"I have heard that before," Clay replied crisply.

He was still seething when he climbed into the carriage and silently took the reins from Shiloh.

"What did he want?" she asked.

"Same old thing—support for making California a separate country."

"Did you make him angry?"

"Doesn't take much to do that."

Shiloh laid her small hand on her husband's. "Don't let him get to you."

"I won't." Clay shook his head ruefully. "It's going to get worse before it gets better. A while ago I told you that we were going to be drawn two ways, between the North and the South. I didn't think about Gladwin and his Empire of the Pacific. It's really going to be a three-way split, and we're right in the middle of the whole mess."

Shiloh nodded. As the shouts and music faded in the distance, she and Clay lapsed into silence that lasted until they pulled up in front of their neighbor's house to return the carriage.

Their two little girls had obviously been watching for them; they dashed into the cold evening without their coats.

"Mama! Papa!" Julia cried, her voice high and shrill. "Ajay got in a fight and hurt his eye! Mrs. Wagner's fixing it."

"What?" Shiloh exclaimed, lifting her long skirt and stepping out of the carriage without waiting for Clay to help her. She saw that both girls had been crying. "Who hit Ajay?"

"Howell, that's who!" Julia exclaimed.

"Howell!" Emily echoed.

"But they're best friends!" Shiloh cried in surprise, following her daughters toward the Wagners' front porch. "What did they fight about? And where's Philip?"

"Philip's with Ajay," Julia replied. "Howell said something and Ajay hit him. Then Howell hit back."

Shiloh rang the doorbell. "Is Howell hurt too?"

"I don't know. Howell's mother came to tell you, but you weren't home, so she told Lizzie."

Mrs. Wagner opened the door. She held Ajay by his left wrist and her eleven-year-old son by his right. Both boys had their heads down, but Shiloh could see that Ajay's right eye was puffy. Howell had a large red spot on his cheek. Philip trailed his older brother.

Mrs. Wagner spoke quickly in obvious embarrassment. "I'm so sorry, Shiloh. The boys got into an argument about this silly thing of South Carolina. By the time I could separate them, Howell had given Ajay a nasty hit over his right eye."

Ajay glowered at Howell. "He said I was a traitor because my father is for South Carolina."

Clay had tied the horse and joined them in time to hear that remark. He sucked in his breath sharply. He had never verbally taken sides.

Shiloh whirled and gave him a warning look. She knew that Clay shared her thoughts: Howell must have formed his opinion from something his parents, likely his father, had said.

"I'm sorry, Mrs. Wagner," Shiloh said crisply. "Is your son all right?"

"Oh, yes. It's nothing serious. I was so surprised when the boys got into it. They always get along so well, you know."

Philip announced, "I stayed out of it."

"That's good," Shiloh told him. She held out her hand. "Come on, Ajay."

She tried to put a protective arm around his shoulder, but he pulled away and ran toward home. The other three children followed.

Clay said quietly, "Mrs. Wagner, I want to thank your husband for loaning us his carriage."

"I'll tell him." Her hands fluttered nervously. "He's not in right now."

Clay and Shiloh nodded and said good night. As they turned away from the door, Shiloh reached out for Clay's hand. She felt the tension there and knew she shouldn't say anything. But inwardly, she fumed.

Clay's right, she thought. *Everybody's going to get caught up in this terrible thing, but why must our children?*

⤞ CHAPTER 3 ⤝

WHILE SHILOH determined that Ajay's eye would suffer no permanent damage, Clay helped Lizzie get the other three children into bed. It took awhile to settle them down, but at last they slept. Later Shiloh and Clay sat close together on the sofa and stared into the parlor fireplace.

After a long silence, Shiloh's inner turmoil forced her to speak. "I'm very disappointed in the Wagners."

"So am I."

"How do you think we should handle this?"

Clay turned from the fireplace and put his arm around

Shiloh. "That's a hard question," he began. "I'm tempted to ignore it and hope it'll blow over and be forgotten."

Shiloh searched his face. "Do you really think that will happen?"

He shook his head. "I know Jess and his wife are from Ohio, just as they know I'm from Texas. But I didn't dream they would judge me by that, any more than I judge them."

Clay stood up abruptly. "What really aggravates me is that I have never said one word to them about what I believe. Not one word! They don't know *what* I support!"

Clay took a couple of agitated steps toward the fireplace. "What gall Jess has! He's never been in a war, but I've been in two, and I've got the wounds to prove it. How could he call me a traitor?"

His anger surprised Shiloh and raised a new fear. He was forty-one, but if civil war erupted, was that too old for him to return to uniform? And if he did, which one would he wear?

Clay wasn't usually secretive, but Shiloh didn't know where his loyalties lay and was reluctant to question him when he was so upset.

Sometimes she wondered if she had been wrong, years ago, in not questioning her first husband more. She wondered if she could have prevented his murder if she had known more. Was Clay now also heading into danger? The possibility sent a shiver through Shiloh. Certainly the situation with South Carolina and Lincoln was far more emotional and dangerous than the political climate had been more than a decade ago. Sighing, she decided that all men were strange when it came to politics.

Shiloh studied Clay with sympathetic eyes. "Jess was totally unfair to you, but it's even worse for Ajay. I don't want our children to get mixed up in this."

"Kids forget and get over things if adults will let them. As long as we live next door to the Wagners, we'll have to be extra careful of what we say or do."

Shiloh thought of someday moving away to the grand house that Aldar had planned for the top of Fern Hill. Aware that her thoughts had drifted, she glanced at Clay.

He guessed her thoughts and said softly, "Nothing lives up there now but wild goats. Someday a way will be found to get building materials up the hill. It's just too steep for horses."

Shiloh smiled and stood, glad that the tension had eased. Clay held out his arms just as there was a knock on the door.

Shiloh mused, "Now who in the world could that be at this time of night?"

"Probably somebody who wants to know if I've heard about South Carolina," Clay replied, heading for the door.

"Please don't be long." Shiloh turned toward the stairs. "I'm going upstairs to get ready for bed."

Clay opened the door to a cadaverous-looking man with a full head of dark hair that flared out behind his collar. His full black mustache accented his straight nose and cleft chin.

Clay had banked with Cyrus Bixby the last year that the Laird and Patton Stage Lines existed. He remembered that Bixby had spoken in favor of Lincoln before the November election.

Clay greeted his visitor. "Hello, Cyrus. Won't you come in?"

Cyrus Bixby stepped into the light and blinked owlishly. "Thanks, Clay. You alone?"

"Shiloh and the children are upstairs." Clay hoped his tone suggested that he wanted to be up there, too, and that Bixby would be brief. Clay motioned toward the sofa. "Please sit down."

Bixby sat uneasily on the sofa's edge. "I'll only be a minute." He nervously cleared his throat. "I suppose you've heard about South Carolina?" When Clay nodded, Bixby commented, "Terrible thing. It'll lead to war."

"I wouldn't be surprised," Clay admitted.

Again clearing his throat and shifting uncomfortably, Bixby said, "I know your Texas roots, just as I'm sure you know I hail from Michigan."

Clay involuntarily stiffened, wondering where Bixby would take the conversation. "Yes?" Clay prompted.

The visitor was clearly uneasy as he approached his delicate goal. "You made your money in this great state of California, which was possible because it's a member of the Union. Dare I be so bold as to assume that you appreciate what this means to you and your wonderful family?"

"I am grateful for what God has given us."

The answer seemed to intimidate Bixby. He licked his lips. "Yes, of course."

Clay waited, watching the light from the fire reflect off Bixby's high cheekbones where the skin was drawn tight.

"Clay, you've heard about the Knights of the Golden Circle, haven't you?"

It surprised Clay to hear a Union supporter mention the secret society. Its purpose was to support states' rights and oppose the federal government in anything that threatened those rights. It supposedly had some six hundred thousand members across the nation, and rumors placed California's membership at more than fifteen thousand.

"Of course," Clay answered, frowning slightly. This wasn't what he had expected Bixby to say.

"Well, since South Carolina has withdrawn from the Union and declared itself an independent commonwealth nation, some of us in San Francisco thought it would be wise to have a countermovement to the knights. Sort of a Union Club to stand up for Lincoln when he takes office."

"That sounds logical," Clay admitted carefully.

Bixby smiled with relief. "I'm glad you see it that way. Those of us who are going to be charter members have made a list of the important men of our city we would like to have standing with us. We would be honored to have you as a member."

Clay turned to stare into the fireplace before answering. "As you know, Bixby, I'm not real good with words. Driving a team of mustangs is more my style."

"You're being unduly modest, Clay," the visitor assured him heartily. "You're a wealthy man, as everyone knows, and that came from having a good head on your shoulders."

Clay wasn't moved by the bold flattery. "I had a lot of help." He glanced up the stairs. "My wife, for one. Her father . . ."

"Ah, yes! Merritt Keene. Another fine man. I haven't seen him lately. How is he?"

Clay turned to face his visitor. "Merritt's been up north helping the new owners of the quicksilver mine get their feet on the ground. He'll be back soon. Now, as to your invitation, I appreciate it, but I don't think this is the time to make any firm decisions."

Bixby scowled and gave his mustache an annoyed tug. "What better time could there be?"

Shrugging, Clay explained, "We'll all know a lot more when Lincoln takes office in March. He's talked appeasement, but what will his actions be when he has power?"

Bixby sensed he was losing ground. He switched to another tone. "I can assure you that he won't be timid like Buchanan. He's afraid to face the facts that the Union must be helped to stay together."

Clay asked mildly, "What will Lincoln do differently?"

"Well, of course I'm not in a position to know, being out here thousands of miles away. But from what he's said, I'm confident he's going to take a firm stand."

"Meaning he'll use force to keep South Carolina in the Union?"

"If that's necessary, I suppose." Bixby missed the subtle tightening of Clay's jaw but caught the flicker of disapproval in his brown eyes.

He remembered the substantial deposits Clay had in his bank. "Of course," Bixby added in a more conciliatory tone,

"I'm sure Lincoln will do all in his power to placate South Carolina, or any other states that may want to follow her out of the Union."

"You said awhile ago that it meant war," Clay reminded him.

"I . . . I spoke out of turn. I don't know what's going to happen."

Clay slowly unfolded his long frame, indicating the discussion was ending. "Well, until we do, I thank you again for your invitation, but I'm going to wait."

Cyrus Bixby also stood, then made one last try. "In the meantime, would you consider making a donation to the cause? Say, something in the neighborhood of a few thousand dollars?"

Clay opened the door. "As I said, I'm going to wait."

The banker stepped onto the porch and hesitated while the crisp January air engulfed them. "You're going to have to choose," Bixby blurted in a sudden surge of patriotism. "Either a man is loyal to the Union, or he's a traitor to his country."

"Good night, Bixby!" Clay said coldly and firmly closed the door.

Later, lying in bed in the dark with his arms around Shiloh, Clay told her of Bixby's visit.

"I'm surprised at him," she confessed, lightly running her fingers along Clay's jawline. She could feel his tense muscles and knew he was still upset.

"I'm not really." Clay's voice was low in the darkness. "Bixby stands for the Union, just as Gladwin stands for the Empire of the Pacific. They both have very strong feelings."

Shiloh saw an opening to ask the question that troubled her. "How about you? Where do you stand?"

"I'm dead set against the idea of Pacifica, but I don't yet have enough facts about this secession business. However, I suspect that other states will follow South Carolina."

The prospect alarmed Shiloh. "You really think so?"

"From what I've heard and read, seven or eight states could withdraw by the time Lincoln takes office in March. He's not like outgoing President Buchanan, who believes he can't interfere. I think Lincoln will act to keep the Union together by force."

"Oh, Lord! I pray that doesn't happen."

"So do I, but if it does, then even more states could secede. There could be upward of a dozen, depending on what border states like Kentucky and Maryland do."

"I can't imagine Americans fighting each other."

Clay added, "Everyone is going to be affected, one way or another. Even way out here on the West Coast, we're going to lose friends."

Shiloh tried to keep the anxiousness from her voice as she asked, "You won't fight, will you?"

"Depends."

The single word sliced through Shiloh's heart.

"But you're past military age! And our children . . . "

"Don't get upset." Clay felt for Shiloh's hand in the darkness and gave it a reassuring squeeze. "Nothing's going to be settled before Lincoln's inauguration. But in the meantime, all sides are going to want something from me."

"Money?" she guessed.

"Money," he agreed. "But I've made up my mind not to choose sides for now."

"Then you'll have everyone upset with you."

"No one will get too upset before Lincoln takes office. After all, nobody wants to take a chance on alienating me and our money. Anyway, you can be sure that Gladwin and Bixby aren't going to be the last ones to approach me. Somebody from the South will be along soon, I suspect."

Shiloh sat up abruptly. "You mean Locke?"

"Why not? He's never been shy about approaching me before. Remember, before statehood, when he wanted California to become a slave state?"

"Oh, yes. I remember." Shiloh stared into the darkness over the bed. "He wanted slaves to work California's vast farming valleys."

"Then when California was admitted as a free state," Clay said, "Locke joined with Denby Gladwin to push for creating a separate nation. Now, with South Carolina leaving the Union, I figure Locke will back the slave states against Lincoln."

Shiloh lay down again, her mind leaping.

She had been quiet for a while when Clay asked in the darkness, "You asleep?"

"No." Shiloh snuggled closer to him. "I was just thinking about Mara and Locke."

"Bad blood there," Clay declared.

"Certainly is. Locke's been fighting her all these years because she dared to buy property next to his downtown. Yet she's been beating him ever since 1850. What's she own now? A whole city block?"

"Close to that, I think. Locke made a huge mistake when he threatened her."

"He hates black people so much that he doesn't always think straight."

"The man's a fool to tangle with Mara that way. I told him so after he admitted that Mara had threatened to ruin him someday."

"She said that?"

"I believe Locke said her exact words were, 'Someday I'll buy and sell you.'"

"Mara must have been very angry to threaten him. She doesn't usually say much; she just does what she feels she must."

Mara, Locke, and South Carolina were still tumbling in Shiloh's thoughts when restless sleep finally caught up with her.

∼⧴∽

While others slept, Mara slipped down the stairs and made her way to a nearby livery stable. She rented a horse and buggy and drove west, skirting the hills that rose as dark hulks against the night.

After checking the road behind her to make sure no one had followed, Mara turned south off of the plank road. The horse's hooves made little sucking sounds in the wet sand. This remote area was still largely undeveloped, remaining much as it had when she first traveled the rural road with newlyweds Shiloh and Aldar.

Mara eased back on the reins as the pale twin kerosene buggy lights dimly illuminated the one-story Spanish-style house. Aldar had bought it from an old *Californio don* as a wedding present for Shiloh. Mara had purchased it from Shiloh when she and Clay had bought their present home. The old adobe house was still furnished but unoccupied except when Mara periodically wanted to get away for a quiet time by herself.

She tied the horse and made her way up the familiar gravel path in the buggy's weak lights. She found comfort in again seeing the solid house with its red tile roof and stout wooden beams. Clay pots hung from the beams by leather thongs. Their once bright spring flowers were dead and lifeless in the cold of winter, but the Chinese man she hired to care for the place would nurse them back to life in the spring.

Mara rounded the corner into total darkness to make her way to the cook house, separated from the main house because of fire danger. She used a large metal key to unlock the kitchen door.

Her fingers easily found the familiar kerosene lantern. She raised the glass, cringing at the dry squeak of the metal parts as they slid up. Lighting the wick and lowering the glass chimney, she picked up the lantern by the bail. With her other hand, she lifted a shovel from the corner nearest the door.

By the lantern's pale yellow glow, she crossed the sandy soil to where it ended in gummy mud. She carefully picked her way, feeling the ground sink slightly under her feet.

Nearing the far end of the property, the posts that supported the split-rail fence seemed to come alive and dance in the light. Mara didn't need to count the posts from the corner but went directly to the one where Samuel's gold was buried.

She exclaimed softly as she slipped and almost fell. Dropping the shovel, she regained her balance. Then, unhappy because the mud sucked at her high-topped shoes, she recovered the shovel, ignoring the now-muddy handle. At the fence, she set the lantern down on the ground.

Only Mara knew what was buried under the posts. She lifted the top rail from its notch in the post and eased it down. The other two rails followed.

As she started to sink the shovel into the earth by the post, Mara remembered the canvas bag. Shaking her head in silent reproof, she took the lantern and followed her tracks back to the buggy.

When she returned to the post, the bag in hand, she started again to reach for the shovel. Then she froze, her eyes on the ground.

In disbelief, she leaned over and lowered the lantern to see better.

Water from the recent rains was slowly seeping into the tracks she had made minutes before. But she also saw other footprints beside hers, tracks larger than her own. These prints were obviously very fresh, for rain water had just started to seep into them.

There was no doubt. Someone had been here while Mara had gone to the buggy.

Instantly, she felt goosebumps of fear on her arms. She turned quickly, staring into the night, but couldn't see or hear anyone.

❧ CHAPTER 4 ❧

B EFORE DAWN, Shiloh drew a quilt over her shoulders, picked up her Bible, and quietly went downstairs. Even early-rising Lizzie was not yet up, but Shiloh didn't mind. She preferred to have half an hour alone to start her day.

She entered the cold kitchen, lit the gas light, and shook the grate in the wood-burning stove to remove yesterday's ashes. As she started the fire to make coffee, there was a gentle knock at the back door.

"Mara!" Shiloh exclaimed quietly, so as not to wake the family. "What brings you here so early this morning?"

Casually Mara answered, "I was out for an early walk and saw your light." She followed Shiloh back into the kitchen where the fire crackled with new life. "Is everybody still asleep?"

"Yes, it's just you and me. I'll put the coffee on."

Mara nodded and sat down at the kitchen table.

Shiloh thoughtfully studied her quiet companion while making coffee. "Something wrong?"

Annoyed with herself for having allowed last night's episode to show, Mara replied, "No. Everything's fine."

The discernment of many years of close friendship made Shiloh say, "I can see something in your eyes."

Mara shrugged. "It's nothing I can't handle."

"You always say that. Don't you want to talk about it?"

"No."

Shiloh wasn't offended by Mara's blunt reply. "Remember when we were growing up? We told each other everything."

Mara smiled. "My memory is pretty good."

"So's mine; we were brought up as sisters, and we've stayed as close as sisters. I think you should tell me what's going on."

Mara sat in silence for a moment, thinking. The girls hadn't drifted apart as they grew older, as most did when one was white and the other was not. Shiloh and Mara had no secrets until young Mara was raped by three white men. She quit going to the local Negro church, and Shiloh suspected that Mara had embraced what is now known as voodoo to get revenge.

Shiloh retrieved two flowered cups from the cupboard. Returning to the table, she sat across from Mara and looked at her pointedly.

"You're not going to let this go, are you?" Mara's tone hardened slightly.

"Only because I care about you. When something bothers you, it bothers me." She hesitated, then asked, "Are you having problems with Lyman Wallace? He's an outspoken southern sympathizer, which means he probably favors slavery."

"No problems with him."

Shaking her head, Shiloh commented, "I don't see how you can even associate with such a man."

"He's helping me get what I want."

"At what price? You know what you're doing is wrong." Shiloh hadn't meant for her voice to sound so sharp.

"That's enough!" Mara flared, her eyes glittering. "I don't have a vengeful God watching my every moment."

Shiloh realized that she had pushed too hard. She softened her voice. "I just don't want anything to happen to you." She reached across and took Mara's hand. "Besides, you've always been there for me. When Aldar died . . ." Sighing, Shiloh finished with a catch in her voice, "I don't think I could have made it without you."

Mara studied Shiloh's earnest face a moment. "I didn't plan to say anything, but something is bothering me." She briefly recounted finding the footprints the night before.

Shiloh frowned. "You didn't see or hear anyone?"

"No. I took the lantern and looked around, but there was nothing except the night and those few muddy tracks."

Shiloh shuddered. "I'm glad you got away safely."

"I had my pistol, so I wasn't in danger."

LEE RODDY

Shiloh scowled at her. "Why in the world were you out there alone at that time of night?"

"I've got a right to walk on my own property any time I want," Mara said defensively, hoping to head off any more questions. "Anyway, it was probably nothing."

"Nothing?" Shiloh exclaimed. "Someone was obviously watching you in the dark, and you say it's nothing?"

"If you're going to give me a lecture, I'm going to leave."

"No lecture," Shiloh agreed, taking a deep breath. "I'm glad you told me. But you can't just forget it. Whoever made those footprints knew you were there, alone, and yet didn't want to be seen. Why?"

"I don't know. Whoever it was didn't follow me from town. I'm sure of that. He must have been hiding around the house."

"But who would do that?"

"Probably a transient who found the house empty and was curious about why I was there."

Shiloh shook her head. "What if it wasn't a transient? What if someone left those tracks to frighten you?"

"Why would anyone want to do that?"

"I don't know, but if I were you, I wouldn't go out there alone again."

"I bought that place from you. It's very special to me, and nobody's going to run me off of it."

Shiloh took a slow breath before deciding, "Then I'll go with you next time."

"No." Mara's tone was final. "You've got a family to think about."

Thinking quickly, Shiloh suggested, "Then take someone else with you. Samuel, maybe."

"I've told you, I can take care of myself." Mara stood. "Don't worry. I'll be all right."

Shiloh rose and skirted the table to put her arms around her friend. "I couldn't stand it if anything happened to you."

"Nothing's going to happen. If you're going to get all upset

34

over little things, I'll stop telling you anything that might distress you."

"Please don't do that!"

"Then quit fretting." Mara broke the embrace. "Thanks for the coffee and for listening." She smiled. "You're very special to me."

On the walk up the hill to the Wallace mansion, Mara remembered that she had heard somebody on the stairs outside her door. She wondered if there was any connection between that and the muddy footprints.

Half an hour later, Shiloh helped Lizzie prepare breakfast, inwardly fretting about Mara. The children trooped into the kitchen just as someone knocked on the front door.

Shiloh said, "I'll watch the bacon, Lizzie. Please see who has come to call at this early hour."

Clay called from the living room where he had begun to build a fire. "I'll answer it."

"Thanks," Shiloh replied. "But please don't get too involved. We'll eat in a minute. Children, please take your places."

Clay walked quickly toward the door, aware of the mouthwatering fragrances drifting from the kitchen.

Asbury Harpending stood outside, his face serious. The good-looking young man had already made and lost fortunes and was wealthy again.

"Sorry to bother you so early, Clay," Harpending began. "But I have something to discuss of the utmost importance. Do you have a minute?"

Clay hesitated. "My wife is just putting breakfast on the table . . ."

"I'll be brief," Harpending interrupted. "I'm sure you've heard about South Carolina?" At Clay's brief nod, Harpending continued, "As you know, I was born and reared in Kentucky. You're from Texas; that binds us with a common heritage. That's why I've come to you."

Clay didn't want to listen to another attempt to persuade

him to take a political stand, especially with breakfast waiting. "I'd rather discuss this later, if you don't mind, Asbury."

"I'll be glad to come back at a more convenient time, but first, let me leave you with some thoughts." Without waiting for Clay to agree, Harpending plunged on.

"I admit that I'm hotheaded about secessionism. Perhaps it's my being from a border state that makes my feelings more intense than yours. I'm willing to spend my last dollar and give my life if necessary to resist the tyrant's yoke that is about to be forced upon us."

Clay, uncomfortable with his visitor's high emotional tone, tried to stem the rising tempo. "I understand your feelings, but I really must ask to be excused."

"Of course. But first, I've made inquiry and learned that you're a man of discretion, one who can keep a secret. Because of that, I would like to invite you to join me and some friends to discuss something of vital interest to us all."

Clay opened his mouth to refuse, but his visitor didn't give him a chance to speak. "Before you can attend," Harpending said, dropping his voice and looking around to make sure no one could overhear, "I need your solemn oath that you will never divulge one word of what you hear or see at the meeting. Agreed?"

"I really don't think . . ."

"This is so crucial that you owe it to yourself to make the pledge and attend the meeting. All it takes is your solemn oath now, and I'll be on my way."

Suppressing an annoyed sigh, yet feeling a tug of curiosity, Clay nodded. "All right. You have it."

"Thank you!" Harpending reached out and vigorously shook Clay's hand. "I'll be in touch. Now, please apologize to your wife for my delaying you."

Clay watched as Harpending mounted his horse and rode off, berating himself for getting pressured into making a hasty decision. But there was something about Harpending's attitude and excitement. Clay headed for the kitchen. He had given his word, and he would keep it.

Shiloh shot a questioning look at him as he sat at the head of the table.

Julia asked, "Papa, who was at the door?"

"A man named Asbury Harpending." Clay met his wife's eyes across the room. "You've met him."

"What did he want?"

"He asked me to attend a meeting."

Shiloh nodded, wanting to know more but knowing that would have to wait. The family joined hands for Clay's brief blessing.

When he finished, Lizzie quickly set plates of bacon and eggs before the family.

Shiloh started to ask about Harpending, but Philip looked at his plate and raised his voice in protest.

"Mama! I don't want eggs!"

"That's what we're having this morning," she replied. "So please eat them without complaining."

"I don't like them," the nine-year-old declared.

Ajay's injured eye didn't stop him from teasing his younger brother. "Mama, you could buy Philip some seabird eggs. Lots of people eat them, especially murre eggs."

Emily asked, "What's *murre?*"

Clay explained, "A murre is a large black-and-white seabird."

"When I first arrived in San Francisco," Shiloh added, "hen's eggs were so scarce that we ate murre eggs. Every spring millions of them come to nest on the Farallons."

Ajay turned to his sisters to show off his knowledge. "Those are the little rocky islands outside the Golden Gate."

"About twenty-six miles outside," Clay added. "Thousands of seabird eggs are still sold here each spring. Now, Philip, eat your eggs."

The boy made a face. "I once saw some of those eggs at my

friend's house. The yolk was almost red, and the whites still looked clear even though his mother said she had cooked them real hard."

"Murre eggs are bigger than a hen's," Ajay said, "and they're shaped funny so they roll in a circle. That's so they won't fall off the cliffs where the birds lay them."

"When your grandfather gets here," Clay said, "he can probably tell you more about murres. He was in the egg business when I first met him."

"When's he coming back?" Julia asked.

"Soon," Shiloh replied, wishing her father had been able to stay through the holidays.

Clay said, "All right now, eat your breakfast."

Shiloh spread her napkin on her lap and looked across the table. "Isn't Asbury Harpending one of those who thinks Lincoln's election is a signal for southern unrest?"

"Actually, he said that's the feeling all over the South."

While Lizzie served hot corn bread, Shiloh asked, "What did he want so early this morning?"

"He wants me to meet some people," Clay replied evasively. He looked for an excuse to change the subject. "Ajay, how's your eye?"

"It's not bad, but it'll feel better when I give Howell one just like it."

Shiloh said firmly, "Ajay, you know that's not the Christian thing to do; besides, he's your best friend."

"He said Papa's a traitor so I must be one too."

Julia peered anxiously from under her red-gold bangs and asked, "What's a traitor?"

Clay thought carefully before explaining. "That's someone who leads another person astray or does something against his country."

"Are you a traitor, Papa?" Julia's blue eyes were wide with interest.

Shiloh exclaimed, "Of course not! Your father is the most honorable man I've ever known."

Philip swallowed hastily and asked, "Then how come Howell called Ajay one?"

Shiloh and Clay exchanged glances before either spoke. "It's hard to explain," Clay replied, "but a lot of grown-up people are very, very upset over some things that don't concern children. It's called politics."

Ajay nodded knowingly. "Politics made Abraham Lincoln president, and an awful lot of grown-ups are mad. But most people are glad. And anybody who doesn't like Lincoln is a traitor. That's what Howell said his papa said. But you like Mr. Lincoln, don't you, Papa?"

"I admire what he has done for the railroads and in other matters," Clay answered carefully. "But he has only just been elected president; he won't take office for almost three months. I'm going to wait to see what he does then before I decide how I feel about him."

"Remember, children," Shiloh added firmly, "everyone has a right to an opinion. That's what this country is all about. But your father is most definitely not a traitor. Don't you forget that!"

After breakfast, Lizzie cleared the table and asked the children to help with the dishes. Shiloh and Clay retired upstairs for a few moments. In their bed chamber, Shiloh stood before the mirror and brushed her hair as Clay, standing behind her, straightened his collar.

He commented, "When I got up this morning, I saw Mara walking up the hill. Was she here?"

"She stopped by, and we had a cup of coffee."

"What was on her mind?"

"She found some footprints on her property that startled her," Shiloh began and told Clay the details of Mara's experience.

Clay dismissed the incident with a shrug. "It was probably someone who saw her lantern and got curious."

Shiloh wanted to believe that. "I hope you're right," she replied and switched the subject. "What kind of meeting does Asbury Harpending want you to attend?"

"He didn't say."

Shiloh raised an eyebrow. "Why didn't you ask?"

"I wanted to join you for breakfast, not talk about meetings. But frankly he rubbed my curiosity bump."

"Are you going?" When he nodded, Shiloh cautioned, "He's got strong southern sympathies; be careful around him. But I guess I'm a little curious too."

Clay hesitated. "Uh . . . I can't tell you about what goes on at the meeting. He swore me to secrecy."

Startled, she whirled quickly to face him. "You don't mean that!"

"I was wrong to agree," he admitted ruefully. "But I did, and I have to honor my word. Don't be concerned. You know I won't do anything against my conscience."

She met his eyes steadily. "I know that, but I don't like mysterious meetings or secrecy, especially now."

Clay hurried to ease the tension he sensed developing. "I wouldn't deliberately do anything to hurt you or take part in anything I don't agree with."

"I know that." She walked to the armoire to select a dress for the day. "But after all these years of marriage, we're facing something new. So I want you to know my thinking."

He crossed toward her. "About what?"

"I love this state. It's not only a beautiful place to live, but it has also given me opportunities that I never dreamed possible when I left Pennsylvania."

He sensed where she was going and tried to head her off. "California has been good to me, too, but let's not get into a political discussion."

"It doesn't have to be a discussion. I just want you to know what I think."

"I know where you stand, Shiloh. You grew up in an abolitionist's home, and you have strong feelings against slavery. But this South Carolina situation isn't about slavery; it's about states' rights."

"I'm sure you believe that, but I feel just as strongly that slavery is a big part of all this." Shiloh put her arms around Clay. Looking up into his eyes, she said evenly, "I will be a good wife in every way that the Bible teaches, but I want you to know how strongly I feel about this."

"I understand," he said, pulling her close and marveling at how she had matured.

Maturity had replaced her childlike innocence almost overnight when Aldar died. Clay had anguished with her, quietly helping in any way he could. They had rebuilt their shattered lives and become a family. But now, in a vague way he could not explain, Clay sensed a threat to that union.

Her voice somewhat muffled against his chest, Shiloh said, "I don't like this tension between us. All around us, common sense is being replaced by wild emotions over something taking place thousands of miles away. We can't let it hurt what we have."

❈ CHAPTER 5 ❈

MARA WAS PREPARING lunch in Lyman Wallace's spacious kitchen when Samuel showed up at the back door. She wiped floury hands on her apron and hurried to let him in.

He swept his cap off with a grin. "Morning, Miss Mara." The handsome runaway slave was Mara's age, yet he treated her with the same deference he would have given his Louisiana mistress years ago. Samuel explained, "I come—uh—came for my money."

"I have it. Come in."

The tall, powerfully built man apprehensively glanced around. "Is he home?"

"No. He had a court appearance." Mara motioned for

Samuel to take a wooden stool by the small preparation table. "Sit down."

She reached for the coffeepot on the back of the stove. "I'm pleased to see that you're still working on improving your speech."

"Like you told me back when I jumped ship and started saving my money, 'a free Negro has to speak better than a slave.' Thanks to you, I do, and today I'm going to start getting my freedom papers. Then I can quit worrying about slave catchers grabbing me and shipping me back to Louisiana, away from you."

Mara ignored the compliment. She filled his cup and handed it to him, aware of the hunger in his eyes when he looked at her.

"You'll need a lawyer," she said, sitting on a stool opposite him. "Try Cornelius Tucker."

Samuel raised his eyebrows in surprise. "Not the one who owns this fancy place?"

Mara gently shook her head. "Take my word for it; you want Tucker, not Lyman Wallace."

Samuel waited for her to explain, but when she didn't, he seemed resigned. "If you say so."

"Good. I'm sure you know that Tucker and Wallace were once law partners."

"I used to clean their offices."

"Did you hear why they split up?"

It was a casual question, and insignificant by itself. However, Mara collected scraps of information. She knew as much or more about what went on behind closed doors as anyone in San Francisco.

Samuel answered, "One day when I was sweeping up the hallway, I heard them arguing. It was something about investing in eggs."

"Eggs?" Mara was surprised. "Why on earth would well-to-do lawyers like them invest in eggs?"

Samuel shrugged. "I don't know."

"Maybe Tucker has a client in the egg business." She paused, then added, "But why would that make Lyman and Tucker split up?"

"Why don't you ask Mr. Wallace?"

"It's not that important." Mara stood up abruptly. "Wait a minute while I get your money."

Upstairs in her room, she locked both the inside and outside doors before removing a brick from the fireplace hearth. From a hole behind it, she retrieved a small canvas sack. She carefully replaced the brick so there was no evidence that it was loose.

Returning to the kitchen, she handed over the sack. "It's all there. Go buy your freedom."

Samuel hefted the sack. "Sure is heavy."

"Gold always is."

Standing, Samuel looked down at her beautiful face and unconsciously licked his lips. "Miss Mara, now that I'm going to be free, will that make a difference between us?"

"We'll see." She tempered the noncommittal reply by suddenly standing on tiptoes and pulling his face toward her with both hands. She gave him a languid, lingering kiss that made him suck in his breath in surprised delight.

When she felt him start to pull her close and felt the bag of gold against her back, she broke away.

"That was nice," she said softly, seeing the hunger in his face. "But now you must go."

"There's no hurry." His voice was suddenly husky.

"Maybe not for you," she said, taking his free hand and leading him toward the door. "But I have work to do."

She felt a sense of triumph, of power, of control as she turned the doorknob. She cautioned, "Don't let anything happen to your freedom money."

Samuel nodded, his breathing irregular. "Miss Mara, I got to have you. I been waiting all these years! I just got . . ."

She broke off his passionate words by quickly placing cool fingers across his lips. "You must go."

"Miss Mara, if it wasn't for him," Samuel jerked his chin toward the interior of the mansion, "would you . . . ?"

Mara interrupted, "As I said before, we'll see. Now, go find that lawyer." Seeing his keen disappointment, she added, "When you get your papers, come show them to me."

After the door closed behind him, Mara leaned against it, aware that her impromptu kiss had stirred her own emotions. Samuel was a mighty good looking man, but he couldn't give Mara what she wanted in life. Still, she told herself, maybe he deserved more than a kiss.

~❦~

Clay kept a small downtown office where he periodically went to check on his varied investments and read every newspaper available. He was there Friday afternoon but couldn't concentrate because his mind was on Shiloh.

He had spent his life with horses and mules and the rough, hard men who managed them. From this background, he had learned to be direct, even blunt, with other men. But with a woman he could not voice his feelings. He loved his wife and children. He tried to show how much he cared, but he longed to put into words what he felt for Shiloh. When he had driven long stagecoach trips, alone on the high seat, he had dreamed of the gentle, loving words he would say to her when he got home. But when he held her in his arms, his heart swelled with such overpowering emotions that he could only manage a rare, "I love you."

After their last conversation, he sensed a lingering tension and knew that she needed his words of assurance. His thoughts were interrupted by a knock on his inner office door.

Gustavus Maynard, Clay's lone employee, entered at his invitation.

"Jefferson Locke is here," the clerk announced, his Adam's apple bobbing.

Clay had expected Locke to call on him, but it wasn't a meeting he welcomed. He thoughtfully regarded his rail-thin clerk for several seconds before answering. "Send him in. I may as well get this over with."

The gray-eyed former lawyer from Tennessee entered with a forced smile. "Thanks for seeing me, Clay," he said, crossing the room to shake hands.

"Sit down," Clay replied. He returned to his seat behind the plain desk and observed Locke. He always wore a rumpled black suit even though he had become one of San Francisco's wealthiest forty-niners by turning land speculator.

"What can I do for you, Jefferson?"

Clearing his throat uneasily, Locke began, "Remember a conversation we had some years back . . . ?"

Clay broke in. "I remember several conversations, including some where you and Denby Gladwin threatened to ruin our stagecoach business."

The blunt reply didn't seem to bother Locke. He made a brief motion with his hands as though dismissing the incidents. "Obviously, that didn't happen. You ended up wealthy. So you got what you wanted, and I'm about to get what I've been after all these years."

Clay waited but didn't reply.

Locke continued, "I told you long ago that any thinking man could see that the issue of slavery would bring on a war between the states."

"The South isn't talking about slavery," Clay reminded him, "but about states' rights."

"The abolitionists will make slavery an issue, so no matter where Lincoln stands on the matter, he'll be forced to act on that."

Clay leaned back in his chair, wondering if Shiloh had any idea how Locke viewed abolition. "If you've come to talk politics," Clay said, "remember that my beliefs don't matter to anyone except me."

"Ah, but you're wrong!" Locke blurted. His eyes widened as he realized from Clay's expression that he had made a mistake.

"I'm sorry, Clay!" Locke leaned across the desk. "I just meant that everyone has to take sides—to stand up and be counted, as it were."

Clay's eyes had narrowed and his jaw firmed. He said nothing as he debated whether to end the conversation by asking his visitor to leave.

Hurriedly, Locke added, "Let me explain. Back in fifty-nine when he served as a U.S. senator from California, David Broderick opposed the extension of slavery. Remember?"

"Yes. David Terry killed him in a duel."

"Right. Terry was California's chief justice at the time. Anyway, when Broderick died, Milton Latham replaced him and joined William Gwin. They were both in favor of slavery."

"And we had two like-minded congressmen," Clay added. "John C. Burch and C. L. Scott."

Locke's crooked teeth showed in his knowing smile. "I always figured you knew more about politics than you let on."

"I read and I listen," Clay admitted, "but my opinions are private."

"I respect that; at least in ordinary times, a man's views are his own. But these are extraordinary times, and when that's coupled with what's going to happen, well, like I said, a man's got to stand up and be counted."

Clay snapped, "Except when I was in the army, nobody told me what to do or think. That still goes."

Locke spread his hands as though surrendering on that point, but he couldn't resist adding quietly, "I don't think a man can forget his roots, especially if they're Texas roots. They run deep."

Clay stood up, indicating the discussion was over.

"Hear me out!" Locke leaped up, almost knocking his chair over. Without waiting for Clay's reaction, he rushed ahead. "You know I've always wanted California to be open to slavery. But that view lost at California's constitutional convention."

Clay nodded as Locke continued, "We lost but we also learned. So we began to do some things that would someday work to our favor."

"I definitely remember that you wanted the Laird and Patton Stage Lines. You said there had to be some means of reaching men all over the state, and that called for an organized staging system."

"That's true, and you eventually provided that."

Through narrowed eyes, Clay pointed out, "We did that in spite of your efforts to buy our line or run us out of business."

"Things change. Gladwin and I parted company. You and your wife succeeded in keeping your stage line. But we pro-slavery advocates also had some success."

"You mean the newspaper?"

"We started that to get the true message out."

Clay's smile warned Locke that he didn't agree.

Hurrying to make his faltering point, Locke urged, "Let me finish. California is firmly politically controlled by people who favor the South, including Governor John Downey."

Clay had met the Irish-born Democrat. He said, "Downey may have some real competition if Leland Stanford runs for governor next fall."

Locke waved a hand to dismiss the idea. "Not a chance. Stanford's a Republican, and California is solidly Democrat. Our officials all favor the South. They only disagree on whether California should leave the Union and form a separate commonwealth, like South Carolina, or just secede outright."

Clay hadn't moved as Locke continued. "If the Union dissolves, Burch favors creating an independent Pacific Republic."

"Like your former friend, Gladwin."

Locke ignored Clay's remark. "Scott would also strongly advocate California's secession and setting up a separate republic."

"Sounds as if those men are more on Gladwin's side than yours," Clay dryly observed.

"No, that's only a first step. Don't you see? Once California is independent, then we can join other states if they form a confederacy with South Carolina, as is being suggested back east."

"That's only speculation," Clay reminded him.

"Not really. Senator Gwin . . . uh . . . do you know him?"

"My wife met him when he arrived in San Francisco in forty-nine. I haven't met him although he lives up on top of Rincon Hill above us."

"Anyway, Gwin's followers are already organized to take control of California's state government. He'll be helped by secret secessionist societies that will be used as a military force."

"The Knights of the Golden Circle?" Clay guessed.

"That, and the Knights of the Columbian Star."

Clay raised an eyebrow. He hadn't heard of the second group.

Locke lowered his voice. "I hear the Golden Circle people have forty thousand armed men in California ready to rise up when given the word."

Clay's lips formed in a silent whistle of amazement. "That's a powerful lot of men. But where would they get the arms?"

Locke smiled knowingly but didn't answer.

There was something about that confident silence that concerned Clay. Maybe Locke knew what he was talking about. Then Clay thought of something that made him shake his head. General Johnston, who also lived on Rincon Hill above Clay, was about to take command of all the army in the west.

Clay asked, "Have the Knights thought about what General Johnston will do if he hears about this?"

Locke lowered his voice. "Of course. Johnston's appointment came about through Senator Gwin's influence! Why did Gwin want Johnston? Because he's a southerner."

"He's also a military officer, sworn to honor the uniform he wears."

"True, but he's definitely pro-South. When he takes command this month, you'll see that he'll make no efforts to stop southern sympathizers, even if they're armed."

Locke smiled confidentially. "Now do you begin to see how it's going to be in California?"

"It's something to think about," Clay conceded.

"Glad to hear that," Locke exclaimed, smiling in triumph. "So, are you ready to join us?"

"I'm going to wait until Lincoln takes office and see what happens."

The surprised look on Locke's face slowly darkened into a scowl. Without a word, he turned and stomped angrily out of the room.

Clay thoughtfully stared after him.

⋘⟡⋙

In the middle of the afternoon, with her duties at the mansion finished, Mara put on her gray bonnet and walked down Rincon Hill toward Shiloh's home. She was curious about what part eggs had played in the dissolution of Tucker and Wallace's partnership and thought Merritt Keene might have some insight. She knew he had gone out of town, but maybe Shiloh knew when he'd return.

Deep in thought, Mara only vaguely noticed a team and carriage moving uphill toward her. She casually glanced at the matched bay team with a Negro in burgundy livery at the reins but didn't recognize the carriage.

The horses' hooves splashed in muddy puddles, and water ran down the gold-striped wheels of the black-bodied phaeton.

Suddenly, the driver pulled back on the lines and the carriage door flew open. "Mara! Is that you?"

She hadn't seen Jared Huntley in a long time, but she recognized him instantly. While some men were beginning to grow beards, as Lincoln had done last November, the auburn-haired man leaning out of the carriage was still clean-shaven.

"Come here," he called, smiling.

Bad memories flooded over Mara. Jared Huntley, an ambitious, greedy liar, had left San Francisco for Sacramento when it became the state capital in 1854. She had heard that he was doing very well in politics and had invested in the first railroad, which began running out of the capital in 1856. She had also learned of Jared's involvement in some kind of paramilitary organization, but it wasn't the Knights of the Golden Circle even though Jared was a Virginian.

Mara kept walking. When Jared repeated his order, she snapped over her shoulder, "You want to talk, you come to me."

Jared glanced up at the black driver as though cautioning Mara to be respectful in her tone.

She continued down the hill.

"Wait!" Jared's urgent tone made Mara stop.

He stepped down carefully, trying to keep his polished shoes out of the mud. As he made his way gingerly toward her, his eyes swept over her appreciatively. "You're an incredible woman," he said softly.

"And you're an idiot." She didn't keep her voice down. The black driver turned to look at her in surprise.

"Now, now!" Jared kept his voice down. "Let's let bygones be bygones."

She regarded him with disdain. "You want me to forget how rudely you treated me? Throwing a coin at me! I am not a common slave, here for your enjoyment!"

"I misjudged you," he admitted, again caressing her with his gaze, "but I've never stopped thinking of you."

"Times have changed, but I doubt that you have," she replied. "It's a waste of time talking to you."

Jared reached out and took her arm when she started to turn away. "I must talk to you privately."

"We have nothing to say. Now, let me go."

"Don't be so hasty! I think you do have reason to talk to

me." He glanced around and lowered his voice again. "I've paid attention over the past few years. Most people don't realize it, but you're becoming one of the most wealthy and powerful women in San Francisco."

Mara was intrigued. She didn't think Caucasians knew or cared about what she did. "Oh?" It was a leading question.

Sensing her interest, Jared nodded and smiled. "I know how you can get that piece of property from Locke."

Mara had spoken about that property only with Lyman Wallace. How did Jared Huntley know? "You seem to know a great deal."

"I know more than you think I do," he replied with a satisfied smile. "You're really an intriguing as well as beautiful woman, Mara. But if you're trying to run me off, it won't work. I'm a very determined man."

"So I've heard. You've come up in the world, and now you're a power behind the scenes in Sacramento."

His smiled widened. "So you *have* thought about me."

"Only to keep track of you. I like to keep on my toes."

"You want that property," he said, his tone brisk and decisive. "Meet me privately, and we'll talk about it."

Her interest rose, but she was cautious. "Just a meeting? Nothing else?"

He raised his right hand. "I promise not to throw another coin at you."

"Let's get one thing straight before I answer," she said firmly. "Don't you ever again do anything to harm Shiloh or her family. If you do, you'll answer to me. Do you understand?"

A frown wrinkled his brow. "Are you threatening me?"

"Just remember what I said."

She saw his face darken in anger and his mouth open. Then he closed it so hard his teeth clicked. His smile returned. "I'll remember. Now, will you meet with me?"

She hesitated, her old memories conflicting with her curiosity. That property was key to her ambition of controlling a vital waterfront area. Ships loaded and unloaded cargo there, at great profit to the owner.

"Well?" Jared said.

Mara nodded. "All right. When and where?"

~ CHAPTER 6 ~

IN THE DARK, Clay reluctantly pulled up at the home of Lafayette Montgomery. Asbury Harpending had given this address for the secret meeting, and Clay had driven by the Montgomery home earlier so he could find it by the feeble carriage lamps.

In daylight, Clay had noticed that the home was large, with several entrances, and stood well away from any other building. At night, with no moon and a white fog bank clinging to the hillsides, an air of mystery prevailed.

Following Harpending's instructions, Clay drove his buggy around to the north side. He heard the nicker of horses and knew other men had already arrived. After tying the mare to a fence post, Clay made his way toward the dark house. A light glowed at the side door.

Clay was admitted by a Chinese servant in baggy blue pants and with a black cue hanging down his back. He bowed respectfully without speaking and led the way down a gas-lighted hallway to a large room. Several men seated around a long table looked up at Clay but did not speak. Clay recognized some of them. All but one was his age or younger. A tall, distinguished man seated at the head of the table appeared to be in his fifties.

The servant closed the door on his way out. Asbury Harpending quickly rose from his place at the table and hurried across the carpeted floor to warmly greet Clay. "Glad you could come," he said, shaking hands. "I'd like to present you to our spokesman."

A second man had risen from the table and followed Harpending. He was about thirty-five with dark hair and probing gray eyes. He shook hands but offered no greeting.

Instead, he said, "I understand that you are a man who can be trusted and that you are willing to take an oath to never divulge what you see or hear tonight. Is that correct?"

Clay nodded, wondering if this was the host, Lafayette Montgomery. "Yes. I came to listen but not to make any commitment. On those terms, I'll take the oath."

"Very well. These other men have already taken the pledge." The spokesman produced a sheet of paper from his pocket. "The servants are all Celestials who speak little English, so you needn't be concerned about them."

Unfolding the paper, the spokesman instructed Clay, "Repeat after me. 'I do solemnly swear in the name of the southern states within whose limits I was born and raised, that I will never by word, sign, or deed hint at or divulge what I might hear tonight.'"

After the pledge, the spokesman seemed to anticipate Clay's next question.

"No names, please." He motioned toward the distinguished man seated at the head of the table. "He is the general. Please be seated."

The general wore a dark suit and had a distinctive military bearing when he stood. For a moment, he said nothing, but let his sharp blue eyes touch the face of each man. His sun-browned face was clean-shaven except for a neatly trimmed yellow mustache. His full head of hair was slightly sand colored.

"Gentlemen," he began with a soft hint of accent, "as you know, our beloved South, the sacred soil of our births, is in dire jeopardy from the tyrant who will soon assume the highest office in the land."

The strong words startled Clay. He was more than willing

to wait and see what Lincoln did about South Carolina's secession, but it was obvious that the general had already made up his mind. A quick glance around the table showed most heads nodding in silent agreement.

The general continued in his quiet but clear voice, "Our mission is to assist our native states in their coming travail. To do that, we will organize for two specific purposes: Each of you shall recruit and organize a fighting force, and each of you shall solicit funds for an extended campaign."

Clay stiffened. He had no intention of getting involved with a military force. Then he relaxed, comforted that he had plainly told Harpending that he had come to listen but not to make a commitment. Still, Clay's apprehension grew as the general spelled out the details.

They were quite simple. The general was in command. He alone would call meetings by word of mouth, receive donations, and plan strategy.

"You are all proven successful leaders," he continued, "and some of you have military experience, most recently as veterans of the war with Mexico."

His gaze rested briefly on Clay.

He had the uneasy feeling that this nameless general knew Clay had been wounded while a member of the First U.S. Dragoons during the Battle of San Pasqual in 1846.

"In addition," the general went on, "California is rich with qualified men," he glanced around the table as though identifying each man by his past, "former Indian fighters and veterans of filibustering expeditions."

Clay silently admitted that was true, but men could not fight without weapons. Where would the general get those? Clay glanced at Harpending, wondering if he was thinking the same thing. But Harpending was so engrossed in the speaker's words that Clay's questioning look went unnoticed.

The general explained, "Now is not the appropriate time to divulge how our mission will be accomplished. However, our success is assured because the federal army is little more than a shadow. We can deal effectively with that."

He motioned to Harpending and the man who called himself the spokesman. "Gentlemen, if you please."

The spokesman reached under the table and produced a large roll, which he carried behind the general. Harpending took one end of it while the spokesman held the other. They spread out a map of San Francisco and the bay.

"At Fort Point," the general said, touching the spot on the map, "there are only about two hundred soldiers." His finger moved on. "At Alcatraz, there are fewer than a hundred. Mare Island has a mere handful."

Clay's uneasiness grew in anticipation of what was surely coming next.

The general's hand swept north and east across the bay. "Thirty-thousand stands of arms are stored at the Benicia Arsenal. Those can be seized, along with militia arms here in San Francisco."

Clay's stomach gave a sickening lurch. The men in this room were planning to organize southern sympathizers to attack federal property.

Isn't that treason?

As the frightening thought seared itself into his brain, a side door opened slightly. The other men at the table were intent on the speaker, but Clay caught a glimpse of a black servant as he quickly drew away from the door.

Nobody else seemed to notice, but Clay frowned, recalling the spokesman's words: *The servants are all celestials who speak little English.* Clay was sure that Negro spoke English.

～≈≫～

While Shiloh helped the children get ready for church, she eagerly anticipated the familiar hymns and comforting words of John Sledger's sermons. The distressing events of the past week had keenly troubled her, but this morning seemed the worst. Something had happened to upset Clay; he had seemed tense after returning from his meeting.

Shiloh tried to shake off her concern while Clay went out to bring the carriage around and she herded their four children out the front door. Emily let out a happy shriek, "Grampa!"

Merritt Keene alighted from a buggy and knelt with open arms for the little girls rushing toward him. Ajay and Philip followed at a more controlled pace.

Shiloh smiled with pleasure as the tall, slender man hugged all but Ajay. The older boy, although glad to see his grandfather, self-consciously held back. The other children showed their obvious delight to see him. His blue eyes reflected their pleasure.

When Merritt stood, he kept one arm around his granddaughter and reached out with the other to give his daughter a hug. She kissed him on the cheek.

"I'm so glad you're home, Papa! When did you get back from Sonoma?"

"Last night, too late to call on you, but I hoped to catch you before everyone left for church."

"You just made it. Clay's bringing the carriage around."

"Good! I'll join you. Now, which of you children would like to ride with me?"

~❧~

Merritt took the larger family carriage and all four children. Clay and Shiloh followed in Merritt's smaller buggy.

"It's so wonderful having him home again," Shiloh said as the horse plodded along the sandy street.

"Yes, it is."

Clay's terse reply surprised Shiloh, and she glanced at him. "Are you all right?"

"Just thinking," he replied evasively. Inwardly, he was in turmoil. After the general had finished, Harpending and the spokesman had urged Clay to make a commitment. He declined.

The spokesman pushed, saying. "You don't have until March to make up your mind."

Clay raised an eyebrow and resisted an urge to say he resented the pressure.

The spokesman glanced around to make sure no one could overhear. Then he lowered his voice and spoke the words that still echoed in Clay's head.

"We will be prepared to strike by the twentieth of this month."

Shiloh's voice broke into Clay's reflections, "Clay, what's going on?"

"Uh? Oh. Sorry."

She looked at him with narrowed eyes. "What happened last night?"

"I can't tell you."

An invisible wall slid into place between them. "I see," she said.

"Please, Shiloh! I would tell you if I hadn't given my word."

"Something has obviously disturbed you, but I respect your decision." She resisted the urge to ask more questions, and Clay said nothing more.

An uncomfortable silence built up between them. Shiloh forced aside her gnawing concern about Clay and looked ahead to where her father and children rode in the bigger carriage.

Shiloh closed her eyes in thought until they reached the church. It was a simple white wooden structure with a steeple. The sanctuary had been made from timbers salvaged from sailing ships that had been abandoned in the harbor. The bell in the belfry once rang on a whaling ship to call whalers back from the sea.

As Clay turned in to the large open yard, Shiloh's spirits lifted at the sight of longtime friends and church members. Some were just alighting from their carriages. Others walked together toward the church's high front steps.

"Good morning, Sister Radcliffe," Shiloh called to a matronly woman as the Patton carriage passed her. She started to look up, then abruptly turned away with a stiffening of her shoulders.

Shiloh told Clay, "I guess she didn't hear me."

Clay quietly responded, "She heard you."

"Then why did she almost, well, snub me?"

"She's from Michigan. Remember?"

"What's that got to do with it?"

Clay warned in a low tone, "South Carolina's secession might change some people's attitudes. I think we just saw an example of that in Mrs. Radcliffe."

Shiloh protested in surprise, "But we're all brothers and sisters!"

"Even brothers and sisters disagree, and sometimes that leads to hurtful feelings, or worse."

"Not in our church!"

"I wouldn't be surprised if many congregations split up before this thing is over. If some people here act differently, don't let it bother you."

But it did bother Shiloh. Clay helped her down near the stairs and guided the horse over to the rail. Shiloh joined her father and the children. "Papa," she said, taking his arm and giving it a squeeze, "I can't tell you how glad I am to see you."

He looked thoughtfully at her as the children ran off to join young friends. "Troubles?"

"No, not really. But I'm sure you've heard about South Carolina."

"Everybody's talking about it."

"What do you think is going to happen?"

Before he could answer, a stout man hurried up, greeted Shiloh and Merritt, then dropped his voice. "Where's Clay? I need to talk to him right away."

Shiloh sighed, thinking that every man in San Francisco seemed to want to talk to her husband. "He's tying the horse," she explained. "He'll be along shortly."

"Good! I'll wait for him. You don't mind going in without him, do you, Sister Shiloh?" He didn't wait for a reply but turned and walked toward the hitching rail.

Continuing up the stairs with Shiloh, Merritt asked, "How long have you known that man?"

"Brother Earl? Oh, three, four years, I guess. He joined long after Clay and I did. Why?"

"He tried to recruit me as a member of the Knights of the Golden Circle."

Shiloh stopped in surprise. "When?"

"A few months ago."

"I've heard about them, but I'm not quite sure what they are."

Her father glanced around before lowering his voice. "Depends on who you ask. I've heard that they were formed in the 1850s to support the South's political goals. I've also heard they plan a 'golden circle' of slave states stretching from South America and Mexico through the West Indies to Florida."

Shiloh suppressed a shudder at the thought, guessing that Jefferson Locke was a member of the Knights.

"I've also heard that the Knights of the Golden Circle are among several secret societies formed by Copperheads. I guess you know they're people in the northern states with southern sympathies. They're supposed to have half a million members."

Shiloh licked her lips, wondering if the meeting Clay had attended last night had anything to do with the Knights of the Golden Circle. If so, what did they want him to do? The possible answer frightened Shiloh. She reached for Clay's hand as he came down the aisle.

They joined Merritt in smiling and greeting other parishioners as everyone made their way to the pews. Shiloh wasn't sure if it was her imagination, but she sensed a change in some of those who shook hands.

Oh, no! she thought, taking her seat. *Not here. What will that do to our church?*

Then she remembered that Pastor John Sledger was also a

southerner. What would his sermon be about? Would it give her the lift and hope she needed? Or would it widen the subtle cracks Shiloh had already sensed in the congregation?

❧ CHAPTER 7 ❧

THE OLD FAMILIAR hymns lifted Shiloh's sagging spirits so that when the preacher rose to begin his sermon, she was receptive. John Sledger more than filled the pulpit at six feet, six inches and three hundred pounds. He reminded Shiloh of a great bear with his massive chest and powerful arms. But Brother Sledger was a lovable bear, and Shiloh cared deeply for him.

When she was a stranger to San Francisco, he had conducted the funeral service for her first husband and had become her friend as well as pastor.

As the choir filed down to sit with their families, Sledger turned his blue eyes on the congregation. There was something strange about his eyes, but Shiloh could never quite decide whether it was their bold, penetrating quality or their reflection of an inner fire. He did not speak, but let his gaze flicker over the congregation until there was a total, expectant silence.

He said quietly, "In the last few days, many of us have realized that our nation faces dark days ahead."

His voice reverberated through the small church like a low rumble that slowly built in power. "But it isn't just our country that's in danger, for each of us here will be tested—tested by fiery trials."

A low murmur swept through the congregation at the frightening implications of those few words.

Shiloh glanced at Clay and saw his jaw muscles twitch. She

clutched his hand while he stared at the preacher. Had Brother Sledger's few words meant something special to Clay?

Sledger continued, "I have been asked where I stand on the issue South Carolina raised when she withdrew from the Union."

He paused. Shiloh waited anxiously to hear his answer. She knew he was a fearless man.

"Two good brothers came to me privately and individually," he went on. "One urged me to support the South, land of my birth. The other wanted me to favor the Union. Each brother quoted Joshua in the Bible, 'Choose ye this day whom ye will serve.'"

Sledger paused dramatically. When he spoke again, his voice rumbled like thunder. "But that Scripture isn't about a country; it's about God. So let me tell you what I told each of those good men: 'As for me and my house, we will serve the Lord.'"

The pastor's voice dropped so low that Shiloh found herself leaning forward to listen.

"God called me to this church. I believe that with all my heart. As your pastor, I try to minister to each of you. I will continue to give you the words He gives me. And I will be with you in your joys and your sorrows, but I am not going to take sides in this political issue."

Sledger let those words sink in before adding, "We are brothers and sisters in the Lord. We are a family, but like all families, we do not always agree on everything. Feelings are running high, so high that it could split this church."

A startled murmur swept the congregation. Shiloh wondered how Sister Radcliffe was reacting.

"We can't let that happen," the pastor continued in a quiet, firm voice. "Let me suggest how to keep our church family together, serving God regardless of which way we as individuals lean politically. Please open your Bibles to the Book of Galatians, chapter six, verse seven. Let's read aloud God's instructions regarding sowing and reaping."

On the drive home, Shiloh tried to compensate for the coolness that had developed between her and Clay earlier.

"I believe Brother Sledger is right," she said. "We must be careful what we plant, because that's what we're eventually going to harvest. If we sow doubt, suspicion, and discord about others in the church, we will reap disharmony and perhaps even a split congregation. Don't you agree?"

"Sounds logical," Clay admitted absently. He sat stiffly erect, the reins in his hands, his eyes fixed on the street ahead of the horse. The ominous words of the night before played endlessly in Clay's mind. *We will be prepared to strike by the twentieth of this month.*

"That applies to us too." Turning in the buggy seat, Shiloh's concerns spilled over. "Did something happen last night that can bear bitter fruit?"

Startled, Clay looked at her before answering. "I've told you that I can't talk about it."

She beat back her silent fears before observing, "That tells me enough to frighten me terribly."

Me, too, he thought, but he didn't answer. Absently he flipped the lines across the horse's back.

"Clay, I want above all things to be a good wife, to be supportive in whatever you do. I love you with all my being, but I also have strong feelings about other things. If Lincoln's election is going to lead to civil war, as so many people think, I don't want it to adversely affect you and me."

"I don't either."

"I told you where I stand," she said. "Of course, I know you were reared in Texas, but I also know you're against slavery. And I'm not at all sure which way you're leaning about states' rights."

"I wish I knew myself."

Satisfied that he spoke the truth, Shiloh declared, "I respect your opinion, and whichever way you choose to go, I will stand with you. I just hope you won't ask me to go against my conscience."

"No man ever had a better wife," he said softly, putting his arm around her shoulder and drawing her close.

His thoughts jumped to his fearful secret. It would be treason against the United States to seize federal property and arms. Some of the soldiers might be killed defending against the attack.

Clay tried to rationalize that he was a civilian, so the military couldn't touch him. But if war came, it would be anybody's guess as to what power the military might take or be granted.

That didn't bother Clay as much as the realization that he possessed knowledge about plans to take over California by force. He was now a party to a plot that nobody outside last night's meeting was supposed to know about, but he knew human nature. Not many people could keep secrets. If this got out . . .

⟨❦⟩

Mara had been intrigued by Jared Huntley's suggestion that he could help her obtain the key property that Locke wouldn't sell to her. On that first Sunday afternoon of the new year, Mara met with Jared at his home. It was one of only six expensive frame houses located on a finger of land jutting out from San Francisco's north shore. Each home had privacy provided by several acres of land formerly called San Jose Point, but more recently, Black Point.

He had shown her around the estate and told her that Jessie Fremont lived in the house nearest the end of the point.

Mara knew that Shiloh would be interested to know that, for she had met Jessie when she disembarked in San Francisco in '49. Jessie periodically led a nomadic life following her famous husband, John C. Fremont, the great pathfinder and defeated 1856 Republican candidate for president of the United States.

"Like it?" Jared asked, coming up to stand beside Mara on the path lined by rose bushes trimmed back for the winter.

"This is the most spectacular view I've seen here, and your home is truly beautiful." Mara raised her face to let the breezes blow against it. In the company of Shiloh and Aldar, she had sailed past this rural area in May of 1849. Then she was penniless. Now she was wealthy and had power that few white women in the city could match.

"You're beautiful," Jared said softly, turning to take her in his arms. "The most beautiful, desirable woman I've ever known."

She placed her hands against his chest and gently resisted.

Jared remembered other encounters. "Don't push me away this time." His voice had dropped to a heavy whisper.

She waited as though debating whether to heed him. She remained temptingly close yet held just enough resistance in her body to let him know she would not easily yield.

"Come live with me," he murmured. "I'll give you whatever you want, more than any other man can give you."

She gave a low, throaty laugh. "I recently became the cook for one of the richest and most powerful men in California. It wouldn't be right to leave so soon."

"Lyman Wallace is a fool! Do you think his wife's going to put up with that arrangement very long?"

Mara was impressed that Jared knew so much about her private life. She said casually, "Malvina's got his name and his money; she doesn't care about me."

"If Wallace told you that, he's a bigger fool than I thought. I knew Malvina before they were married. She's a proud woman. Someday all the whispering and rumors will get through to her, and she'll make him pay for his blatant indiscretion. Taking you into his home, right under her nose, is an affront she won't always tolerate."

Mara gently freed herself and looked around. It was one of the most scenic spots in San Francisco. To her left, the sun was already sliding down the western sky beyond the Golden Gate. Alcatraz Island sat proudly in the bay. Beyond that, to the north, Marin's hills rose in their splendor.

Jared stepped close and slid his arms around her waist. "Come live with me."

This time she did not resist. "I heard your divorce is final."

He shrugged. "Over a year ago. But I've never stopped wanting you. Never."

Mara knew from experience that lying came easily to Jared. "What happens to us when you feel the need to again play the respectable, married man like everyone else?"

"Why, you'll stay on, of course."

Mara considered that with pursed lips. She didn't believe him. However, she couldn't let that keep her from achieving her objective in meeting with him today.

"How about it?" Jared asked eagerly, holding her tight and looking down into her flawless face. "I want you. I wanted you the first time I saw you. You may not remember, but I told you back then that I'm a very determined man."

"I remember. But so far, you've not succeeded."

"I haven't given up. What do you say?"

"On what terms?"

He smiled in appreciation. "You're a very practical woman, Mara. Beautiful, practical, and blunt. So, on your terms: You live with me and keep me happy; the rest of the time you're free to come and go as you want."

Mara pulled free of his arms and turned to watch a schooner on the water. She heard the sails smartly snapping in the breeze. "When you asked me to meet you, you said you could help me get a piece of property from Locke."

"That's right."

She asked, "What makes you think I'm interested in any property Locke owns?"

"I make it my business to know things. I know that Locke has refused to sell. I also know that with that piece of land and what you already own, you'd control a large section of the waterfront. Ships loading or unloading will have to pay your price."

Jared shook his head in wonder. "Someday you'll own half of San Francisco, but very few people will know that. Will you be satisfied then?"

"Ask me again when I have it."

~❧~

On Monday, Clay had lunch alone in the dining room of a small hotel near his office. His thoughts were still in turmoil over what he had learned at Lafayette Montgomery's home. Through discreet inquiries, Clay had learned that Montgomery owned a small fleet of ships that hauled lumber along the coast. He was also an outspoken southern sympathizer with reclusive tendencies. That's why Clay had never met the man.

For several minutes, Clay stared at the bill of fare while his mind wandered. He could not remember the wording in the oath of allegiance he had taken when he joined the military years ago. However, he recalled enough to know that if anyone ever found out what he knew, the federal government could charge him with treason.

Everything he had, from money to his good name, was at risk. It would be acceptable if he had made up his mind to support South Carolina and other states' rights to secede. But his decision was still at least three months away. Regretting that he had attended the meeting didn't help, Clay reminded himself. His real concern was what to do now and how to ease the tension between himself and Shiloh.

"Good afternoon, Clay."

Hearing his name jerked him out of his reverie. Clay looked up to see Cyrus Bixby and a man in blue uniform passing the table.

"I'm glad I ran into you," the banker said. "I want to invite you to a meeting. But first, you gentlemen should know each other. General, may I present Clay Patton, one of this city's most successful and respected citizens? Clay, this is Brigadier General Albert Sidney Johnston."

Clay rose quickly, glancing at Johnston's single star denoting his rank. "How do you do?" Clay said formally, shaking the extended hand. He added quickly in a friendly manner, "We're neighbors, General. I understand you have a home on Rincon Hill. I live in South Park. Welcome to San Francisco."

"Thank you." The new top commander of the army in the west was in his late fifties but still had a full head of blond hair with no sign of gray. He was nearly as tall as Clay but heavier and had a commanding presence. "I am honored to meet you, Mr. Patton."

"Won't you sit down?" Clay asked.

"Thank you, no," Bixby replied quickly. "The general and I have some business to discuss."

Clay nodded in understanding. He was relieved but tried to not show it.

Bixby added, "Clay, there's a new preacher in town by the name of Thomas Starr King. He's going to speak Wednesday evening at our new Union Club. I invited General Johnston, but he can't make it. Would you do me the honor of attending as my guest?"

"I would be pleased to accept," Clay replied. He felt that this would give him an opportunity to hear a federal spokesman.

The three men shook hands all around before the banker and the general continued toward a table in the far corner. Clay stared thoughtfully and uneasily after them.

What would Johnston do if he knew about the planned raid on federal property?

Clay wished he knew the answer.

Back at the Wallace home, Mara had begun dinner when Samuel arrived. With some annoyance, she admitted him.

"This is a bad time," she announced brusquely.

"I know," the big black man confessed, "but I just had to talk to you right away."

Something in his face made her soften a bit. "Come in. But please be brief."

"I will," he promised. "I tried to wait, but my insides is so tore up I just couldn't."

The desperation in his tone kept Mara from asking him to sit down. Instead, she looked into his serious, dark eyes and asked, "What is it?"

"First off, I saw that lawyer, Mr. Tucker, and he says I'll soon be a free man."

That obviously wasn't what concerned Samuel, so she said, "I'm proud of you, Samuel." Gently laying her hand on his arm, she was aware of the strength in his biceps through his jacket. "You've worked very hard for several years to buy your freedom."

Samuel's voice dropped. "I didn't work hard to just get my freedom papers for me. No, not just that." He gently took both of her hands and pulled them to his chest. "I asked you away back to jump over the broom with me, but you . . ."

"Wait!" She broke in, pulling her hands free. "I care very much about you, Samuel, but I can't marry you."

He didn't answer for several seconds. "What about that kiss? The last time I saw you, you kissed me; I didn't try to kiss you. You just did it on your own."

Shaking her head, Mara tried to explain. "That was an impulsive act to show you that I am very fond of you. If I gave you the wrong impression, I'm very sorry."

Mara saw the disappointment in his eyes and heard the anguish in his next words. "I got to have you. I just got to!"

He again reached for her, but she stepped back. "Please don't make this any more difficult than it is already."

His voice shot up. "I got such love for you that there ain't nothing I wouldn't do for you! I respected you all these years and didn't take you the way I wanted, the way I could. I waited. It was very hard, but I did. I never wanted to marry nobody but you. Never. I earned my freedom money, and I got money saved. I'm a good man, Mara. So tell me why you won't marry me?"

The simple, honest words stirred her. She tried to think how to answer without further hurting his pride and hopes. "Samuel, I can't explain it, but I just want us to be friends."

"Friends!" The word seem to explode. "Just friends?"

She nodded. "Please. That's very important to me."

For the first time she could remember, his eyes slowly turned cold. "It's because I'm black, and you're half white. You can have what I can never give you. Is that it?"

"Please, Samuel . . ."

"I've watched you over the years, moving from one rich white man to another, always leaving one for a richer one." There was bitterness in the words. "You only recently got this big house and Mr. Wallace, but already, you got your eye on that bigger place on Black Point!"

So Samuel had followed her.

"Please don't talk that way."

His eyes narrowed in anger, but with an effort, he forced it away. "So that's the way it's going to be, is it?" he asked, his voice normal again.

She didn't reply but looked him in the eye and saw something she didn't like.

He nodded, understanding her silence to mean he had his answer. "I hoped this wouldn't happen, but I had to think what I would do if it did. Now I need to ask you something."

She waited without speaking.

"I want you to make something for me."

Relieved, she said, "Of course. What?"

"I want two of your voodoo dolls. Men dolls."

Startled, she shook her head. "Samuel, I can't . . ."

"You just said you would!" he broke in harshly. "If I can't have you, is it too much to ask for the dolls?"

She knew Samuel didn't realize how vital a part suggestion and fear played in making the dolls seem effective. The intended victim had to know about the dolls so the power of imagination could conjure up frightening results. Mara had never revealed that to anyone and never would.

"I'll make them," she said in a barely audible voice, "but won't you tell me why you want them?"

"I thank you for making them, but I can't say why." He turned toward the door. "I'll be by in a few days to get them."

Mara desperately wanted to ease Samuel's pain and disappointment. She followed him, frantically trying to think of something to say that would salvage their friendship.

"Please," she began, but he cut her off.

"One more thing," he said coldly, opening the door. "There's something else you should know." After glancing around, he leaned down and whispered in her ear.

When he finished, she drew back in surprise. "You're sure?"

"It's the gospel truth," he solemnly declared, then closed the door behind him.

Mara momentarily stood in stunned silence. Then she reacted. Dinner would have to wait. She whipped off her apron and ran upstairs for her coat.

❧

Helping Lizzie prepare dinner, Shiloh was startled when Mara opened the back door and hurried into the kitchen, breathing hard. Shiloh exclaimed, "Mara, what on earth . . . ?"

"Clay home?" Mara interrupted.

"Not yet."

"The children?"

"Getting washed up. Why?"

"I must talk with you right now."

"Upstairs," Shiloh suggested, and led the way, leaving Lizzie alone by the kitchen stove.

In her room, Shiloh closed the door and raised her eyebrows in surprise when Mara reached down and locked it.

"I probably shouldn't tell you this," she began, still catching her breath. "But I thought you should know."

"Know what? For goodness' sake, you're frightening me!"

"There's going to be an uprising by southern sympathizers who will seize all the federal arms and supplies in San Francisco and Benicia at the same time."

Shiloh stared in disbelief. "What? That's treason!"

Mara nodded, but before she could give details, Shiloh wanted confirmation. "How do you know?"

"Samuel has a friend who drove his employer to a meeting. He was supposed to stay in the carriage, but it got so cold he slipped inside the house to get warm. He listened at a door."

Shiloh's initial surprise gave way to calm reasoning. "Who was there? Anybody we know?"

"Samuel's friend didn't know anybody. He just saw a bunch of well-dressed men around a long table listening to another man."

"Did he hear when this will happen?"

"Yes. About the twentieth of this month."

Shiloh took a couple of quick, agitated steps, her mind whirling. "Their plan could succeed because it will be a total surprise. California will fall to the insurrectionists because they'll have control of all the arms and military supplies. Oh, I wish Clay were here!"

"Do you know where he stands?"

Shiloh shook her head. "Not really."

"After I heard about this, I tried to think of what would happen to me and some of my friends if a bunch of armed pro-slavery men got control of California."

Shiloh hadn't even considered that possibility. She saw and shared Mara's concern. At the very least, such men would eventually learn about Mara's real estate holdings and her quiet wealth and seize it. Mara had a double motive to bring Shiloh this news.

Shiloh said, "Whether they turn California into an independent nation as Gladwin and some others want or secede from the Union, armed and dangerous men will rule California. The state we know will be lost."

She hesitated, then added hopefully, "Clay will be home any minute, and he will know what to do."

"But you can't be sure which way he'll go."

"You're right." If she told Clay, would he see the secret plan as sedition, or would he favor the raids? She confessed, "I don't know what he would do, but I've never kept anything from him. I don't want to start now."

Mara looked doubtful. "There must be somebody else. Maybe your pastor?"

Shiloh considered that. "I trust Brother Sledger, but he's from the South, so maybe he would rather not be involved. So there's nobody else . . . wait! Maybe I could speak with General Johnston."

"I don't know," Mara protested. "I heard Lyman Wallace and some lawyer friends talking a few nights ago in the back parlor. They say Senator Gwin got him appointed, and you know that Gwin is pro-South. They could be in this together and be part of the plot."

When Shiloh nodded in agreement, Mara continued, "One of Lyman's friends laughed and said that it wouldn't surprise him if Johnston and Gwin are planning to take California out of the Union and send all our gold and other supplies to the South."

Wild thoughts tumbled over each other as Shiloh considered what to do. She said, "If I tell the general, and he is a party to this, he won't risk having me tell anyone else. What would happen to me or to Clay and the children?"

"There's certainly some danger in telling the general. But I guess there's danger in doing nothing and letting California fall into the hands of armed men who are against the Union."

Nodding, Shiloh said, "*You* could tell the general."

"He might not believe me. But he would you."

"I suppose so. Oh, this is a terrible predicament! I've got to think and pray about this."

"Don't take too long," Mara warned. "The twentieth is coming fast."

❧ CHAPTER 8 ❧

SHILOH STOOD at the front door, anxiously watching for Clay. *What's keeping him? He should be home by now.*

Feeling the need for guidance, Shiloh went to the kitchen and asked Lizzie to watch the children. Then she retired to her bedroom and knelt by the side of her high bed. She finished her silent prayer with anguished questions. *If I don't tell anyone or do anything, and if the plot succeeds, would that make me a party to treason? But if I tell Clay, what will he do? Help me to make the right choice, please!*

She rose and settled in an old hickory rocking chair by the window. Opening her Bible, she tried to read but found it difficult to concentrate. The enormity of what she knew threatened to overwhelm her.

Her rampaging thoughts were interrupted by the doorbell. *Clay! Oh, thank God!* She leaped up, calling down, "I'll get it!"

She started downstairs before realizing that Clay would not have rung the bell.

When she opened the door, she saw Cyrus Bixby in the gathering dusk.

He whipped off his hat. "Sorry to bother you, Mrs. Patton, but your husband asked me to tell you he won't be home tonight."

Shiloh's hand flew to her mouth. "What happened? Is he all right?"

"He's fine, and so's your father. They came by the bank a little while ago. Clay said a courier had just arrived from Sonoma. The quicksilver mine is on fire."

"Oh, my! How terrible!"

"Yes. The courier said the new owners wanted Clay's assistance because he knows the mine better than anyone. So he and your father left immediately for Sonoma."

Shiloh shook her head in bewilderment. "He didn't even come home to pack!"

"He said there wasn't time. They had to catch the last ferry of the day."

Shiloh recovered her composure enough to invite Bixby in. He followed her in and took a seat in front of the fireplace. Shiloh sat on the edge of her chair and urged, "Tell me everything, please."

"I don't know much more," Bixby replied. "Your father was with Clay at his office when the courier arrived. You know my office is right next door, so . . . "

Shiloh interrupted. "Do you have any idea how serious the fire is?"

"I'm sorry, no."

"How long will they be gone?"

"I would guess that depends on how serious the problem is at the mine. Probably days, at least."

Shiloh silently groaned in disappointment, but she understood Clay's reason for rushing off. The new owners had made a substantial down payment but still owed a large balance for the mine's purchase. If it was severely damaged, the new owners might default. This would not only cause the Pattons to lose all the money they expected but would also leave them with a burned-out and potentially worthless piece of property.

Shiloh fell silent as dismay engulfed her.

She heard Bixby say reassuringly, "I'm sure everything will be all right, Mrs. Patton."

She replied absently, "Thank you."

He stood, gripping his hat. "I'd better be going. Sorry to bring you such bad news."

"You were very kind to come tell me." Shiloh arose to face her guest. "I appreciate that."

"I had run into Clay at lunch today where I had the opportunity to introduce him to General Johnston."

The name yanked Shiloh back to another problem. *With Clay and Papa out of town, I have nobody I can tell—except maybe the general. But can I trust him?*

"I've heard so much about General Johnston, but I haven't met him although he's our neighbor. What do you think of him?" Shiloh motioned for her visitor to resume his seat.

"I'm very impressed," Bixby said as he sank back down into his chair, mindful that this woman and her husband had substantial funds in his bank. "When I first heard that he was to head up the army in the west, I did some research on him. You know, in hopes the bank would be chosen to secure some of the army's payroll or other finances."

"Of course," Shiloh said, smiling in understanding.

"The editor at the *Bulletin* is a friend, so he helped me compile some information about the general."

Shiloh waited expectantly, alert to whatever she could learn to help her decide whether to trust the general with her disturbing secret.

"He was born in Kentucky in 1808, so he's going to be fifty-three this year. He graduated from West Point in twenty-six and served in the infantry during the Black Hawk War. He left the army when his wife got sick, but after she died about twenty-five years ago . . . "

Shiloh broke in. "He's a widower?"

"He remarried and has children. Anyway, he went to Texas, enlisted as a private in the Texas army, and became a senior brigadier general. He resigned after a disagreement with General Sam Houston."

"Clay served under Houston when he was eighteen."

"Really? I thought Clay fought in the Mexican War."

"He fought in that war too. He was wounded at San Pasqual."

"I didn't know that." Bixby focused on Shiloh's eyes before commenting, "He has served our country well."

Shiloh sensed the hidden meaning. "Yes, he has. But he's a very private kind of man who doesn't say much." She smiled encouragingly. "You were telling me about General Johnston."

"Oh, yes, where was I? Well, when the war with Mexico broke out, Johnston rejoined the army as a major. In fifty-seven, when it seemed the Mormons were about to rebel against the United States, Johnston was sent to Utah."

"I remember reading about that, but I don't recall hearing about Johnston's involvement."

"He was in charge and was very successful. As you know, it ended without bloodshed. He's a brilliant military man. No wonder he's now in command of the Department of the Pacific."

Everything she had heard encouraged Shiloh toward telling the general about her awful secret. But she needed to know where he stood. If he was for the South, he would be the wrong man to tell.

Delicately, she began, "I heard some rumors . . ."

Bixby interrupted. "The town is full of rumors, like the one about Johnston having pro-South leanings."

Shiloh was delighted that Bixby had voluntarily mentioned the subject. She asked with forced casualness, "Do you think he has?"

"I have no way of knowing." He changed the subject. "Mrs. Patton, I don't want to presume on our friendship, but your husband should seriously consider becoming a charter member of the Union Club."

"Clay thinks everything through carefully, and I don't try to influence him in such decisions."

"I see. Well, guess I'd better be going."

After he had gone, Shiloh remained by the closed door. *The general sounds like a very fine man, but which side of this political situation is he really on? Do I dare tell him about the raid?*

~≈⊱~

Clay and Merritt stood by the ferry's railing facing the chill breeze that blew against their cheeks. The paddle wheels churned up the water on San Pablo Bay, carrying them north across San Francisco Bay toward Sonoma. To their left, Marin's stark hills marked the western horizon with the Pacific Ocean just beyond. Faint lights ahead on the far shores helped Clay locate Benicia. It was on the north shore where the land closed down on an arm of water leading to the Carquinez Strait.

Clay wished he could call on Merritt's experience to resolve the conflicts that raged in him. He had sworn secrecy about the planned attack on the Benicia Arsenal, but he could talk about another matter.

"What do you make of the secession?" he inquired.

"It'll probably lead to war. Crying shame too."

"Sure would be. But if it happened, who would win?"

"Technically, the North. In reality, neither side."

Intrigued, Clay turned to face Merritt. The wind ruffled his graying hair. "Why do you say that?"

"I've been in business all my life, and I've learned the importance of reading, listening, and analyzing. So what I say is based on an estimate of how many states may actually secede. Just counting those, but not border states that may or may not secede, gives us a rather clear picture. Unfortunately, a lot of people don't or won't see it."

Meaning me? Clay silently wondered, but he said, "I'm interested in the picture you see."

The older man looked soberly into Clay's eyes. "I'm glad. Now, let me see if I can make it clear." He leaned against the rail and took a deep breath.

"The South is mostly agricultural, with slaves working much of the land. I doubt the South could put more than three-quarters of a million white men in uniform.

"By comparison, the North will have up to four million men of military age, so it should have no trouble using at least half as fighters."

"Really?" Clay read a lot, and he listened to knowledgeable speakers, but he had not known the numbers his father-in-law had just given. "Are you saying the South would be outmanned at least two-to-one?"

"At least, and that's not even counting the possibility that Negroes could be put in northern uniforms. If war comes, the North would have adequate numbers of well-equipped troops plus well-mounted cavalry. Southern troopers would mostly have to provide their own horses."

Clay sadly shook his head. "I hate to think how many good men would get killed."

"That doesn't count how many will die of disease. As in all wars, disease usually claims about twice as many lives as military action."

Clay took a long, slow breath, remembering the wars he had fought in.

Merritt continued, "But there's another important reason why the North would probably prevail. Quite simply, the North is highly industrialized, so it automatically has the resources necessary. It also has manpower trained in running railroads, manufacturing, and shipbuilding. The South doesn't have such men."

"Shipbuilding?"

"That's vital. It will give the North the ability to blockade Southern ports and slowly starve the South into submission."

Such thoughts had not occurred to Clay. He was a proven businessman, yet in the present situation, he was thinking emotionally, as were many people. Many men, especially southerners, had passionate ties to their home states.

Clay agreed with his father-in-law. "I fought in two wars; I understand the importance of material and supplies."

"Then you know that in a war, you can't always get what you need from one state, or even several. You need unlimited supplies."

"I learned that the hard way." Clay didn't often speak of when his troops of dragoons had engaged the formidable *Californio* lancers at San Pasqual in Southern California, but the memories came flooding back. When the lancers' superior horsemanship cut off escape for the Americans, Clay and his surviving dragoons were reduced to existing on mule meat until reinforcements arrived.

Salt spray and the January breeze stung Clay's face when he looked squarely at Merritt. "If all that you say is true, then it seems clear why you believe the North would win. What did you mean when you said that neither side could actually win such a war?"

"Think about it, Clay. Americans fighting Americans, brothers choosing different sides. As in all wars, there will be pillaging, raping, burning, and battlefields covered with the bodies of the finest young men of this country. That's terrible enough, but to win, one side will have to invade the other's territory."

Clay remembered the old military adage, *the best defense is a good offense.* Defenders rarely won; victory usually went to the offense.

"Eventually," Merritt continued, "the invaders will bring those horrors of war to the unguarded women left behind while their gallant men are off fighting and dying elsewhere."

Clay took a slow, deep breath. "You paint a mighty grim picture."

"I've not even begun to hint at the enormity of what such a war will bring. It will take decades; maybe a century, to rebuild this country, regardless of whether it remains one nation or ends up in two broken and shattered halves."

Both men fell silent as the ferry continued across the bay. Clay stared toward Benicia, thinking about the planned attack.

But now he was troubled with the new thoughts Merritt Keene had envisioned. Clay frowned, wondering if his father-in-law had spoken his mind to help Clay decide against supporting secession.

He thought, *That war will be thousands of miles from here, but will we have our own war here in California if Harpending and his friends try to seize federal property?* He suppressed a shiver, thinking about what could happen to everything he had, including his family.

～～

Malvina Wallace pushed her way into the kitchen where Mara dried the last of the breakfast dishes. Mara's eyebrows shot up in surprise. Lyman's wife usually avoided the servants except to give orders, and she had never come to the kitchen since Mara had moved in.

In persuading Mara to move into her quarters, Wallace had privately assured her that she would have no trouble with his wife. Mara had no concern about any woman, but she preferred to avoid problems with this tall, gray-eyed woman who wore fashionable hoop skirts.

Malvina said coolly, "I have a question that you may be able to answer for me." Her stern features were accented by her gray hair, which she parted in the middle and drew tightly over her ears.

Mara dried her hands and straightened her apron. "Yes, Ma'am," she said politely. She knew Malvina objected to her presence.

"Because you're a Negro," Malvina explained, "I thought you might know someone who has some knowledge of something my husband found at his office."

Mara asked casually, "What is it?"

Malvina unwrapped a napkin, exposing a doll about a foot long with a hatpin thrust through the left chest.

Mara recognized it at once and wasn't surprised that Samuel had lost no time in placing it where Lyman Wallace would find it.

"About a year ago," Malvina explained, "for a short time, I employed a servant named Mattie who had come from New Orleans. She mentioned the existence of a Negro society down there." Malvina lifted her eyes from the doll to Mara's face. "I believe she called it vaudo, something like that."

"I've never been to New Orleans," Mara said easily.

"I didn't think you had, but I thought perhaps some of your colored friends might have mentioned this practice to you."

It was obvious that Malvina suspected Mara knew something about the voodoo doll, but Mara said, "I don't recall any of my acquaintances being involved in whatever this 'Negro society' is that you mentioned."

"That's too bad." Malvina held up the doll. "As you can see, the clothing indicates this is a representation of a man. I assume the pin is a warning of some kind."

"I suppose it could be."

Malvina sighed. "My husband has sometimes been threatened because of his law practice. He's even been challenged to a duel. But I've never seen anything like this before. He wasn't even going to show it to me because he says it's insignificant. But when I saw it at his office, I thought I would ask you about it."

"Sorry I can't help you."

"Well, no matter." Malvina started to leave, then stopped. "Would you like to know what Mattie said colored people do in this vaudo?"

"I have to finish the dishes . . ."

"They'll wait." Malvina dropped her voice. "I heard that the members swear on pain of death not to tell what goes on. But men and women strip down to their bare bodies and dance around a large snake. Mattie told me that this represents the devil. They worship him."

Malvina shuddered. "Can you imagine?" Without waiting for a reply she added, "In our white man's religion, Satan is represented as a serpent in the Garden of Eden. Did you know that?"

"I had heard that, yes." Mara was tempted to say that she had attended church regularly until she was about thirteen, and she had never before heard that Christianity was a white man's religion. But she didn't want to continue her discussion with this woman.

"Well," Malvina said, "I thought I'd ask." She turned and walked away with the doll.

Mara returned to drying dishes. She didn't think that Malvina really believed her innocence, but that did not bother her. She turned her thoughts to Samuel. Did he think the voodoo doll would actually cause Lyman Wallace's death?

She wondered what Samuel had done with the second doll. Did he think doing things like that would cause Mara to change her mind and marry him?

He had acted very strangely lately. Shaking her head, she decided to have a talk with him soon.

※

In midafternoon, Mara walked down the hill to Shiloh's home. While Lizzie made tea, Shiloh and Mara sat in the front parlor and watched the children playing through the window.

Mara observed, "Ajay and his friend seem to be playing together very well. Have they forgotten their fight?"

"Clay and I decided that the boys would just have to learn to get along. Clay talked to Jess, and he agreed, but they both insisted the boys not discuss anything political they overhear adults say."

Mara nodded and turned toward the stairs. "Is your father home?"

"No, he and Clay had to make an emergency trip to Sonoma. There was a fire at the quicksilver mine. Clay and Papa felt they had to be there."

"I see."

Shiloh looked closer at her friend. "You sound disappointed. Did you want to see Papa about something?"

"Nothing important. I was beating some eggs for a cake and remembered that he used to be in the egg business up north. I wondered if he might have an answer to a question I had."

Shiloh asked with an amused smile, "Why are you interested in eggs?"

"Not just any eggs, seabird eggs."

"Oh, yes, the kind that Philip finds so distasteful. Papa will be back in a week or so, then you can ask your question."

Lizzie brought the tea on a tray. Mara caught her disapproving look, but Shiloh didn't seem to notice.

As Lizzie returned to the kitchen, Shiloh asked, "Have you seen any more mysterious footprints?"

Mara laughed. "No, not a thing. My imagination must have been playing tricks on me."

Both women fell silent, sipping their tea and gazing into the fireplace. Each seemed reluctant to bring up the planned insurrection.

Finally, Mara glanced toward the kitchen and leaned toward Shiloh. "Have you decided what to do?"

Shiloh waited until she heard Lizzie rattling dishes in the kitchen before replying. "I wanted to talk to Clay, but he took off for Sonoma before I had a chance to."

Taking a sip from her cup, Shiloh added in a whisper, "But I don't dare wait until he returns."

"You're going to risk telling the general?"

"I don't have a choice. I can't talk to Clay, so I've got to handle this alone, and that frightens me terribly. If I do nothing, the state will fall into the hands of armed bandits. I hate to think what will happen then."

"I don't know, Shiloh. It could be very dangerous. Suppose the general is in on the conspiracy. Where will that put you?"

"He wouldn't do anything to me," Shiloh declared firmly, then added doubtfully, "Would he?"

"I don't know him, and I don't have any contacts who do, so I can't even guess."

"But suppose he isn't in on the plan? Suppose he's loyal to the uniform he wears? He could stop the raids before they start, and nobody would be hurt."

Mara thoughtfully considered that, then cautioned, "That makes sense, but there's something else. Even if the general is not part of the conspiracy, somebody might see or overhear you. There's no way of knowing what that person or his friends might do. You and your whole family could be in jeopardy."

"I've thought of that. But I have a plan. Nobody will know that I've seen him." She got up and paced a few steps. Returning to her chair, she explained, "I'm going to take some bread and salt, the traditional welcoming gift, and call on him at his home."

"When?"

"Tonight, after dark, when the children are in bed and Lizzie's busy with her sewing. I'll say I've come to welcome our new neighbor to the neighborhood. Then I'll get a sense of whether to say anything to him about the raids."

❧

About the time Mara expected Shiloh to head up Rincon Hill toward the general's home, Mara left the Wallace mansion for a solitary walk. She had no fear as she moved along the street illuminated by gaslights. She kept to the boardwalk that would take her across from General Johnston's home.

She had only gone a short distance when she became aware of footsteps behind her in the darkness. She slowed her pace so that whoever was behind would pass her. She was surprised when she heard those footfalls also slow. Without stopping, she casually glanced back.

The footfalls ceased, but she saw no one. She started on again. So did the steps. Calmly, not really concerned but curious, she kept walking.

Samuel? she asked herself. Maybe he had also made the footprints near her secret fence post bank. No, he was too respectful of her, Mara told herself. He wouldn't do that. But who else could it be?

To determine if she was being followed, Mara crossed the street toward the pale illumination cast by a gaslight. The steps followed. She moved on, unhurriedly, as though unaware or unconcerned. She continued on and waited until her pursuer had time to walk close to the light. Whirling quickly, Mara caught a glimpse of a man leaping into the shadows.

Her heartbeat increased, but she forced herself to resume walking at a natural, unhurried pace. Now she had no doubt. She was being followed. But by whom, and why?

❧ CHAPTER 9 ❧

MARA FORCED herself to walk naturally on the dark, deserted street as she looked around for a way to lose her pursuer.

Beyond the glow of the gas streetlamp ahead of her, she made out the faint outline of several large trees. She could slip unseen into the shadows there.

Moments later, hidden, she felt positive that she had made her move without being seen. Pulling up her long skirt, she retrieved the small single-shot derringer strapped above her ankle. The steady footfalls drew closer.

Suddenly the sound changed from steady walking to a

slower, more cautious approach. *He's trying to figure out where I went,* Mara told herself. *Well, he'll find out soon enough.* She palmed the weapon and calmly waited.

She had made enemies of people like Jefferson Locke. But she didn't think he or any of the influential men for whom she had acted as "housekeeper" or "cook" would follow her. She had argued with the banker, the judge, and the state senator, especially when she moved on to a man of greater power, but each discarded lover had eventually let her go on fairly comfortable terms.

Whoever followed her tonight now advanced very slowly. It sounded like he was about twenty feet away. Mara gripped her gun and waited. *Another few feet . . .*

The footsteps stopped. She waited impatiently and listened hard but didn't hear anything for a couple of minutes. *What's taking him so long?*

After another minute or so, she slowly crouched so that she was less likely to be seen. Then she carefully peered around the tree trunk. *He's gone!*

She glanced in every direction, probing the shadows. She saw no sign of movement, heard no sound.

Mara remained in her crouched position, derringer in hand, for another five minutes. Only then did she stand and continue her walk. The footsteps did not come again.

Mara again felt a slight tingle of fear as goose bumps trickled down her arms.

<hr>

The darkness would hide Shiloh's identity. She put on her best velvet bonnet and took her hospitality basket in hand. Climbing Rincon Hill, she rang the doorbell at General Johnston's home. She warned herself to sound neighborly and try to judge the man. If she had any doubts, she would not tell him about the insurgents' planned arsenal raids.

She expected a servant to answer the door, so when it swung open, the presence of the giant of a man startled her. Even though he wore casual clothes instead of uniform, Shiloh knew instantly who she faced.

"Good evening," he said politely.

Flustered at his unexpected appearance, Shiloh thrust her basket toward the general. "Here," she said, "freshly baked bread and salt. Welcome to our neighborhood."

"Thank you." In reaching out to accept the gift, he shifted so the gaslight inside the room illuminated his blond hair and face. The first word that came to Shiloh was *noble.*

"Uh . . ." she began, gathering her wits and looking beyond him, "I was expecting . . . uh . . . oh! I'm Mrs. Patton, Shiloh Patton. My husband, Clay, and I live down the hill with our family, in the South Park area."

"My name is Johnston," he said simply. "Won't you come in, Mrs. Patton?"

"No, thank you." She managed a smile. "I just wanted to bring you this little basket. It's an old tradition—giving bread and salt to new neighbors."

Shiloh silently scolded herself for acting like an embarrassed schoolgirl. But she was somewhat awed by the size of the man and his dignified bearing.

"That's very nice of you," Johnston said. "Your thoughtful gift is most appreciated."

Nodding, Shiloh hesitated. "Well," she began uncertainly, "I hope you have a wonderful stay in San Francisco."

"Thank you. It's a beautiful city." He cocked his head. "Patton? Clay Patton, you said?"

She nodded.

"Ah, yes! I remember him. Cyrus Bixby introduced us at lunch."

"Yes. He's a banker." Shiloh silently castigated herself. Of course the general knew Bixby's occupation, and he probably had expressed his pro-Union feelings to Johnston.

An awkward silence built as Shiloh grappled with whether to trust the general. The big man's royal bearing impressed her. She decided that she had to take a chance.

"General," she said, dropping her voice and looking around but seeing no one, "I have some information that may interest you."

He studied her earnest face in thoughtful silence for a moment. "I'm alone this evening, but won't you please step inside out of the cold, Mrs. Patton?"

She shot an anxious glance around, then entered. She shook her head when he invited her to sit down. Standing by the door, she quietly admired the house with its dark furnishings.

"I'll only be a minute," she began, and quickly repeated what she had learned from Mara.

The general stood without comment until she had finished. Then he asked quietly, "How reliable do you consider this intelligence?"

"I have no reason to doubt any part of it."

"I see. You said this meeting took place in the home of someone known as Lafayette Montgomery?"

"Yes, but I have no idea if he was present, and I don't know who the other men were."

"And you've told me everything?"

Shiloh wasn't sure he believed her. "I'm sorry, General Johnston, but that's all I heard." Eager to convince him, she plunged on. "I hope you understand that I have never before done anything like this. I would have just told my husband, but he had to make a business trip out of town—an unexpected business emergency. I had no one else I could trust to bring this information to your attention."

"But you do believe this meeting took place?"

"Yes. Oh, I know it must not sound logical to you, but I thought I had to take the risk of coming to you, even though I . . . " She broke off, horrified that she had almost spoken about his suspected southern sympathies.

"Uh . . . that is, well . . . " she stammered then thought of something that might appeal to his honor. "I know that graduates from West Point are men of great integrity."

He gave a slight bow in acknowledgment of the compliment.

"Anyway," she finished forcefully, "if I didn't do something and those men succeeded, I would feel responsible for allowing California to fall into the wrong hands. I couldn't do that."

"I understand." He regarded her with steady, penetrating eyes.

She turned and reached for the doorknob. "I know that the one name I gave you isn't much, but I do hope that you will check on it."

He said quietly but firmly, "I shall."

"And you won't reveal to anyone that I told you?"

"You have my word."

Shiloh said good night and hurried into the darkness, hoping she had done the right thing. Yet she could not shake a lingering doubt that maybe she hadn't. What if Johnston was part of the conspiracy? Had she put herself in some kind of danger? She shivered, but not from the cold.

❧

Although Mara had not heard the footsteps again, she had hurried enough so that she was slightly breathless when she reached the Wallace mansion. She walked toward the enclosed back stairs that led to her comfortable quarters.

"Mara." The man's voice made her whirl in surprise. "It's Jared."

She had recognized his voice. "Don't ever do that again," she warned as he emerged from the shadows.

"Sorry," he replied quietly, moving toward her. "I have news I thought you would want to hear tonight."

"You shouldn't come here," she said reprovingly, keeping her tone low but firm.

"It's all right. Malvina is at a concert, and Lyman has gone to a meeting of the Knights of the Golden Circle."

"Just the same, don't ever come here again."

89

"Now, now," he said, "don't be so difficult." His words took on a hard edge. "I brought good news. Do you want to hear it, or shall I leave?"

Briefly reflecting, Mara asked, "Is it about that property?"

"Yes."

"Well?"

"He'll sell it to me tomorrow. As soon as the deed is transferred from Locke, I'll pass it on to you."

A slight sigh of relief escaped Mara's lips. "Thank you."

He chuckled. "That's all? Just 'thank you'? I have my carriage around the corner. We could go have a private celebration, just the two of us."

"Not tonight. Now, you must go."

She sensed more than saw him tense in the darkness. "I'm giving you what you want," he said, his voice thick with desire. "Is it too much to expect you to show some gratitude?"

She fought down an impulse to coldly tell him what she felt. But if he wasn't going to buy the property until tomorrow, she had to be nice to him.

Smiling, she said, "Why don't we plan a little private celebration for later? When you have Locke's signature on those papers, send a courier to my kitchen. Give him a note saying that the package I ordered has arrived in case Malvina or someone else is there. I'll meet you at nine o'clock that same night at Black Point."

When he nodded eagerly, she bade him good night and continued on up to her quarters.

Mara didn't expect Jefferson Locke to show up at the kitchen door the next afternoon. She hesitated when she went to answer the loud knocking and saw him through the glass.

"Let me in!" he yelled, his face dark with anger.

She glanced over her shoulder, making sure that Malvina wasn't close enough to hear. "I'm busy," she said through the door. "I can't talk now."

He kicked the door hard. "You'll hear what I have to say, you black witch!"

She jerked the door open and ordered firmly, "Stop that! And keep your voice down!"

"After I signed those papers, Huntley told me he was turning them over to you. Is that true?"

"That's none of your business! Go away."

In fury, Locke replied, "No nigra can talk to me that way!" He drew back his right hand to strike her, but she stepped back quickly and slammed the door in his face. She rushed into the kitchen, hearing him angrily turning the knob.

She reached into a drawer and whirled around, leveling her derringer at him.

He stopped abruptly, eyeing the weapon. "You wouldn't dare." Doubt and fear had replaced his anger.

"Try me," she said with such cold calmness that Locke stood still.

Slowly, he lifted his eyes to meet hers. "There are ways to deal with high-and-mighty nigras like you."

"Is that a threat?" Her tone was challenging.

He slowly backed up to the open door. "Just remember what I said."

When he had gone, Mara quickly hid the little gun before Malvina rushed in.

"What was all that noise and shouting?" she demanded.

"A produce peddler didn't like that I refused to buy his vegetables."

Malvina was plainly suspicious. She examined the door where it had been kicked then straightened up and faced Mara. "Don't let it happen again." As she closed the door, she made an annoyed clucking sound.

"Here comes another of your black friends. Get rid of him and tell him to stop coming around. I won't have my servants turning this home into a social gathering." She swept grandly across the room, adding over her shoulder, "And tell them I don't want any more of those silly dolls left around. Do you understand?" She didn't wait for an answer.

Mara let it pass. Malvina's power over her was limited to threats. She might wheedle and threaten her husband when they were alone, but Malvina couldn't force Mara out of the house.

Samuel whipped off his hat when Mara came to the door. "I'll only be a minute," he began.

"You know you shouldn't be here."

"I know, but I got to ask you something. How long does it take those dolls to work?"

Mara tried to sound understanding. "It takes more than just leaving a doll someplace. You have to have the power."

"You mean, you got the power, but I don't?"

She chose to not answer directly. "What did you do with the second one, Samuel?"

He dropped his eyes. "I'd rather not say."

"You can't keep it from me."

He raised his gaze to meet hers. For the first time, she saw defiance there. "I can try."

Mara didn't want to press the issue. "Please go."

She saw disappointment replace the defiance and added quickly, "Mrs. Wallace was just in here, very angry about your coming around so often."

"I can't help it."

She heard the plaintive truth in his words and recognized the old hunger softening his features. "Please try to understand my situation, Samuel."

"I try," he confessed, "but it's hard." He replaced his hat. "But you got to understand me too. I worked all these years to get money for my freedom papers. I worked and I waited because of you . . ."

She broke in, "Please stop, Samuel!"

"I'm going to say it." There was a fierce determination in him. "I don't care what you say, but I'm not going to give up. I'm going to have you, for always, no matter what it takes."

Mara watched him walk away with his head high and shoulders squared. She realized he still had some fear of her powers, but he wasn't as compliant as before.

Getting his freedom papers has changed him, she thought. *I'm not sure I like that.*

❧❧❧

Shiloh laid her sewing aside to answer the doorbell. A young army officer in a dark-blue uniform stood before her.

"Pardon me," he said, "is this the Patton home?"

"Yes, it is."

"I have a message for Clay Patton."

It took Shiloh a moment to overcome her surprise. "He's out of town. I'm Mrs. Patton. I'll give him the message when he returns."

"Thank you, but my instructions are to deliver the message to no one except Mr. Patton. When do you expect him to return?"

"I'm not sure. A few days. Is something wrong?"

He sidestepped the question, saying only, "I will return in a few days."

As he started to turn away, Shiloh asked quickly, "May I ask who sent the message?"

When the soldier continued to walk away without answering, Shiloh shook her head. *He's pretending he didn't hear me. But why would anyone in the army want to see Clay?*

❧❧❧

Shortly after eleven o'clock two nights later, Mara stood at the seaward-facing window of Jared Huntley's large bedchamber on Black Point. She gently fingered the deed that he had presented her with.

Jared came up behind her and slipped his arms around her. "You were incredible," he whispered, nibbling at her ear. "Absolutely incredible."

93

She half turned so he could see her smile in the soft glow of the gaslight. "Takes two, you know."

"It could be like this all the time." He pulled her closer. "When will you move in?"

She stiffened slightly but didn't answer.

He caught the change in her and turned her to face him. "What did that mean?"

"What are you talking about?"

"You know perfectly well!" His tone took on a harsh edge. "You've got what you wanted from Locke. I got it for you, just as I said I would. But when I mentioned moving in just now, you suddenly got tense. I asked you a straightforward question. I'd like a similar answer. When will you move in here?"

Mara stepped away, carrying the deed. "There are some problems . . ."

"Problems?" his angry voice asked. "What problems?"

"Locke came to see me," Mara explained quietly. "He was furious."

"What did you expect? He found out too late that I didn't want the property for myself. When I told him what I planned to do, he yelled that you were deliberately trying to ruin him."

Mara well remembered her threat of years ago that she would someday buy and sell Locke. She told Jared, "I'm simply following my plan. I needed that piece of property to go with what I already have. It's just business."

"Not to him. Don't you see? He feels very superior to all Negroes, and especially you, a woman . . ."

The sudden snap in Mara's eyes stopped Jared in midsentence. Too late, he realized his mistake in revealing that he, too, considered her black. She had long ago made it plain that Caucasian society labeled her as Negro, but she was also half white. He knew that the unfairness of society's label drove Mara.

"I'm sorry, Mara," Jared said quickly, reaching out to her. "I didn't mean . . ."

She cut him off with words as sharp as a knife. "Oh yes you did! Remember when you first wanted me, but you couldn't bring yourself to kiss me? I thought you had changed, but you haven't." She walked deliberately across the room to her clothes.

"Wait! What're you doing?"

"Guess." The word was acid.

He took a few quick strides and seized her arms. Spinning her around, he thrust his face close to her flawless one. "I see it now! You got what you wanted, and now you're making an excuse to walk out on me!"

"You're blind, Jared," Mara said calmly, not drawing away from him. "You're absolutely blind, and maybe I was too. I thought you had changed, but you haven't."

Her quiet, self-assured manner infuriated him more. "Don't try that kind of reasoning on me! You and your plans! You devised this whole thing, didn't you? You used me to get what you wanted, and you're walking out. Well, I'm not giving you up. Do you understand that?"

"Don't shout at me!" Her voice rose for the first time as she broke away and reached for her shoes. "I am not a possession that you can give up or keep!"

She saw him raise his hand and tried to duck, but he struck quickly. She went down hard. As from a great distance, she heard his voice.

"We'll see about that!"

CHAPTER 10

CLAY AND MERRITT disembarked from the mid-morning ferry on their return from Sonoma and hurried out to the street to hail a hackney.

Because he was anxious to get home, Clay didn't notice Denby Gladwin until it was too late to avoid him.

"Clay, where you been keeping yourself?" the stout man waved his ever-present cigar stub and waddled up to Clay and Merritt.

"Out of town on business," Clay replied a little briskly. "We'd like to hire a carriage and get home. So if you'll excuse us . . ."

"How is Shiloh?" Gladwin interrupted, falling into step with the other two men.

"She was fine when I last saw her."

"Glad to hear that." Gladwin's tone changed, "Clay, I owe you an apology. The last time we met, I said some rash things because we didn't agree."

"Apology accepted." Clay said quickly.

"Good!" Gladwin turned to Merritt. "Seeing as how your friend isn't going to introduce us, I'll do it myself. I'm Denby Gladwin. You are . . . ?" He left the question incomplete.

"Merritt Keene." He extended his right hand. "Shiloh's father."

"*The* Merritt Keene?" Gladwin vigorously shook hands. "I've heard about you. You've done right well for yourself in business, so I hear."

"I eat regularly," Merritt admitted.

"You know who I am?" Gladwin asked, matching the other men's steps although Clay had greatly increased his stride.

"Of course. You're in favor of California splitting off from the Union and becoming a separate nation."

"Our numbers are growing too. Have you read the papers about some statements our elected state officials have made about favoring a separate nation?"

"I've read them all very carefully."

"That's good, very good, because the time is rapidly coming when we break away and become the Empire of Pacifica. That's really going to happen, Merritt."

Gladwin's enthusiasm made him rush on. "When it does, a

good businessman can sell Pacifica's rich resources to whoever has got the money to pay for it. With the war coming, we can supply both North and South with whatever they need. A man of vision like you can make more money than he knows what to do with."

"Thank God, I have no money needs."

"Money and power go together, you know. How would you like to be a civil official, like a judge?"

Merritt stopped and looked down at the shorter man. "Mr. Gladwin, none of those things tempt me. Now, I must get home to my grandchildren."

Clay and Merritt got into a hackney, leaving Gladwin staring angrily after them.

"Don't mind him," Clay advised. "The last time I saw him, he wanted me to make a donation to his cause. When I wouldn't, he told me I'd regret it. Which I haven't."

Merritt turned to look back. "Men with such dreams are generally thought to be insane. That makes their threats all the more dangerous; that is, if they ever get a chance to make their dreams come true."

"Well, there's no telling what's going to happen here when Lincoln takes office. But I'm confident of one thing: California's not going to become a separate nation, not if I can help it."

He raised his voice to the driver, "Can you go a little faster, please? We're anxious to see our family."

Upstairs, Shiloh heard Ajay shouting from next door. *Oh, no!* she thought, *he and Howell are fighting again!*

She was halfway down the stairs when the front door burst open and Emily and Julia rushed in. "Mama! Mama! They're coming! They're coming!"

It took Shiloh a moment to shift her thoughts.

"Who's coming?"

"Papa and Grandpa! Come see! Come see!"

Grabbing a shawl from the coat rack by the front door, Shiloh rushed outside and saw her father paying the driver.

Moments later, Clay had his arms full of little girls. An army officer who had followed the carriage up the hill dismounted and tied his horse to the post.

Shiloh whispered quickly to her husband, "He was here a couple of days ago looking for you."

"Oh? What did he want?"

"He wouldn't tell me." She turned to her father for a hug and a kiss on the cheek. Together they watched the soldier approach. He nodded politely to Shiloh and her father before turning his attention to Clay.

"Mr. Patton?" he asked, stopping in front of him.

"Yes, lieutenant, I'm Clay Patton." He shifted his youngest daughter so her head wasn't in his vision. "What can I do for you?"

"I have instructions to personally deliver this to you." He extended a sealed envelope.

Clay reached past Emily and accepted it. "Who's it from?"

"The contents will be self-explanatory," he said evasively. "My instructions are to wait for your reply. I'll be near my mount." He again nodded to Shiloh and walked away.

All four children clamored for their father to open the envelope. He kissed the top of Emily's head and set her down. Facing the officer, he said, "Lieutenant, I'll be back in a minute."

He and his father-in-law started toward the house. Clay looked questioningly at Shiloh.

She clearly saw from his expression that he had no idea why the letter had been delivered. She ventured an opinion. "Maybe it's from General Johnston. I met him the other night." She hesitated, then added, "I took a fresh loaf of bread and some salt up to his home to welcome him to our neighborhood."

"If it's a thank-you note, then why wouldn't it be addressed to you? And why would he request a reply?" he mused as he entered the front parlor.

"That does seem a little strange," she admitted.

"Maybe it's not from the general," Merritt suggested, "but if you'd open it, we wouldn't have to guess."

Nodding, Clay opened the envelope and removed a single sheet of paper. He read aloud, "'Your presence is requested at two o'clock on the afternoon of January 18th at the Presidio on a matter of utmost urgency.'"

Clay looked up at his wife and father-in-law before adding, "It's signed 'Albert Sidney Johnston, commanding general, Army of the West.'"

Shiloh saw a flickering shadow of thought reflected in her husband's face. "What is it?" she asked anxiously.

He paused before answering while rejecting the first thought that had leaped to mind. *Nobody knew about that meeting at Lafayette Montgomery's house.*

Shiloh broke into his thoughts. A frightening possibility had suddenly come to her. "Please, Clay. Why do you think he wants to see you?"

Clay took a quick breath and forced a smile. "Perhaps he wants to talk to me about the state. After all, he's probably heard that I've driven a stagecoach over every mile of California."

Shiloh nodded. "I suppose that's possible."

"I'd better go tell the officer that I'll be there."

When Clay closed the door behind him, Shiloh quickly turned to her father. "Did you see the look on his face when he read that note?"

"You noticed it too?"

"I certainly did. Something's going on, but I don't think he's going to tell us what—at least, not yet."

"That's probably because he doesn't want us to worry. So let's make it easy on him. Ask me about our trip."

When Clay returned, Merritt was telling Shiloh about the fire. "The mine is already back in production, and everything's going to be all right."

Shiloh nodded, not really listening. She glanced at her husband.

He smiled and put his arms around her. "Your father's right," he said confidently. "Everything's going to be fine."

Shiloh wanted to believe him, but doubts like rats' teeth began gnawing at the back of her mind. She wanted to tell him about her conversation with the general, but she didn't feel right about doing so in front of her father.

She suggested, "Clay, would you come upstairs for a moment?" Turning to her father, she added, "I'm sure Lizzie would make you a cup of tea if you want."

"I'd rather go spend some time with my grandchildren," Merritt replied, and headed toward the sounds of the children at play.

Clay gave Shiloh a squeeze, saying, "It's sure good to be back here with you."

"I miss you so much when you're away," she agreed. As they started up the stairs together, she added, "There's something I need to talk to you about right away."

"I guess we both have some catching up to do. I want to give you the details on what we found at Sonoma."

"I'm anxious to hear about it, but . . . " She interrupted herself at the sound of the doorbell and raised her voice. "Lizzie, will you see who that is?"

Shiloh heard the front door open, followed by Mara's voice, "Anybody home?"

"Come on in," Shiloh called. "Clay just this minute got home, so I need a few minutes with him. Papa's in the backyard with the children. You can either visit him for a couple of minutes or have a cup of tea. We'll be down in a bit."

"There's no hurry," Mara called back.

When Mara entered the kitchen, Lizzie turned from where she was rolling out a piecrust.

"Umm-umm!" she exclaimed, staring at Mara's swollen face. "Looks like you done been kicked by a mule."

Mara kept walking, passing the servant on the way to the back door. "I had a little accident."

Lizzie laughed knowingly and turned her attention back to

the pie crust. "I know somethin' about them kind of accidents. Umm-umm, do I? But my man only done that once. I made it mighty plain that . . ." She left her thought unfinished as the back door slammed. "Guess she don't want to hear," she added aloud to herself.

Mara crossed the backyard toward the four children and their grandfather. He glanced up as Mara approached.

He explained, "I was just telling them about the trip their father and I took to Sonoma. Do you want . . . ?"

"Oooh!" Julia interrupted, staring boldly at Mara's face. "That looks awful!"

Mara forced a smile, but she was sorry she had come, even though she really needed to talk to Shiloh. "I bumped into a door. It looks worse than it is."

"Those doors can be mighty hard on a person," Merritt replied, rising. "You young ones run along for now." At their protestations, he added quickly, "Later, we can open the presents I brought from Sonoma."

That prospect sent the children scampering off.

"Want to take a walk?" Merritt asked Mara without looking at her.

"That would be nice." She fell into step with him, heading around the side of the house. "I didn't expect to see you," she explained. "Especially with this." Gingerly, she touched her bruised face.

He nodded and took a few steps before speaking. "I hope you won't mind a friend giving you a bit of advice."

Mara didn't want a lecture, but she was too fond of the older man to stop him. "I don't mind."

Turning to lock his eyes onto hers, he said gently, "When a door does that to a person, it's wise to never go near that door again."

"Don't worry. I intend to stay away from that door forever."

Merritt smiled warmly and gave her a light pat on the shoulder. "I always knew you were an intelligent woman."

That gave her an opportunity to change the subject.

"Thank you, but there's something I know little about, but you may be able to enlighten me."

"That's very flattering." He gave her another smile. "What would you like to know?"

"Remember when Shiloh and I first saw you?"

He chuckled. "I'll never forget, although I must confess I remember Shiloh more clearly than you."

"I certainly understand that. Anyway, you were so surprised to see her that you dropped the eggs you were carrying. Remember?"

"Oh, yes. They splattered on my daughter's dress. Of course, at the time, I didn't know I had a daughter."

"Shiloh tells me that you used to raise chickens and sell eggs around Sonoma."

Merritt looked at Mara with questions in his eyes. "That's true. I've done a lot of things in my life, including that. But why are you interested in eggs?"

"Not just any eggs, seabird eggs."

They had reached the street and turned downhill, moving slowly, comfortably together.

"Oh, yes, seabird eggs. That's quite a story." He spoke slowly, remembering. "I arrived in San Francisco in forty-eight, right after James Marshall discovered gold at Sutter's Mill but before the Gold Rush started. I was doing a little farming, including raising chickens for eggs, but when the miners started pouring in, nobody could meet the demand for eggs."

"So you started selling seabird eggs?" she guessed.

"It wasn't my idea, but I got in on it. A pharmacist named Robinson began selling seabird eggs to bakeries and restaurants. Then some other men formed a little company to gather the eggs on the Farallon Islands. You know where they are?"

"Yes. We sailed past them on the way to the Golden Gate back in May of 1850."

"They're not much to look at, just a bunch of barren rocks nearly thirty miles offshore, and there's almost no place to land.

That isolation makes it perfect for the millions of seabirds that nest there every spring.

"Apparently nobody bothered the birds for centuries until the Gold Rush miners poured into here by the thousands. They created a huge market for the eggs. It's still a profitable business because there aren't enough laying hens to meet the demand."

Mara's interest was aroused. "How profitable?"

"Well, back in the early fifties, it was still a small operation: a few hundred thousand eggs gathered each year. Now, I hear that at least half a million murre eggs are taken each year. Maybe a million. And that doesn't count petrel eggs."

Mara's eyes widened in surprise. "That many?"

"Yes, and with no end of demand in sight. Egg pickers gather the eggs in huge sacks hung around the front of their bodies. The eggs sell for about six bits up to a dollar six bits a dozen."

She figured rapidly in her head. "If we divide a dozen into five hundred thousand eggs, that's . . . something over forty-one thousand dozen. Is that right so far?"

"I thought I could do numbers pretty well in my head, but you're ahead of me. But that does sound about right."

Mara stopped and closed her eyes to better visualize her figures. "Let's round it off at forty thousand dozen. Multiply forty thousand times a dollar and six bits. That comes to . . ." She opened her eyes in surprise. "Seventy thousand dollars. Can that be right?"

"Sounds logical. And there's no end in sight. But, of course, there's always a squabble from people who want to get in on this with those who got there first and don't want to give up that kind of money."

Mara repeated wonderingly, "Seventy thousand dollars a year." She cocked her head. "Why did you get out of that business?"

"Too many headaches for the small part I owned. You see,

the government built a lighthouse out there but didn't pay enough for the keepers to endure the isolation, the winter storms, and so forth. So the lighthouse keepers started to sell eggs to augment their salaries and got greedy. Naturally, the government didn't like that because they wanted them to focus on caring for the light, not on gathering eggs."

He shook his head. "I'm afraid that someday there's going to be an egg war and somebody will get killed. So I sold out and have made a reasonable living doing other things with less risk."

Mara's eyes were bright when she said, "I'd love to visit the islands."

"There are lots of seals and sea lions to see too. And something else. Once I watched a bunch of seals swimming rapidly toward land. One seal fell behind. Then something almost exploded from behind it. I caught a glimpse of a huge fish with a high dorsal fin. It was gone faster than I can tell it. So was the seal."

"Shark?" Mara asked.

"The captain told me later that it was a great white shark—probably fifteen, maybe twenty feet long."

Mara wasn't perturbed. "If I promise to stay out of the water, will you try to find someone who will take me out there someday?"

Merritt slowly shook his head. "I would rather not. It's just too dangerous. You see, it's not just what's in the water that's hazardous. There's really no easy place to land, and waves up to twenty-five feet pound those rocky shores. A person's boat can be swamped."

"But men have gone ashore to get the eggs."

"Oh, yes. It's risky, but it's done all the time in good weather. Once you're ashore, you could fall from a cliff and break your neck on rocks below or drown if you fall into the ocean."

"I'd still like to go. Will you help?"

"I really can't, Mara. It's too risky, and I don't want anything to happen to you."

"You're very kind and thoughtful. But as Shiloh must have told you, I'm used to getting what I want."

Smiling fondly, Merritt replied, "I wish I could talk you out of it."

"You can't."

"I probably shouldn't tell you this, but I have an old friend named Manton Briggs. He's still active in the business. You'll find him on Market Street near First. But he can't take a boat out until spring when the storms are over and the birds fly in to make their nests."

Merritt added, "If you talk to him, tell him I tried to discourage you from going out."

"Thank you." She gave him a grateful smile, reflected even more radiantly by the excitement already stirring within.

⬥⬥⬥

Clay stared in disbelief at Shiloh. "You what?"

She cringed at the sudden anger in his tone. "I wanted to tell you before you left."

"You should have waited until I got back!" He towered over her, his face flushed. "You had no business going to the general like that!"

Surprised and hurt at his reaction, Shiloh protested, "I didn't know when you'd be back. I thought I was doing the right thing. Anyway, it shouldn't make you angry."

He turned and paced the bedroom floor. "You've just created an awful problem for me!"

"How could I have . . . ?" she began, but he spun around and gripped her shoulders hard.

"It doesn't matter! You shouldn't have done such a thing!"

"You're hurting me."

"Sorry." He released her and stepped back. "I didn't mean to." He lowered his voice and held out his arms. "I'm just shocked."

She came to him, leaning her head against this chest. His

heart thudded rapidly against her ear as he pulled her tight. Then, abruptly, she guessed the truth.

She jerked away. "Oh, no! You were at that meeting! The night you went out without telling me where!"

"Shiloh . . ."

"Of course! I was blind! Oh, why didn't I think of that before I went to see the general? You were with Lafayette Montgomery when he and the others plotted to seize the arsenals. That's . . ."

She stopped, shaking her head violently. "No, you wouldn't. You couldn't! You were going to wait, to ask questions, to attend meetings. But *not* meetings like that!"

"I had no idea . . ."

"General Johnston must think you're a . . . a . . . " She couldn't say the loathsome word that sprang to her mind. She backed away from Clay, looking up at him in total disbelief. "No!" Her face contorted and scalding tears blurred her vision. "No!"

"It was a mistake to go there." He stepped toward her, but she backed away. "I didn't have any idea what was going to happen. If I had, I never would have gone!

"Never! Please, Shiloh! Believe me! This is going to be difficult enough without you turning against me!"

The words stung like a slap. "I'm not turning against you!" Her voice began to break. "I'm just hurt and . . . disappointed . . . and frightened. I . . . "

She left her sentence unfinished as Mara called from the foot of the stairs. "Shiloh, if you need more time with Clay, I'll see you another time."

She struggled to control her voice and whispered to Clay, "I can't talk to her right now."

Clay nodded and stepped to the door. "Mara, we're right in the middle of something important. Can you come back later?"

Mara gingerly touched her bruised cheek before replying. She wanted to talk with Shiloh, but she understood that a husband came first. "Of course," she called up. Turning toward the outside door, she added, "It'll probably be tomorrow before I can return."

"Thank you, Mara," Clay replied, and closed the bedroom door.

Shiloh dabbed at her misty eyes with a handkerchief. "I'm sorry you thought I was turning against you."

"I shouldn't have said that," Clay admitted. "I spoke out of turn." He reached out.

Wordlessly, she clung to him while the tears flowed.

He held her for a long time before whispering in her ear, "I'm sorry for raising my voice. I love you. I wouldn't hurt you for the world."

She raised her tear-stained face for his kiss. "I know. Now we've got to figure out what might happen when you meet with General Johnston."

Clay breathed a long, shuddering sigh. "A general has no authority over me as a civilian, but if there's an insurrection, the rules may change. I don't know for sure. But he must already know what he's going to say at that meeting; he may not want to hear why I was there."

Shiloh forced herself to ask calmly, "What . . . what's the worst that could happen?"

Drawing a slow breath, Clay said thoughtfully, "It primarily depends on where Johnston stands politically."

Hesitating, Clay reminded himself that the plan presented was treason against the United States government. Clay didn't agree with the plan, yet he could be judged guilty by association.

Shiloh prompted. "You mean, whether he's a southern sympathizer or not?"

"Exactly. He was born in Kentucky but has lived a long time in Texas, so he could truly favor the South. In that case, he might not do anything. Before our meeting on the eighteenth, I hope I'll get an opportunity to tell him what really happened. But he may not listen."

"You're not in the military." She stepped back to look up into her husband's eyes. "You told me that a general has no authority over you."

"Civil authorities would cooperate with the military in a case like this. There are two terrible crimes in any country: murder and rebellion against the government."

"But you're not planning to join in the rebellion!"

"I know, but I could still be accused of being a Copperhead, or worse. I could handle that, but I can't stand the thought of how it will affect you or our children. Somehow, I must clear myself."

Shiloh felt herself sinking in fear. Desperately, she asked, "You said it depends on where Johnston stands politically. What if he's not a southern sympathizer, but is loyal to the North?"

Clay didn't answer for several seconds. "Then I guess it's even more important to make him believe the real story of why I was at that meeting."

"I hope you can," she said.

He took her hand. "Let's put that in our prayers."

❧ CHAPTER II ❧

A LIGHT RAIN fell against Mara's bedroom window that night when she heard Lyman Wallace's code knock on her door. She closed her eyes and groaned. *Oh, no! I don't want him to see my face like this!*

She thought of not answering in hopes that he would think she had gone out, but she realized he could see the faint glow under the door from the gas lamp.

Quickly making a decision to stall, she called, "Just a minute." She turned down the light before opening the door an inch or so and hid her bruised cheek behind it. "Not to-night, Lyman."

"I just want to talk," he said in a low voice. The pale light from behind Mara illuminated his clean-shaven, grim face.

He pushed on the door, but she held it firmly. "I just can't tonight, Lyman."

"Don't tell me 'no'!" he growled, pushing harder against the door, forcing Mara to step back. The light hit her face. An expletive escaped him. "Who gave you that?" he demanded harshly. He stepped into the room and turned her face toward the lamp.

"I had an accident."

"You think I'm a fool, Mara? Who hit you?"

She closed the door and walked away from the light. "Nobody you know."

"Why did he do it?" His voice rose slightly. "No, let me guess. You've been sneaking around behind my back. What's his name?"

"It's not important."

"It is to me!" Wallace crossed quickly to confront her. Fury showed in his eyes. "I told you when I saw that big black buck that I would not share you with anybody! You said you understood, remember?"

She nodded. "Samuel hasn't bothered me."

"Then who?" He raised his voice. "I ought to give you more of the same. I put you up here, give you the best of everything, and this is how you repay me! Who is he?"

Mara stalled, fearful that if she mentioned Jared's name, Lyman might challenge him to a duel. Dueling had long been outlawed in California, but men still fought outside of town. Lyman Wallace had once challenged a fellow attorney named Gilkrist. They had met at sunrise a few miles south on the peninsula. As Gilkrist took aim, his hair-trigger pistol had discharged prematurely, and the ball had harmlessly struck the ground. Lyman had calmly shot Gilkrist in the heart. It was tempting to think of Jared losing his life for striking her, but Mara preferred to fight her own battles.

Wallace demanded, "I've got to know!"

Mara met his gaze with calm deliberation while her thoughts whirled. In a measured voice, she said, "I'm not going to tell you."

Lyman's tone turned cold. He warned, "I'm only going to ask one more time."

Her gaze never wavered. Tilting her chin up defiantly, she said, "Then what? You'll hit me too?"

He raised his hand. "I should. You deserve it!"

"Do what you want. I'm not going to name him."

He lowered his hand and clenched both fists. "Then I'll find out for myself," he warned through clenched teeth, "and take care of him. In the meantime, take your possessions and get out!"

"What?" Mara cried in disbelief. Never before had any man rejected her. She had always been the one in control, the one to leave.

"You heard me! Out!"

"Tonight? It's raining!"

"I don't care!" He stormed angrily toward the door. "Go to a hotel, or go to him! That'll make him easier to find. But get out—now!" He jerked the door open. "If you're still here in half an hour, I will physically throw you out!" He stormed down the enclosed stairs, leaving the door open.

Anger surged in her throat. In blind fury, she seized a book off the table and ran after him. She hurled it at him, but it hit the stairwell wall and flopped harmlessly to the bottom of the stairs. Lyman Wallace didn't look up; he disdainfully exited in silence.

For a long moment, Mara stared after him, breathing hard. She pressed both hands to her temples where blood furiously pounded against her fingers. *He can't do this to me.* She turned from the stairwell, seething, and slammed the door.

Early the next morning, Clay was the first customer at the downtown hotel restaurant where he had met General Johnston. If Johnston didn't come in for breakfast, Clay would try again at lunch or ask Bixby how to arrange a meeting.

Clay had rejected the prospect of calling at the Presidio because he knew military security might prevent him from seeing the general. Clay had also concluded that only as a last resort would he risk breaching etiquette by calling uninvited at Johnston's home.

Taking a seat where he could watch the door, Clay picked up the bill of fare as Cyrus Bixby entered.

"Morning, Cyrus," Clay said, standing quickly. "I was just thinking about you. Please join me."

"Thanks." The banker approached and shook Clay's hand. "You heard the latest news from back east?"

Clay shook his head. "I just got here."

The banker pulled out his chair. "The Pony Express arrived late yesterday with a report that secessionists have seized Fort Moultrie in Charleston Harbor near Fort McHenry."

"No!" Clay sat down hard, fearing the impact this might have on his upcoming meeting with General Johnston. "They didn't!"

Nodding emphatically, Bixby explained, "They took Union military property, and you know what that means."

"I can guess," Clay replied thoughtfully. "The federals won't stand for that. They'll want it back."

"Right! On the other hand, the rebels can't afford to let that happen."

Rebels! Clay cringed at hearing the word applied to secessionists. "Sounds bad," Clay admitted.

"There's more," Bixby continued, "Mississippi has voted to secede."

It shouldn't have surprised Clay, but he shook his head in disbelief. "When?"

"January ninth. The pony brought that word too. Florida,

Alabama, Georgia, Louisiana, and Texas are expected to soon follow."

Stunned, Clay stared at Bixby while the waiter poured coffee for both men.

"President Buchanan has already declared the federal government could not forcibly prevent the secessions," Clay mused, "so he probably won't act because his term is almost over. But when Lincoln takes over on March fourth . . ."

"The first shots of the war have already been fired," Bixby interrupted. "A ship called the *Star of the West* loaded with relief supplies for Fort Sumter . . ."

"That's a federal fort."

"Yes, but South Carolina has a battery on Morris Island, which is close by. They fired two rounds on the ship. It turned and sailed away, but you can be sure that's just the beginning. It's a terrible thing, but the Union can't let the secessionists go unchecked."

That news increased Clay's anxiety about Johnston. With war now a certainty, he had probably already made up his mind whether he would remain loyal to the blue uniform he wore. The prospect chilled Clay.

Bixby took a sip of coffee. "You were in the army. What do you think will happen next?"

Clay mused a moment before answering. "Two states can't take on the federal government, so South Carolina and Mississippi will probably wait until others join them."

"So the real hostilities won't begin until spring? Armies like to have the winter behind them."

"That's the way I see it," Clay admitted. "Meantime, judging from what happened at Fort Moultrie, more Union military installations will be seized. Buchanan will just sit out the rest of his presidency."

"He's going to leave the problem for Lincoln?"

When Clay nodded, Bixby declared, "I wonder whether General Johnston will be called back east or stay here."

Clay grasped the opening. Lowering his voice, he said, "You know him better than I do. Do you have any idea which side he favors?"

"Well, he just accepted another invitation to attend a Union Club meeting with me. Would you like to come too? Everybody liked Thomas Starr King so much we invited him back. What do you say?"

Clay nodded. "Sounds good. When?"

"This Friday, the eighteenth at seven thirty. Can you make it?"

He could, if all went well in the afternoon meeting with Johnston. If it didn't . . . Clay forced that thought aside.

Trying to remain hopeful, Clay told Bixby, "Let's plan on it."

⁂

The morning air was brisk and inviting, and Shiloh joined her children outside to take advantage of the lovely weather. As Philip playfully chased his sisters, Ajay and Shiloh laughed in delight.

Shiloh noticed Mara walking toward them and started to welcome her, then her eyes widened in surprise. "Mara! What happened to your face?"

"That's what I wanted to talk to you about yesterday."

"Let's go inside and talk. Ajay, would you keep an eye on your sisters and brother?"

Once they were settled in the parlor, Mara announced, "Lyman threw me out."

Shiloh sucked in her breath. "Did he hit you?"

"No, but when I wouldn't tell him who did, he got angry and told me to leave. I spent last night at the old house."

Shiloh critically studied Mara's face. "Then who did that?"

Shrugging, Mara explained, "It's not important."

"Not important? Anybody who'd hit a woman could do something worse!"

"He won't do it again, so let's forget about it."

"Well, if you don't want to talk about it, why are you here?"

Mara smiled at Shiloh. "I just needed to be with you a while, like in the old days."

Shiloh sighed. If Mara didn't want to talk about who had hit her, she'd find another subject. "All this political unrest reminds me of when California was admitted to the Union."

Mara chuckled. "Wasn't that something? The steamer *Oregon* came through the Golden Gate with a huge banner stretched across her whole length." She raised her hands as though pointing out the words, "'California admitted.'"

Shiloh's face lit up with the memory. "Flags flew, and people fired cannons, danced in the streets, and built bonfires at night. Oh, what a glorious time!"

Shiloh's voice softened. "No wonder I love this state so much."

"Where else could a woman like me, born a slave, become a wealthy woman?"

"This state has been very good to all of us."

Mara's eyes shone bright. "Remember in September of 1850 when Governor Burnett took a stage to San Jose to let the people at the capital know about being admitted?"

"Clay tried to get Governor Burnett to ride in one of our stages, but Burnett chose a Hall and Crandall stage."

Laughing with delight, Shiloh continued, "That didn't stop Clay. Remember how he raced Bob Crandall's stagecoach those fifty-some miles from San Francisco? Ajay was barely six months old."

Mara smiled as she remembered. "We really flew with those mustangs running their hearts out. So many people along the way rushed out to see what was going on. Remember that?"

"Oh, I'll never forget! The men took off their hats and waved, and you and I swung our bonnets out of the windows. Everyone shouted, 'California is admitted to the Union!'"

Both women fell silent. Crandall's stage had beat them by a few minutes. However, the newspapers had picked up the story of the baby racing the governor. That publicity had helped to establish Clay's stage line as one of the top three in the new state.

Shiloh surprised herself as a tear slid down her cheek. She gently brushed it away. She had seen California born and learned to love it as her own. Would she now see it die?

Mara stood and pulled Shiloh to her feet. "Thanks for a good laugh. I've got to be going."

Shiloh glanced at Mara's bruised face. "Please be careful."

"Nothing's going to happen to me."

"I hope you're right," Shiloh replied. Then she hugged Mara and let her out. When Shiloh had closed the door, she added under her breath, "But I'm frightened for you."

❧ CHAPTER 12 ❧

THE MOMENT Clay came home that evening, Shiloh read the disappointment in his face. He quickly changed his expression as the children joyfully welcomed him home, and he swept Emily up in a bear hug. Setting her down gently, Clay put his arms around Shiloh and whispered in her ear, "I didn't get to see him, but I'll keep trying."

"It'll work out." She tried to sound confident.

"I think I know how he got my name."

Shiloh's eyebrows rose as she asked, "How?"

"Indirectly because of you."

"Me?" Shiloh's voice shot up in alarm. "But I didn't even know you were there."

"Wait!" Clay put up his hand to check her words. "Let me explain."

Shiloh took a deep breath and nodded. "I'm listening."

"You gave Johnston all he needed when you told him that Lafayette Montgomery was involved."

"The meeting was held at his home."

"Right. Johnston must have talked to Montgomery."

"But you said you didn't know Montgomery. Does he know you?"

"He doesn't have to. He just had to have heard my name from someone at the meeting."

"I thought everyone had been sworn to secrecy."

"Yes, but most people can't keep secrets. Military officers are very skilled at getting one little piece of information from someone and another piece from someone else. All the pieces eventually fit together."

"Does that mean that the general knows about everyone who was there that night?"

"It sure seems likely."

"Then he must also know that you weren't a party to their plans." Shiloh's eyes lit up with hope. "He must already know that you had nothing to do with the plot to seize government property."

"The only one who knows I'm innocent is Asbury Harpending. If Johnston didn't talk to him, anybody else who was at that meeting would logically have concluded that I *was* a party to their plans."

"Then you have to make sure that Harpending tells the general the truth."

Clay shook his head. "I've thought about that and decided to stay away from him."

Shiloh protested, "But he could go see Johnston now, tell him what really happened, and maybe you wouldn't even have to attend the meeting on Friday."

"I don't want to be seen with any of those men." Clay's firm tone told Shiloh not to argue. "I'm going to keep trying to see Johnston so I know he gets the plain truth. I want to spend some time with the children, but after dinner, I'm going to walk up to the general's house. I know invading his privacy might make him angry. But you went to his home and he was nice to you. Perhaps I can at least get him to make an appointment."

Shiloh heaved a weary sigh. "I hope this doesn't just make things worse."

❧

Dusk had barely given way to darkness when Mara entered the small kitchen behind the main house she had bought from Shiloh. She lit the wall-mounted kerosene lamp to illuminate the stove area then reviewed the meager food supplies in the open cupboard.

The sound of a heavy foot on the step outside made her whirl toward the door. She plucked a knife from the small preparation table.

"Who's there?" she called through the solid door.

"It's me, Miss Mara."

"Samuel?" She opened the door a crack to confirm her guess. The big man stood there, hat in hand.

Mara asked, "What are you doing here?"

"I had some news, so I went by that mansion. You weren't there, so I got scared and went looking."

With a light laugh, Mara said, "You've found me, and I'm fine." She held the door open. "Come in."

He started to enter, then stopped, his eyes dropping to her hand. "You going to use that on me?"

She smiled and tossed the knife onto the table. "I wasn't sure who was at the door. I was just going to start dinner, but that can wait." She reached up for the lamp. "Come into the parlor and tell me your news."

Samuel nodded in acceptance and hung his hat on the peg behind the door. "At that other place, a new servant girl said you was gone but didn't know where. Then that white man, he heard me and ran me off."

Samuel interrupted himself as Mara lifted the lamp from its

mount and the light fell on her face. Staring at her bruised face, Samuel's voice rose angrily. "Did he do that? Is that why you left?"

"No, Lyman didn't do this."

Samuel bent to look closely at her injury. "If he did, I'll . . ."

"You'll do nothing!" Mara said firmly. "He didn't do it. Now, sit down and tell me your news."

The big man waited until Mara sat down before lowering himself into an old hickory rocker.

"I got a chance to make some extra money later this spring," he began. "That lawyer who's handling my freedom papers introduced me to a man who owns part of a seabird egg business. He says I can make real good money gathering eggs off some islands out in the ocean a ways."

Intrigued, Mara prompted, "Really?"

Samuel explained, "It's a short season, but the pay is better than anything I've done so far."

"Who is this man you met?"

"His name is Manton Briggs."

Mara nodded, recognizing the name Merritt Keene had given her.

Samuel continued, "Mr. Briggs says the pay's good because there's some risk in climbing around on those rocks out there. They're sometimes slick, and the wind can be high, so it's easy to fall. But I figure it's worth a try."

"I've heard about those eggs. I want to go out to the islands so I can see everything for myself."

Shaking his head, Samuel cautioned, "I wish you wouldn't, Miss Mara. I don't think I could live if anything happened to you."

Touched by the simple declaration, Mara also felt concerned that Samuel cared so much for her. She spoke gently, "You mustn't talk like that."

He exclaimed, "I can't help it. You're all I got in the world!"

"No, Samuel." She said bluntly. "I've tried my best to tell you where you and I stand."

"I know that, but I can't help myself. Like I said before, I'm going to keep hoping that you'll change your mind."

He stood abruptly, his voice rising, "I know I can never give you what those rich white men can, but I can give you something they can't." His voice softened as he added fervently, "I can give you a heart full of real love, and I'd do anything for you. Anything!"

"Please, Samuel!" She stood quickly and put her fingers to his lips. "Don't say such things."

She felt him tremble before he gently reached up and removed her fingers.

"I'm never going to give up because I can't." He abruptly turned away, snatched up his hat, and walked into the night.

Mara closed her eyes, touched by his devotion.

❧

Clay had called at the general's home, but a servant had informed him that the general had gone out.

Though he pretended not to be concerned, Shiloh sensed Clay's frustration. She persuaded him to let her join him for breakfast in hopes of lifting his mood.

As they walked toward Market Street, Shiloh lifted her eyes toward San Francisco's lofty Fern Hill. She said softly, "We've accomplished all of Aldar's dreams except for building a grand house up there. It seems so wrong that he can't enjoy them."

Clay followed her gaze but didn't reply. Aldar had been his friend, but if he was alive, Shiloh would still be Aldar's wife. He sometimes felt private moments of guilt because he had so much.

Shiloh continued in a soft, thoughtful way. "I would like to visit his grave again sometime soon."

"I'll hire a carriage and we can go there now."

Shiloh shook her head. "No, not right now. Not until this situation with the general is finished." She added with a touch of embarrassment, "I know it's silly, but when I go alone, I sometimes talk out loud. Not to Aldar, but to God. I ask Him to tell Aldar how things are. Is that wrong?"

"If it helps you to feel better, I can't see any harm in it."

Shiloh took Clay's arm and gave it a squeeze. "The things we've accomplished seemed so impossible, but because Aldar thought they could be done, we found a way."

Lifting her free hand, she added, "But I still don't know how we'll ever be able to build a house away up there."

"We'll find a way. I read about a young Scotsman named Andrew Hallidie. He has invented a wire rope that's so strong he thinks it can pull a little horse car up these hills. Maybe we can get building materials up there someday.

"I know it sounds impossible, but who knows? Very few people believed in Theodore Judah's dream—in fact they call him Crazy Judah. But he's already built a rail line out to Folsom. I'm convinced that someday rails will connect the East and West Coasts."

They had turned up Market Street when a stray dog suddenly darted from between a parked dray wagon's wheels. Instantly, a larger yellow cur chased after him and caught up with him in the middle of the street.

"Stay here!" Clay instructed Shiloh as he dashed toward the snarling and snapping dogs. Clay yelled at them, feeling sorry for the smaller animal. Suddenly, a third dog charged from an alley and hurled himself into the fight.

The big dog that had begun the attack tucked his tail and ran. Clay smiled as the last dog began to lick the smaller one's wounds.

Shiloh came up and took Clay's arm. "I've never seen anything like that."

"I recognize this little hero. He's a stray that hangs around and begs for food. People call him Bummer. I think the other dog is Lazarus."

"Oh, Ajay has talked about him. That's the dog who follows Emperor Norton around town."

"Speaking of his royal majesty," Clay remarked, jerking his head toward a small group of men ahead, "there he is, surrounded by his subjects."

"I've heard so much about him. Could we get a little closer so I can see him better?"

"Of course." Clay took her hand and hurried her along. "Just remember, he's very serious about being emperor."

The group parted so that Shiloh had her first full view of the man who called himself "Norton I, Emperor of the United States and Protector of Mexico." He stood under a tricolored umbrella with a certain royalty dignity even though his regimental blue uniform showed its age. His epaulets were tarnished, and a wilted flower sagged from his lapel. His beaver hat with a feather cockade was a little sad with time, but all the men around him treated him with respect.

Clay continued, "He dropped out of sight for a few years after he lost everything trying to corner the rice market. Then one day he got the editor of the *Evening Bulletin* to run an announcement in which he proclaimed himself emperor of the United States."

"Sort of like Denby Gladwin would like to be head of the Empire of Pacifica," Shiloh mused.

"Not quite," Clay disagreed. "Gladwin and his separate-nation advocates have all their mental faculties. Anyway, the paper ran Norton's little proclamation. That's how it started."

As Clay and Shiloh approached San Francisco's most famous character, he caught sight of Shiloh. Bowing gallantly, he said grandly, "Welcome to the court of Norton I." Straightening, he extended his free hand.

Somewhat flustered, Shiloh took it, then smiled at the

benign-looking man. "Thank you," she said. Then, glancing around and seeing the encouraging looks on the onlookers' faces, she added, "your majesty."

He again bowed to her, his beaver hat tipping slightly forward over his eyes. "You may proceed with your day's activities," he said gravely, and turned back to continue his conversation with the group of men.

Walking on with Clay, Shiloh glanced back. "What a delightful character!"

"San Francisco is a unique place," Clay admitted. "Where else could you find people who would treat such an unfortunate man so well?"

At Shiloh's questioning expression, Clay explained. "A printer provides Norton with scrip with a face value of fifty cents. All the stores and restaurants honor it even though it's worthless. Not that Norton needs real money. He is admitted to any theater when there's a vacant seat. For a man who has lost it all, he still has a lot."

Shiloh didn't reply until they reached the restaurant where Clay opened the door. "I wish we could solve our problems as easily."

"Only a few more days and we will," Clay assured her.

Shiloh nodded, but doubts still clung to her.

The next few days were filled with frustration. Clay tried to see General Johnston at the Presidio but, without a pass, was turned away by soldiers at the gate. A second evening call at the general's home again found him out.

On the morning of the eighteenth, Shiloh and Clay rose after a restless night. Neither mentioned the importance of the afternoon meeting with General Johnston.

As the family gathered for breakfast, Merritt knocked on the back door then stepped inside without waiting for Lizzie to admit him.

After greeting everyone, Merritt pulled a chair to the table. "All set for tonight, Clay?"

"Tonight?" Clay repeated, confused. Then he nodded in understanding. "Oh, the Union Club meeting. Yes, I'm ready."

Clay glanced at Shiloh, and she realized that his thoughts had been only on his meeting with Johnston.

Merritt said, "I heard this Thomas Starr King isn't mincing any words about where he stands on secession."

"I think his talk this evening with be interesting," Clay replied.

Merritt shifted his attention to the children. "It's going to be a pretty nice day. How would all of you like to go for a ride to the beach and have a picnic with your . . ."

He was interrupted by four happy cries of acceptance. Turning to his daughter and son-in-law, he announced, "I guess that leaves you two alone for the day. Think you can find something to do by yourselves?"

Shiloh rose quickly and came around the table to kiss him on the cheek. "You're wonderful, Papa."

"Don't you forget that," he said with a broad smile before turning to the children. "Now, where do we want to go and what should we take to eat?"

Fifteen minutes before two o'clock, Clay and Shiloh arrived at the Presidio. Shiloh had helped Clay choose his best clothes and cravat.

When he had dressed to her satisfaction, she stood back and nodded approval. "General Johnston will take one look at you and know you're innocent," she declared. "Then you can breathe easily tonight when you hear King speak."

The day had dragged, but finally the meeting with the general was about to begin. Clay wrapped the reins around the buggy whip socket and turned to look at Shiloh. He waited until she glanced up.

"I'm sorry that I didn't get to talk to Johnston," he said quietly. "But I will be all right."

Nodding, Shiloh agreed, "I'll wait where I can see you come out again."

He took her face in his hands and kissed her tenderly. Then, wordlessly, he turned and walked toward the sentry. He heard the buggy wheels crunch on sand as Shiloh pulled away.

Clay reached into his suit pocket and produced the general's summons.

"Clay!" The man's voice startled Clay.

Asbury Harpending, leaving his two companions to join Clay, asked, "What're you doing here?"

"I think you know," Clay replied coolly.

The younger man frowned. "Know what?"

Clay stalled, glancing at the other two men. He recognized them from the meeting at Lafayette Montgomery's home. "You're all together?"

"Yes, of course." Harpending glanced around and lowered his voice. "Do you know them?"

"I met them at Montgomery's, but I don't know their names."

Harpending leaned closer to Clay. "It's just as well. You see, there's been a problem since that night. That's why we're here."

Clay had to ask. "What happened?"

Harpending continued quietly, "Do you know Edmond Randolph?"

"I've met him." Clay was thoroughly puzzled but eager to learn more. "He's a very respected attorney here in the city. Originally of Virginia, as I remember. He's been outspoken in supporting the South. Why?"

"He's a member of our committee, but he is also very close to General Johnston, both professionally and socially." Harpending shot a nervous look around. "Without any authority from our committee, Randolph said something to Johnston."

Clay raised his eyebrows in surprise.

"Nobody knows what he said, but Johnston replied in such a way that it made Randolph absolutely furious. In his anger, he committed an incredible indiscretion."

Harpending paused, scowling deeply. "Some of our members saw Johnston and reported back that our cause is lost."

Clay struggled to grasp the significance of this unexpected development. "Lost?" he repeated.

"So it seems. However, after discussion at several meetings, it was decided a committee of three would call on Johnston. In a social way, I mean, so that some firm idea could be gained about what our future should be."

Clay forced himself to take a quiet breath to hide the hope he suddenly felt. "So you and those two," he slightly inclined his head toward the other men, "are the committee?"

"To my joy, yes, I was among those chosen. But," Harpending hesitated, studying Clay's face, "why are you here?"

Without a word, Clay handed over the general's note.

The younger man read it, frowning thoughtfully. "That's the same time our committee is to have an audience with the general. I don't understand why you were summoned."

"Neither do I," Clay admitted.

"Well," Harpending said, "I guess you'll soon find out. I'd better get back to the other committeemen."

"Wait!" Clay impulsively reached out and caught the other man's elbow. "You must know how very surprised I was at what happened at the meeting the other night. If I had known its purpose, I never would have gone."

"I was impulsive, I admit. I apologize. After we finish with the general, I'd like to meet with you on another matter."

Clay looked at Harpending in disbelief. "What makes you think I would want to discuss anything else with you?"

"Because the states of our birth are in dire peril."

"Stop!" Clay held up both hands, palms outward. "I told you once that I'm not going to make any decisions until after the inauguration. And I'd like you to undo the injustice you did me."

"Injustice?"

"Yes! Letting me blunder into that meeting. When we meet

with General Johnston, I want you to tell him the truth about that."

Harpending's eyes narrowed. "Tell him yourself."

Clay started to make an angry reply but noticed the sentry's approach. The officer announced, "The general will see you gentlemen now. Please follow me."

Clay licked his suddenly dry lips, wondering what the next several minutes would do to his life.

～§ CHAPTER 13 §～

CLAY, HARPENDING, and the two members of the Knights of the Golden Circle were ushered into General Johnston's office. All four visitors stood until he politely invited them to be seated.

Settling well forward in his chair, Clay anxiously glanced around the room. Under the American flag a large map covered the wall behind the desk. Clay's eyes flickered across the map then focused on the sites he knew the three men seated beside him had intended to seize. Fort Point was armed with two hundred soldiers, not even a hundred at Alcatraz, and only a few at Mare Island. The biggest prize was the Benicia Arsenal across the bay where the Knights expected to confiscate thirty thousand arms.

The general began speaking casually. "I have heard foolish talk about a scheme to seize the strongholds of the government that are under my charge."

Clay squirmed as Johnston continued.

"I have prepared for emergencies." He paused, his eyes boring into each visitor's face by turns. "I will defend the property of the United States with every resource at my command and with the last drop of blood in my body."

Still speaking in an offhanded manner, he added, "If you wish, you may tell that to our southern friends."

There was no threat in Johnston's words or manner, yet his meaning was so powerful that the four men facing him sat stiffly silent.

Clay tried to think how to convey his innocence, but the general nonchalantly glanced out the window. "It's going to be a very pleasant day, isn't it, gentlemen?"

The three Knights of the Golden Circle, in obvious relief, commented on the weather. Clay merely nodded, wondering if he had been fretting for nothing these past days. His thoughts raced with how best to explain why he had been at the clandestine Knights meeting. He preferred to speak privately to Johnston, but that opportunity was quickly slipping away.

The general said good-bye to the men then added, "Mr. Patton, would you remain a moment, please?"

Surprised, Clay merely nodded. Harpending gave him a quizzical look before walking down the hallway with his two companions. The general closed the door and motioned for Clay to again be seated. Clay obeyed, feeling pleased that he would have an opportunity to clarify his involvement yet a little concerned over why he had been singled out to remain behind.

Shiloh waited impatiently in the buggy. Two of the men who had gone in with him came out, but Clay and Asbury Harpending did not.

What's going on in there? Shiloh wondered.

She was startled by a man's voice: "Hello, Shiloh."

She spun around in the seat. "Jared! I didn't hear you approach."

Smiling, he rested his foot on the high step, making the buggy tip slightly toward him. "I suppose that's because you were concentrating so hard on watching for your husband."

A quick frown flickered across Shiloh's brow. "Have you been spying on me?" she asked a little sharply. Old, unpleasant memories of Jared's behavior streaked through her mind.

"Not spying," Jared assured her with a disarming smile. "I happened to be driving by a while ago when you dropped Clay off. I'm on my way back, and I stopped to see if I can be of any service to you."

"No, thank you." Shiloh hoped her tone carried enough coolness to discourage further conversation.

"Then perhaps you could do something for me?"

The thought surprised Shiloh. She lifted an eyebrow in a silent question.

"You have a great deal of influence with Mara," Jared explained when she did not speak. "I would appreciate your saying a good word to her on my behalf."

Shiloh replied coldly, "I don't think anything I might say would favorably influence Mara about you."

Undaunted, Jared tried again. "Some of her friends don't have her best interest at heart."

"And you do?" Shiloh looked back toward the Presidio gate, vainly hoping to see Clay. "I cannot help you, Mr. Huntley."

Jared shrugged at the use of his surname. "Please listen to me. I'm in a position to hear and know many things going on in high places."

"So I have heard." Shiloh let the frost in her tone show she was through with the discussion.

"Allow me to say one more thing, then I'll leave."

She turned to give him a stern look. "If it were up to me, Mara would get rid of all the men in her life and settle down with a decent one."

Jared stood in momentary silence, meeting the firm resolve in Shiloh's eyes with his own. Finally he said, "These are uncertain and difficult times. Mara needs someone like me to see her safely through the days ahead."

Shiloh scowled down at the lawyer. "Is that a threat, Mr. Huntley?"

He smiled pleasantly, "I just wouldn't want anything to happen to Mara or to your husband. Good day."

Shiloh watched him stride away. He approached a carriage, and a driver in livery jumped down from his seat to open the door. Jared didn't look toward Shiloh while the driver closed the door, returned to his seat, and drove off. Shiloh tried to shake off her alarm. Had Jared threatened them? Or was that just another of his lies? Impatiently, she glanced toward the Presidio. *What's keeping Clay?*

Deep in thought when he left the general's office, Clay couldn't wait to tell Shiloh some of the thought-provoking comments Johnston had made about what he had studied as a West Point cadet. Johnston had offered no opinion but had merely pointed out what he had been taught and what Thomas Jefferson and James Madison had said on the issues now threatening to engulf the country in civil war.

Clay had walked about halfway down the hall when Asbury Harpending shoved himself away from the wall. "I've been waiting for you," he announced. "As I indicated before the meeting, I would like to talk with you on another matter."

Clay kept walking, forcing the younger man to fall into step with him. "We have nothing to say to each other."

"Look, Clay, I'm sorry about what I said awhile ago. I'm a little hotheaded."

"It doesn't matter." Clay approached the outside door. "If you'll excuse me, my wife is waiting."

"I understand." Harpending took a couple of quick steps to open the door. "You were in there with the general for a long time."

"That was his choice," Clay replied, exiting the building.

"I figured that, since he invited you to stay behind." Harpending matched Clay's step again. "Did it have anything to do with me?"

Clay increased his pace. "Not a thing."

"I know you're in a hurry, but please listen to me for a minute. I wanted to talk to you about . . ."

Clay interrupted. "I do not have time to listen."

The younger man's face flushed at the rebuff.

"You have time for this. I'm going to meet with certain high officials from the South. When I return, I expect to have letters of marque."

"I don't know the term," Clay admitted.

"I will have authority to arm ships and use them to seize other vessels off the California coast in retaliation for what the Union will undoubtedly do to the South."

"You're talking piracy."

"We prefer the term *privateer;* it's not the same thing at all. Pirates are individuals whose ships attack any prize on the seas. Privateers are government-sponsored ships that are armed to prey on another country's vessels."

Intrigued, Clay stopped. "Millions in California gold are shipped annually from here to the East. You propose to intercept that bullion and turn it to your own purposes."

"To *our* purposes, Clay. That is, the South's, where both you and I were born and to which we owe allegiance."

"When I signed up for the army years ago, I took an oath of allegiance to the United States, not to my native Texas." Clay had thought about that oath a lot recently.

"Times are different now. Soon you'll see countless officers still on active duty resigning from the army to support their native states. They have a right to then swear allegiance to the states that gave them life. After all, there's nothing in the Constitution that gives the federal government power over the rights of individual states."

Clay pursed his lips, recalling General Johnston's private comments. "I think I see what you mean. Your armed vessel would lie in wait for, say, the Pacific Mail's SS *Oregon* and seize her gold shipment."

"Wars cannot be fought without money. California's bullion may be what tips the scales in favor of the Union unless that gold is intercepted and diverted to the South."

Clay nodded. He knew that the Pacific Mail ships could

carry more than a million dollars in gold to the Philadelphia Mint.

"Why are you telling me this?" Clay asked.

"Two reasons. You have money, and it takes plenty of that to properly outfit a clipper schooner. We would like you to join us in this venture. And I believe you will stand with the South when the time comes."

"You're assuming an awful lot. How do you know I won't tell the revenue service about our conversation?"

Shrugging, Harpending explained, "You're a man of integrity, a true southern gentleman whose word is his bond."

Annoyed, Clay replied a little sharply, "I haven't given you my word on this conversation."

"I know, but I have inquired about you, and I feel satisfied that my confidence is well placed."

Clay couldn't resist asking, "Suppose you're wrong?"

"I don't expect to be. You don't need to give me an answer until I return. Meanwhile, think about it."

When Shiloh finally saw Clay, Asbury Harpending was with him. Countless questions buzzed through her head as Clay approached the buggy.

While he hoisted himself into the seat beside her, she nervously asked, "What happened?"

"General Johnston warned Harpending and the others that he had heard talk about a scheme to seize federal property and that he wasn't going to let it happen."

"That's all?"

"That's it. No threats. Just a flat statement."

"What's going to happen now?"

"My guess is that Harpending and the others will ponder that very question."

"And then?"

Clay took the reins and clucked to the horse. "I don't know, but at least I'm out of it."

"Did you tell the general that you wouldn't have attended

that meeting at Montgomery's home if you had known what they'd discuss?"

"He already knew."

Shiloh looked sharply at Clay as he guided the horse along the street. "How could he?"

"Same way he found out who was there, I suppose. Anyway, Johnston asked me to stay after our meeting. I started to tell him why I was at the Knights' meeting, but he stopped me. He knew I wasn't a member of the Knights of the Golden Circle or in on the plot to seize government property."

"That took all this time?"

"Oh, no. He casually mentioned the Kentucky and Virginia Resolutions, which were passed in 1798 and 1799."

"What are they?"

"As Johnston explained it, the Kentucky Resolutions were written by Thomas Jefferson. They said that the federal government had no right to exercise powers not specifically delegated to it by the Constitution."

"Really?"

"Really. Not only that, the resolutions state that if the federal government did assume such powers, the states had a right to judge the constitutionality of the government's acts."

Shiloh shifted uneasily. Clay had just learned from very high civic authority that the South's actions were legitimate. This could persuade Clay to support policies she strongly opposed.

"The Virginia Resolutions," Clay continued, unaware of her sudden concern, "were written by James Madison. They aren't as strong as Kentucky's, but they have been considered important statements on the theory of states' rights."

Shiloh's sense of concern rose. "Why did Johnston tell you all this?"

"I don't know. Maybe he just sensed that I was very interested."

"Because you were born in Texas?"

"I didn't tell him that."

"Maybe you didn't have to. He already knew a lot about

you. Maybe he was testing to see where you stand on the question of states' rights."

"That's possible. What really intrigued me was his mention of a textbook used at the U.S. Military Academy, *View of the Constitution* by a lawyer named Riyal. The only line I remember went something like, 'The secession of a state from the Union depends upon the will of the people of such state.'"

Shiloh exclaimed, "Are you serious?"

"He showed me a copy of Riyal's writings. It clearly said that it depends upon the state itself whether it will continue as a member of the Union."

"He learned that at West Point?" Shiloh asked. In a low, fearful voice, she added, "Has that helped you make up your mind?"

"Not even Jefferson and Madison are going to make me choose until I see what Lincoln does in March."

Shiloh took a deep breath. As she quietly let it out as a long, slow sigh of relief, she thought about her conversation with Jared and of seeing Clay with Harpending after the meeting with the general. But she didn't want to discuss either now. She needed to mull over what impact the general's words might eventually have on Clay.

❧

Working at the kitchen range, Mara heard footsteps outside. She quickly retrieved her derringer from a drawer and slipped it into her apron pocket. Its weight comforted her as she answered a knock at the door.

"Evening, Mara," Lyman Wallace said, the light from indoors falling on his face.

She remembered how he had curtly ordered her out of his house. Abruptly she stated, "I'm busy," then started to close the door.

"Wait! Please!" Wallace didn't try to block the door but simply held up his hands. "I've come to apologize. May I come in?"

Mara's free hand touched her face where Jared's blow had landed. She hesitated, before reminding Lyman, "You said some terrible things to me."

"I know," he answered contritely. "I was wrong."

She opened the door wider. "Come in."

He followed her to the small parlor next to the kitchen. Waiting until Mara took a chair, he seated himself beyond the box stove, which glowed with pleasant warmth.

"Please be brief, Lyman."

He tried a smile. "As a counselor, I need to build my case."

"As the judge and the one in charge here," she shot back, "I will give you one minute for your presentation."

He laughed, throwing back his head. "You are a delight, Mara! Direct and honest. Very well, I want you back. Will you come?"

"Why should I?" She said it harshly, intending to keep control of the situation.

"Several reasons. You and I have made a lot of money together when I've represented you in negotiations where . . ." he broke off, aware that he had been about to make an unpardonable mistake.

"Where my color would be a concern," she finished for him. "I know full well that some people will not sell or buy from me because of something beyond my control."

"That's the practical reason. For another, how about this: I miss you and want you back."

It had been a good arrangement, Mara knew. Except for his impulsive action in throwing her out, they had gotten along well. "Go on," she said.

"I haven't been able to sleep or think about anything else since you left."

Mara tried to not be annoyed that he could not bring himself to say *I love you,* or even, *I care for you.*

"Malvina hates me, not that I blame her. I've had my share of people resenting me, but she goes out of her way to try to humiliate me. She spoke to me once about her 'white man's religion,' as though I had never heard of God. But I bet I learned as many Bible verses when I was a girl as she did."

"It doesn't matter what she thinks; she moved out."

Surprised, Mara exclaimed, "Why?"

"Something about a silly doll that turned up in my things. She insists that it's some kind of magic. She had a Negro servant from Louisiana some time back, and according to what she said, that doll is supposed to mean I'm going to die. Of course, I laughed at such a stupid idea. That set her off. We got to quarreling more and more. So she left."

Mara guessed, "You also told her that you wanted me to come back, didn't you?"

"I always did say you are a very discerning woman, Mara. Yes, that made her pack and leave." Lyman paused, looking intently at Mara across the stove. "Will you come back?"

"I don't know." Mara stood. "I'll think about it."

Rising, Lyman asked, "When will you decide?"

"I can't say." She led the way back into the kitchen and the outside door.

"Don't take too long."

She whirled on him. "Don't tell me what to do!"

Anger surged across his face. He opened his mouth to reply, then closed it with a click of teeth. "I'm sorry."

Mara turned away so that he couldn't see her satisfied smile.

─⊰ঽ⊱─

Feeling much more at ease after his meeting with General Johnston, Clay happily joined Cyrus Bixby to hear Thomas Starr King. Clay and the banker broke off greeting other men to find seats down front before the hall filled up.

Clay's thoughts flickered back to the earlier events of the day. He wasn't sure what to make of Shiloh's concern about Jared Huntley's veiled threats.

Bixby broke into Clay's reflections. "How much do you know about King?"

"Very little. I heard he arrived here last June. He's a power-ful speaker who says what he thinks."

The banker raised his voice slightly so Clay could hear above the hubbub of voices. "Well, King began teaching when he was sixteen and was a schoolmaster at nineteen. He reads French, Spanish, Latin, Italian, and a little Greek."

"That's pretty impressive."

"There's more, of course. For eleven years he was minister of Hollis Street Unitarian Church in Boston. The congregation increased fivefold during that time. When King came to San Francisco, the local church had a thirty-thousand-dollar debt. By Christmas, he had done a fabulous job of paying off the debt."

"He obviously gets things done," Clay admitted.

"I think if he had been in California sooner, Lincoln would have won here by more than 711 votes."

Clay nodded, believing Lincoln had carried California only because Stephen Douglas and John Breckenridge split the Democratic Party by each claiming to be the nominee.

Clay glanced at the stage as two men walked on and took chairs. The slender, clean-shaven, quite boyish-looking man sat to the right of the stage.

"That's King on the right," Bixby whispered to Clay.

He nodded and settled down to listen.

❧ CHAPTER 14 ❧

CLAY HAD come prepared to listen with an open mind. Thomas Starr King stood at the podium looking young, fragile, and not at all like a man who, at a hundred and twenty pounds, was already regarded as a heavyweight in political power.

At King's first words, the audience hushed expectantly. His voice was rich, a golden flow that gently gathered the listeners and gradually swept them along as he built from point to point.

He spoke bluntly, saying war seemed to be coming but calling it "a geographical wrong, a moral wrong, a war against the Constitution, against the New Testament, and against God."

Cyrus leaned over and whispered to Clay, "That's putting it pretty strong. I like that."

Clay didn't reply but continued to listen. King brought applause with his assessment of the coming insurrection. "Rebellion sins against the Mississippi; it sins against the coastline; it sins against the ballot box; it sins against oaths of allegiance; it sins against public and beneficent peace; it sins worst of all against the cornerstone of American progress and history and hope: the worth of the laborer and the rights of man. It strikes for barbarism against civilization."

Clay did not join in the applause. As it died down, he was vaguely aware that the man sitting to his right was staring at him. Clay avoided meeting his eyes.

Speaking of the president of the Confederate States of America, King cried, "To my soul and conscience, he is a representative of a force of evil. His cause is a pollution and horror. His banner is a black flag."

Clay stirred in his seat while King continued about Jefferson Davis: "I would pray for him as one man, a brother, in his private affectional and spiritual relations with heaven. But as president of the seceding states—of the brigand forces, organic representative of the powers of destruction within our country—pray for him? As soon as for Antichrist! Never!"

The pro-Union throng exploded in thunderous applause. Clay did not join in even when he felt Cyrus Bixby's eyes on him. Clay thought about what Thomas Jefferson and James Madison had written about states' rights to secede.

It seemed to Clay that states had a perfect right to withdraw from the Union, yet King's audience clearly did not agree. When he built to his closing, "I pledge California to a northern republic and to a flag that should have no treacherous threads of cotton in its warp," the audience broke into thunderous applause. The boyish speaker with the spell-binding voice waited to conclude his remarks.

As the clapping finally died down, King cried out, "God bless the president of the United States and all who serve with him the cause of a common country."

Men leaped to their feet, shouting and clapping and thumping each other on the back. Clay found himself standing, stirred so deeply he could not speak or even look at the banker next to him. Instead, Clay stared in awe at the beardless little man who had impacted the entire city of San Francisco with his pro-Union message. Someone down front leaped on the stage and called out, "Three cheers for Thomas Starr King and Abe Lincoln!"

When the echoes died away, Cyrus turned to Clay. "Did you ever hear anyone like him?"

"Never," Clay admitted. He started to follow the banker toward the aisle when someone tapped him on the shoulder. He turned to face the burly, red-faced man who had sat to his right.

"I didn't see you clapping, Mister. You a secesh?"

"I came to listen and learn," Clay replied mildly. He started to turn back toward Bixby, but the belligerent man grabbed his arm.

"We don't like Copperheads in this town."

He glanced down at his captive arm then looked into the other man's angry brown eyes. "I'm not a Copperhead." Clay's voice was calm, but he felt his blood start to race.

"You sure as blazes don't act like no real American!"

Clay faced his challenger with deliberate coolness. He had learned to stay even-tempered when dealing with occasional bellicose passengers riding his stagecoach.

"You have a right to your opinion," Clay said softly; his words were barely audible. He slowly pulled his arm from the other man's hand, saying, "I have a right to mine. Isn't that the American way?"

For a moment, the burly man hesitated, then he slowly lowered his eyes from Clay's dominant gaze. Without another word, Clay turned away and followed Bixby outside.

"Sorry about that, Clay," Bixby apologized. "Emotions are running pretty high these days."

Nodding, Clay agreed, silently adding to himself, *And it's going to get worse.*

After making sure the fires were safely banked in the heating box stove and the kitchen range, Mara reached for the kerosene lamp for the walk to the main house.

Glancing out the window, she froze at a shadowy movement in the shrubbery outside. Could it be the same person who had left muddy footprints by the fence post or followed her though the night near Lyman Wallace's mansion?

Calmly she decided to do without the light. She blew out the lamp on the wall bracket. In the darkness, she palmed her derringer. Then, instead of going out the kitchen door, she crouched low and entered the small parlor. Staying low so she could not be seen through the single window, she scurried into the tiny bedroom at the far end of the building. Quietly, she stood up, opened the door, slipped outside, and ducked around the side of the building.

Again bending so she was even with the shrubbery, she neared the kitchen area. She stopped and listened, her hand steady on the small but deadly weapon.

Her straining ears caught a faint sound of movement. She eased around the corner and froze. Mara could just discern the outline of someone standing near the door.

"Don't move!" she commanded, bringing up the gun.

She heard a sharp intake of breath from the shadowy figure. Straightening up, Mara took a few quick steps forward.

"Mara? Is that you?" Jared asked over his shoulder.

"What are you doing here?" she demanded, reaching up with her free hand to touch her bruised face.

"I've got to see you." He started to turn around, but Mara stopped him with a quick warning.

"Don't move a muscle unless I tell you to." She closed the distance between them and shoved the derringer's blunt barrel against his back. "Now, answer me."

"I've come to warn you about something. Please, can we go inside to talk?"

"After what you said and did to me the last time, I should pull this trigger and tell the authorities that I thought you were trying to kill me."

"They'd say you were justified, too, but you're not going to do that because you're in danger and I'm the only one who can help you."

Mara hesitated, then laughed softly. "Why should I believe you? You're a liar through and through, and always have been."

"Not this time. Believe me! Do you want to hear what I came to tell you, or will you pull the trigger and let Locke get you?"

Mentioning that name had the desired affect. "I'll listen," Mara decided. "Walk ahead of me, but don't make me nervous."

Mara lit the table lamp and picked it up with her left hand but kept the derringer in her right. "In there," she said, motioning toward the small parlor.

She set the lamp on a small writing desk under the window. Pale yellow light illuminated Jared's face.

"Talk," she commanded, sitting across from him.

"A friend who's in a position to know told me today that Locke is losing everything."

"How do I know you're not lying?"

"Because I want something in return for the information I have, and I don't want to make you any more angry."

With a sardonic laugh, Mara exclaimed, "You've got even more nerve than I thought. No man ever hit me before, and no one will ever do it again, especially you."

"I'm sorry, Mara. I lost my head."

"You're liable to lose more than that before I make you finish paying for what you did. I owe you for that. So before I decide to settle that right now, give me the whole story about Locke."

"He overextended his credit in buying some property that he can't sell, and his creditors are hounding him. If he goes under, he's going to blame you."

"I suppose," Mara said with thinly veiled sarcasm, "he told you this, so you know it's true?"

"He was drinking with some men and a friend of mine overheard him. Believe me, I'm convinced it's true."

Mara regarded Jared with suspicion. "What am I supposed to give you in return for this information?"

"Move in with me."

She stared across the room, then threw back her head and laughed.

"Don't do that!" The ugly edge in his voice stopped Mara. "No man can stand to have a woman laugh at him."

She glared at him. "What will you do? Hit me again?"

With a visible effort, he brought his anger under control. "Not while you're holding that gun." He tried to make his tone light, but Mara continued to glare at him.

"You'd better go," she said, rising.

He hesitated, then also stood. "There's something else you should know."

"Oh?" She suspected he was going to lie in a desperate effort to change her mind.

"Your friend, Shiloh . . ." he began, but Mara cut him off by demanding sharply, "What about her?"

"There are two secret societies of armed men in this state plotting to seize federal property, especially weapons."

"I know about the Knights of the Golden Circle."

"As of today, they're probably going to disband in California."

That was news to Mara. "Why would they do that?"

"Ask your friend Shiloh."

Mara frowned. "How in the world would she know?"

Jared seemed pleased that he had learned something before Mara. He replied, "Some Knights of the Golden Circle were called before General Johnston today. He warned them that he knew of their plans and wouldn't let it happen."

"You expect me to believe you have contacts inside a general's office?"

"Ask Shiloh. Her husband was at that meeting."

That startled Mara. She knew Jared wouldn't have told her a lie about something she could easily check. "I will," Mara decided. "What's the other secret society you mentioned, and what does it have to do with Shiloh?"

"The other group is called Knights of the Columbian Star."

"You're making this up!"

"Absolutely not! This group has avoided publicity, but I know it has at least sixteen thousand men ready to rule by force and push California out of the Union."

"To form a separate nation? That sounds like Denby Gladwin's Pacifica idea."

"It's similar, and he may be involved. But instead of remaining independent, this plan calls for California to join the Confederacy."

"What's this got to do with Shiloh?"

"They're going to invite Clay to join them, and if he doesn't . . ." Jared shrugged.

"Don't play games with me, Jared!"

"They plan to spread rumors that he has joined and take other steps to force him in."

Mara's dark eyes snapped angrily. "If you're lying to me. . . ."

"I'm not," Jared broke in. "The Star people need Clay's money to support their cause. Ask Shiloh about his meeting with the general. When you find I'm right about that, then maybe you'll believe me about the Star movement. I'll come back in a couple of days for your answer about moving in with me."

Mara started to protest that she never would do that but decided to keep silent for the moment. She let Jared leave then sat by the box stove, deep in thought.

~⚬~

Shiloh rose before the children awakened and had breakfast with Clay. He wanted to spend a few hours at his office even though it was Saturday. Shiloh sat alone in the kitchen with a final cup of coffee and reflected on the day before.

They had agreed things had turned out well with General Johnston. Shiloh hoped that Clay's reaction to last night's rousing speech by King would help move him toward supporting the Union. For the first time since news came of South Carolina's secession, Shiloh saw possibility.

Mara arrived at the back door. Shiloh saw with a single glance at her friend's face that something was wrong.

"What is it?" Shiloh asked anxiously.

"That coffee smells good. Any left?"

Shiloh nodded. When both had settled with their cups, Shiloh repeated her question.

Mara parried with one of her own. "Did Clay meet with General Johnston and some members of the Knights of the Golden Circle?"

Startled, Shiloh looked across the table. "Yes, but how did you hear about that?"

"Jared came by the house last night. He told me." Mara sipped her coffee before asking, "Is it true that Johnston warned the Knights that he wouldn't let them seize control of federal property?"

"Johnston apparently said it very casually, so it didn't sound like a threat. But there's no doubt that's how the members of the knights took it." Hesitating, Shiloh added, "Is that why you're here so early this morning?"

"Partly that, and partly because Jared said Clay is being targeted by another group."

"He's not going to join anybody until after Lincoln takes office." Frowning, Shiloh asked, "What's the name of this second group?"

"Jared says they're called the Knights of the Columbian Star."

"I've never heard of them."

"They keep out of sight, but there are at least sixteen thousand of them. They're probably tied in with Denby Gladwin in his Empire of the Pacific. Jared says their real purpose is to first form a separate nation, then join the South."

Shiloh leaned back in her chair. "We both know that Jared Huntley can't be trusted."

"He's an accomplished liar, all right, but I think he's telling the truth about this."

"Even if he is, it doesn't matter. Clay is very firm in his decision not to make a choice for the present."

Mara carefully set her cup in the saucer before asking, "Suppose he was forced?"

Shiloh smiled. "You know my husband. He can't be pushed."

"Jared seemed to think that Clay might be set up in a trap so that it wouldn't matter whether he was actually involved."

Shiloh leaned forward and cradled her cup. "Are you trying to frighten me?"

"You know I wouldn't do that. But I believe Jared in this instance. He's pinning some high hopes on this information."

"I don't believe Clay's in any danger," Shiloh said stoutly. "But I'm not so sure about you. I hope and pray that you'll stop what you've been doing before something terrible happens."

"The old sow-and-reap thing again?" Mara pushed her chair back from the table and stood up.

"Wait!" Shiloh quickly rose and came around the table to

keep her friend from leaving. "We could always talk about anything. Please don't go now!"

"I've said what I came for. Warn Clay to be careful."

Shiloh followed Mara to the door. "If I didn't care so much about you, I could probably keep from commenting on how you live."

Mara opened the door and looked out. It was raining lightly. "I know that," she said, turning back to face Shiloh.

"Don't leave while you're angry."

"I'm not really angry, but I've experienced things you never have. I've had to fight for what I want the only way I can."

After she left, Shiloh struggled to keep from crying. She returned to the kitchen and sagged into her chair. She and Mara had often disagreed over the years, but neither of them had ever walked out before.

In the churchyard Sunday morning, Clay dropped his family off near the front steps. The children ran off to join their friends while Clay tied up the horse. Shiloh noticed a matronly woman slowly stepping down from her husband's carriage.

"Sister Radcliffe," Shiloh said, remembering the cool attitude she had received at their last meeting. "How are you this morning?"

The former Michigan resident glanced disapprovingly at Shiloh. "I'm fine." She hurried as fast as her stout body would permit up the church stairs.

Just like last time, Shiloh sighed. *I guess she's made up her mind about Clay and me.*

She looked around, hoping to find her father in the crowd, but instead, Earl Quesenberry bore down on her.

"Good morning, Sister Shiloh," he said with a friendly smile. "It's good to see you."

"Thank you." She remembered her father telling her that Earl had tried to recruit him as a member of the Knights of the Golden Circle.

Earl lowered his voice. "Could I speak to you privately for a moment?"

"I'm waiting for my husband to join me."

"Then I'll be brief." Taking a quick glance around, Earl spoke in a subdued tone. "I know that you grew up in an abolitionist's home, but Clay is southern born."

Shiloh tried to hide her dismay that he had brought politics to the church.

"Brother Earl, I try to stay out of . . ."

He interrupted. "I know you can't vote, but you can certainly influence your husband. Whatever your personal feelings, I think it's in your best interest that Clay goes along with us."

Blinking in surprise, Shiloh said, "That sounds ominous."

"The way the situation is deteriorating in the East, men are going to die for what they believe. This is not about slavery but about loyalty to a man's state of birth. And the central government has grown out of control, become too powerful. I hope you will consider this as friendly advice: Be sure Clay's on the right side."

Shiloh stared in disbelief as the man joined the crowd entering the church. She turned to look for Clay and moaned inwardly at the sight of William Judd earnestly talking to him. Shiloh was sure about what the southern-born man was saying to her husband.

"Morning, Shiloh," said a man behind her.

She turned, saying, "Good morning. How is the Fratken family this morning?" She recalled how reserved the former Maryland couple had seemed the last time she had seen them.

"Quite well, thank you, Sister," the slender bakery owner replied. He turned to his wife, "Dear, would you excuse us for a moment?"

Shiloh wanted to protest as the other woman left them alone, but her husband had already begun to speak confidentially.

He began, "Shiloh, Clay can't sit on the fence much longer. Some friends and their wives were over at our house earlier this

week, and we realized how vital a part a woman plays in helping her husband choose the right course in difficult situations."

"Wait!" Shiloh held up her hand. "I think I know what
you're going to say. So let me save you some time. I have very
strong personal feelings about our country, but my husband is
the only voter in our family. I love him dearly, but he must
make up his own mind about such things. Now, if you'll excuse
me, he's coming."

Clay's long legs carried him to Shiloh's side. "Sorry I was
delayed," he said. "William Judd wanted to share his views on
supporting the Confederacy."

Shiloh slipped her arm through Clay's as they walked
toward the church stairs. "I got it from both sides: Earl
Quesenberry wants me to get you to support the Union, and
John Fratken wants me to get you to side with the South."

Clay shook his head. "It's hard to believe that right here in
our church there are such strongly divided opinions. Well, at
least we know John Sledger is going to preach tolerance and
understanding."

"Thank God for that. But the way things are going, I wonder if this congregation will put up with neutrality for long?"

Mounting the stairs, Clay said, "I wouldn't be surprised if
some members started walking out. If that happens, you can
be sure the church will split."

The thought distressed Shiloh. "I pray that nothing like
that happens."

"Me, too. But we won't know for sure until after the
inauguration."

With a heavy heart, Shiloh turned her thoughts toward
worship as she entered the church. *We can only wait,* she
thought. *And pray.*

But she had grave doubts about what would happen in the
spring.

~ CHAPTER 15 ~

I N LATE April, Clay had just closed his office for the day when San Francisco erupted into bedlam. He stepped out onto Market Street and saw men running along, shouting wildly.

He called to a wide-eyed man puffing toward him, "What's going on?"

The runner did not stop but yelled as he passed. "The Confederates have fired on Fort Sumter! President Lincoln has called up troops!"

For a moment, Clay stood in stunned silence, unwilling to believe that it had started. His eyes swept the incredible sight of thousands of excited men pouring into the streets.

The Monumental Fire Company's bell clanged as though the ringer were deranged. The frenzied bongs sounded nothing like the call to fight one of the city's frequent conflagrations.

Someone began singing "Yankee Doodle," as a couple of women rushed from a nearby building holding their ribboned bonnets on their heads with one hand and waving American flags with the other. Men spilled into the streets like hordes of runaway cattle, forcing wagons and carriages to pull over and stop.

It struck Clay that it seemed more like a joyous Fourth of July celebration than the start of war between the states. He shook his head in dismay as a driver struggled to curb his frightened horse. Clay grabbed the animal's bridle to help control it. When the driver leaped to the ground, Clay recognized Cyrus Bixby.

"Thanks!" he exclaimed, securing the horse to a hitching post. "Everyone's gone mad!"

Clay nodded and raised his voice to be heard above the swirling humanity. "Is it true?"

"Oh, yes! On April twelfth, Fort Sumter was fired on. Three

days later, Lincoln announced that an insurrection had occurred and called for volunteers to serve ninety days."

Clay asked, "How do you know?"

"I read the newspaper account the mail brought earlier today."

Clay asked, "Can you tell me more details?"

When Bixby nodded yes, Clay began to push his way through the throng toward his office with Bixby in tow.

Clay wished the transcontinental telegraph was complete. But the last newspaper account he had seen said that the Bee brothers, working west from Sacramento, had not even crossed Nevada with their stub of line.

Inside his office, Clay sat behind his desk and motioned for the banker to take a seat across from him. "Tell me everything you know, Cyrus," he said, dreading what he would hear.

"Well, as you know, seven states seceded before Lincoln took office."

When Clay nodded, Bixby continued, "The Washington Peace Convention failed to preserve the Union, and so Confederate States of America were formed. They started seizing federal forts while President Buchanan was still in office, and he let them get away with it."

"But Lincoln won't. I didn't think he would."

"He had no choice. He tried appeasement, but when the Confederates fired on Fort Sumter, he called for troops."

"So the war has started," Clay mused sadly.

"It was inevitable. So many states have seceded from the Union. There's nothing yet on whether the border states will stay in or follow the secessionists."

"The border states are all slave states," Clay recalled. "If they go out, it's possible the Confederacy could end up with fifteen states."

"You really can't count on the border states," Bixby cautioned. "They'd be better off, from a practical viewpoint, to stay out. That way, they can sell arms to both sides."

Clay sat silently contemplating the odds between the Union and Confederacy. He remembered what his father-in-law had said about the other factors that made it almost certain the North would triumph.

Bixby leaned forward. "You said you wouldn't make any decision until after Lincoln took office. That's nearly eight weeks ago. What are your thoughts now?"

Clay didn't answer right away. He pushed his chair back and walked to the window overlooking Market Street. Dusk had settled over the throngs of men and women.

One man had climbed onto a carriage and was waving his arms, his mouth moving in an impromptu but doubtless impassioned speech. More American flags had been raised. So had two Palmetto flags. One flapped from a second-story window. The other was waved defiantly by an ardent southern sympathizer who had climbed partway up a gaslight post.

As Clay watched, another man shimmied up the standard and struggled to knock down the defiant symbol of South Carolina. Both men fell, and the Palmetto symbol fluttered after them. Before it touched the ground, several hands grabbed it and threw it to the boardwalk where it was viciously trampled.

"San Francisco is no place for a Copperhead," Bixby said.

Clay had been so absorbed in his thoughts that he hadn't noticed the banker join him at the window.

Taking a slow breath to steady his swirling emotions, Clay turned from the window. "I've got to get home. Shiloh will be anxious to hear what's happened."

"You've got to choose," Bixby warned as they walked to the door. "I hope you make the right choice."

~❧~

Shiloh met Clay at the door. "I heard," she greeted him, her eyes wide with concern. "Papa brought the news."

Clay kissed her and held her close, not saying anything as the enormity of what was happening continued to overwhelm him. He saw his children standing with their grandfather and Lizzie, all silent and solemn, their eyes clinging to his.

"What now?" Shiloh whispered, tilting her face up to him. "What's going to happen?"

"I've been thinking about it on the ride home," he admitted. "I'd like to discuss that with you and Merritt, but first I'd better reassure the children."

⁂

Samuel borrowed a horse from a friend and spurred up Rincon Hill to bring the news to Mara. He hated the fact that Mara had moved back into Lyman Wallace's mansion. A Palmetto flag sagged on the front porch.

At the back door, he knocked nervously, hoping that the lawyer wasn't home.

"Samuel!" Mara exclaimed when she opened the door. She instantly saw the excitement in his face and asked, "What happened?"

He respectfully whipped off his hat. "War started back east." He had been caught up in the downtown excitement and was breathing a little heavily. "I heard talk after the Pony Express brought the word. Seems like every person in San Francisco has gone into the streets."

Mara held the door open. "Come in and tell me all about it."

Samuel glanced furtively beyond her. "You alone?"

"I have the run of the house since Malvina left." Mara led the way toward the kitchen table. "Lyman won't be home for a while. He has a meeting tonight."

"Miss Mara, you know I feel plumb uncomfortable, being here. And you should too."

"Don't start that again!" She spoke sharply. "Tell me about the news."

Declining the chair she offered, he stood, hat in hand, and repeated what he had heard. All the time, his eyes flitted from her face to the darkened interior of the house and back to the windows.

"There's not much to tell. I just heard people shouting and

carrying on. Seems like President Lincoln called for volunteer soldiers after the South started shooting at some northern fort. Sumter, I think it's called."

"That's very bad news," Mara said. "A lot of people are going to get killed."

"I'm just glad it's way back on the other side of the country."

"We won't escape the turmoil, even from this distance. There will be lots of pressure on Shiloh and Clay. I'm glad he's too old to have to fight," Mara paused, then added, "but you're not."

Samuel laughed. "They don't want my color in their armies."

"They might." Mara watched the surprise on Samuel's face. "If they kill off enough white soldiers, they'll come looking for any man who can carry a gun, regardless of his color."

With a groan, Samuel turned around in anguish. "I been a runaway slave all these years, doing my best to keep slave catchers from getting me. Now, just when I'm about to buy my freedom . . ." He spun back to face Mara. "That ain't right if they try to make me fight! No, not right at all!"

Mara said gently. "I wouldn't concern myself about it right now, if I were you."

"I won't do it, Miss Mara! I just won't!" The sudden realization of what could happen made his voice rise.

"You're not listening. I said . . ."

"I know! I heard you!" he uncharacteristically interrupted. "I couldn't stand to be far away from you." He took a couple of quick steps and gently took her hands. "Marry up with me. Now, before something terrible happens and we can't!"

She freed her hands and stepped back. "Please don't start that again."

"I can't help it. I ain't never going to give up asking you until you say yes!"

She sighed heavily. "I can't seem to make you understand that I think the world of you as a friend, but marriage, no; it can't be."

His features clouded angrily. "It's him, isn't it?" He jerked his head indicating the mansion and the man who owned it. "I know you like nice things and all, but how do you take them from a man like Wallace? Everybody knows he favors slavery. If it was up to him, folks like you and me would never be free. You got no business with a man like that."

"I know what he is," Mara replied abruptly. "But I'm a free woman, and I don't want you talking like this."

Samuel ignored the warning in her tone and said bitterly, "As long as he lives, you're going to be his and not mine. Is that what you're saying?"

"I'm nobody's, Samuel." Mara put steel in her words and enforced it with her eyes. "But I prefer this arrangement because it gives me what I want."

He didn't answer for a long time but looked hard at her through eyes narrowed to angry slits. "Your dolls don't work," he exploded.

It took her a moment to realize Samuel was referring to the two voodoo dolls she had made for him months ago.

"I know you left one for Lyman, but what about the other one?" Mara asked.

"I'm saving that."

"Oh? Why?"

He shrugged. "I got my reasons." His fury had blown itself out. He turned toward the door. "Well, I got to be going."

"Wait—some time ago you mentioned having a job gathering seabird eggs this spring. When are you going to do that?"

"Mr. Briggs said the early part of May."

"Briggs? Oh, yes. I'm going to ask him if I can go along on one of those egg-gathering trips."

Samuel opened the door. "I don't think you should. He says it's mighty dangerous on those islands."

"I'll take my chances." She tried to erase the remaining tension between them. "Thanks for bringing me the news about the war."

She closed the door and walked away, but when she glanced back, she saw that he was still standing outside, thoughtfully looking through the glass at her.

❦

Clay left the children with Lizzie and joined Shiloh and Merritt in the parlor.

"Are they going to be all right, Clay?" Shiloh asked as he sat down beside her.

"I think so. Ajay was concerned about his friend next door. I reminded him that he and Howell had been getting along just fine and told him that they shouldn't think about what grown-ups are saying and doing. Just be friends, as always."

Shiloh leaned close to her husband. "I wish grown-ups could always be friends. I'm tired of people on both sides trying to get me to influence you to support one side or the other."

"Emotions always run high when there's a possibility of war, and it gets worse when war starts," Clay said, remembering his own military experiences. "Now, I'm afraid, it will really be difficult. I don't mind for myself, but for you and the children . . ."

"For everyone," Merritt interrupted. "Speculation has been rampant for days. First, there was the rumor that General Johnston had sent his resignation to Washington. Now it's confirmed. Just a few days ago, General E. A. Sumner replaced him. He's a strong pro-Union man."

"What's going to happen to General Johnston?" Shiloh wanted to know.

When Clay shrugged, Merritt said, "I talked to an editor at the newspaper. He said privately that they're waiting for confirmation that Johnston and some of his officers conspired to set up a Pacific Republic."

"Denby Gladwin's old dream!" Shiloh exclaimed.

Her father reached out and lightly touched the back of her

hand. "Don't blame him alone. Many men have had that idea. But in this case, rumor has it that forming the republic is just the first step to withdrawing from the Union. The second step is to have California join the Confederacy."

"Gladwin won't like that," Shiloh commented. "But what do you think will really happen?"

Clay took both of her hands in his and held them tightly. "It's hard to say, but I've heard another rumor."

"About what?" Shiloh asked anxiously.

Clay looked at his father-in-law. "Maybe you've heard something about a Home Guard?"

Merritt nodded. "There's a plan to form the State Home Guards along the organizational lines of the Vigilantes of 1856."

"Vigilantes?" Shiloh's voice rose. "They scare me."

"The Vigilantes were necessary," Clay assured her. "Crime was out of hand." He broke off suddenly, wondering if Shiloh guessed that he had felt compelled to join them to help restore law and order to the city.

"But what would they do now?" Shiloh asked, pulling her hands free and facing Clay. "This isn't a lawless city anymore."

"Shiloh," her father said gently but firmly, "the guards will form to repel a possible naval attack on our harbor."

She broke in, "But why would eastern states send ships around the Horn over thousands of miles to attack San Francisco? They'll need all their ships back in the Atlantic and in the Gulf of Mexico."

"Neither the North nor South would use regular eastern seaboard warships off of California's shores," her father pointed out. "It could even be the English who send naval vessels if they saw a chance to seize California while the rest of the nation is tied up in civil war."

"Oh," Shiloh said, nodding. "I remember how hard they tried to take both California and Oregon as their own colonies a few years back."

"There's another possible source," Merritt continued. "Privateers, either Union or Confederate raiders—depending on whether California secedes—that would target steamships carrying California's gold to the east."

Merritt turned his gaze on Clay, who wondered if his father-in-law knew about Asbury Harpending's plans.

Quickly, Clay said, "How can anyone believe General Johnston conspired against the Union? He did stop the Knights of the Golden Circle. Johnston could have done nothing and let those men seize the federal arsenals and take over the state."

His outburst surprised Shiloh. She had never known him to speak with such conviction about the current situation.

"What should we do?" she asked, afraid of the answer. "Now that the war has started, you must take a stand, one way or another."

"I thought," Clay began, "that when Lincoln took office, I would know inside myself what's right. That didn't happen. And now . . . I still don't know."

Merritt pointed out, "Shiloh's right. You're going to be under pressure to choose."

"I'm not going to let outsiders affect my decisions!" Clay snapped.

"Don't get upset at us," Shiloh said soothingly. "We need to talk about this, but first, let's take some time to clarify our thinking."

⁂

On Sunday, Shiloh felt comforted by Pastor Sledger's pulpit plea for brotherly love, tolerance, and understanding. But that comfort shattered when, on the way home, the Patton family's carriage neared Calvary Presbyterian Church on Bush Street.

"Something's happened!" Shiloh exclaimed, pointing ahead. People had spilled into the street and seemed fairly agitated.

Clay said, "I know the pastor there: Dr. William Scott. I believe he's from New Orleans."

"Stop and ask what's going on," Shiloh urged.

Clay halted the carriage, then called to three men talking on the curb. "Anything wrong?"

An elderly gentleman with silvery hair stepped over to the buggy and looked up. "In the opening prayer, Dr. Scott prayed for Jefferson Davis."

"Oh dear. What happened?" Shiloh asked fearfully.

"Split the congregation," the older man explained. "Some men walked out. When we came outside after services, somebody had hanged Dr. Scott in effigy."

Shiloh exclaimed, "They what?"

"Most of us don't care for Jeff Davis," the silver-haired man continued, "but pastor has a right to pray for any man."

Clay agreed then thanked the man and eased the carriage through the crowd in the street. Shiloh stared back in disbelief.

Turning to Clay, Shiloh asked, "What in the world is happening to people? In a church! Imagine! Well," she declared stoutly, "Nobody would dare do that in our church!"

"I hope you're right," Clay said soberly. *But,* he added silently, *I'm not so sure.*

❧ CHAPTER 16 ❧

SHILOH AND Clay retired after the children had gone to sleep. Shiloh crossed to the flowered basin and poured water from the matching pitcher to wash her face. Casually she mentioned, "You've been awfully quiet this evening. Do you feel like talking?"

Clay removed a clean nightshirt from a drawer of the high dresser. "I'm concerned. Men who support both sides of this war will really begin to push me to join them. I guess what they really want is our money. I'm just not sure where my loyalties lie."

"If you want to sort out your thoughts, I'll be glad to listen."

"Thanks." Clay sat on the edge of the bed and removed his shoes. "But first, I'd rather know what you're thinking."

She turned around and leaned against the marble-topped washstand. "You know where I stand. I believe President Lincoln is doing what he thinks is best to keep the Union together. Papa and I spent some time talking about him after lunch.

"Papa says that even though Lincoln is not an abolitionist, he does consider slavery an injustice and says it's evil. He opposed extending it to other states."

"But this isn't about slavery," Clay said a bit impatiently, yanking off his socks. "It's about a central government getting too powerful and about states' rights. I read through the Constitution today. The Tenth Amendment says that the powers not delegated to the United States by the Constitution, nor prohibited by it to the states, are reserved to the states respectively, or to the people."

"Papa's been reading a lot too. He's also talked to his friends at the newspaper. Both he and they believe the Constitution created a sovereign union of states, and states can't withdraw."

Clay shook his head. "I respect Merritt very much, but both of you grew up in the North. Being from Texas, I see the South's side. The Constitution is a voluntary compact between sovereign states, but it's not absolute in power. So states *can* withdraw from that union."

Shiloh didn't like the sharpness that had crept into his tone. She walked over to stand in front of him. "Can't we talk about this without you getting upset?"

"I can't help it." Clay slid his arms around Shiloh's waist. "I keep thinking of what General Johnston said about the writings of Jefferson and Madison and about the text the cadets at West Point used. I tend to agree with all of them. States do have the right to secede if they want."

Shiloh tried to keep impatience from her voice. "The North

doesn't see it that way, and apparently neither does the general who replaced Johnston."

"Edwin Sumner. From what I hear, he's regular army and a staunch Union man." Clay stood up and took off his shirt. "As soon as he took over Johnston's command, Sumner brought troops down from Oregon. He also moved some soldiers up from Fort Mojave near Los Angeles."

"Do you think Papa is right? Will they arrest Johnston?"

Clay slid the nightshirt over his head and sat down again. "Makes sense. He's considered a brilliant general. Charging him with treason could prevent him from heading down South to fight for the Confederacy." Clay's voice took on an irritated tone. "Johnston might favor the South, but I don't believe for one second that he ever betrayed his oath of allegiance."

Clay hung his pants across the back of a chair. "This whole thing makes me angry. If Johnston wanted to betray his uniform, he could have let Harpending and the Knights of the Golden Circle grab the arsenals and other government property. I was there when Johnston told Asbury Harpending and the others, in no uncertain terms, that he wouldn't stand for that. So what did Johnston do that was treasonous?"

Shiloh frowned. "If Johnston resigned from the army, he's a civilian, isn't he?"

"Yes, when his resignation is accepted by the army."

"If they can arrest him as a civilian, what's to keep them from arresting others—even you?"

"Don't talk nonsense, Shiloh!"

She looked up, startled, and stared at him, frightened at what was happening.

~≈≈~

Shiloh's anxiety drove her to seek counsel with John Sledger the next day. She was somewhat embarrassed to share such personal feelings, but she felt desperate enough to make the trip to the pastor's modest home.

His wife, a large, friendly woman, made tea for them, then left them alone in the parlor.

"You look troubled, Sister Shiloh," the big man said, holding the tiny cup with a huge hand.

"I am," she admitted, leaning toward him.

The pastor put down his cup, took Shiloh's hand, and bowed his head. When he completed his brief petition for guidance, he looked expectantly at his visitor. "Now tell me about it."

"I'm concerned about how I can honor my husband, as Paul the apostle taught, and yet help Clay to see that his thinking could get him—in fact, our whole family—in terrible trouble."

"You mean his thinking about the war?"

"Yes." She repeated part of last night's discussion with Clay. "How can I honor God and my husband when I feel so strongly that he should support the Union?"

Sledger shifted his considerable bulk in his chair before answering. "You and Clay are going through the same kind of soul searching that everyone is. Civil war pits brothers against brothers and fathers against sons. Some will possibly face each other on the battlefield. They're the only ones allowed to vote in this country, so each has to follow his own conscience."

He paused, considering Shiloh's tight, concerned features. "A wife cannot vote, and she is in a different position spiritually, according to the Bible."

"That's very true. This morning I looked up every verse I could think of about husbands and wives. I want to support my husband, and I will, even though it will be hard. He doesn't see things the way I do. But I must respect that."

"Do you mean he's made a firm decision?"

"No, but he's talking more and more about states' rights. Please understand, Brother Sledger, I will support him in whatever he decides to do. But I feel strongly that I should do everything in my power to help him see the other side of this terrible situation before he makes a final choice."

Shiloh leaned forward, adding, "He said something last night that frightened me. Do you think it's possible that the military will arrest civilians during wartime?"

"Your father and I had a brief discussion on that very subject yesterday."

Shiloh took a deep breath. "You did? I suppose I should have gone to him instead of you."

"You did the right thing, Shiloh," Sledger interrupted. "Your father is a very knowledgeable man in worldly matters. He's well read and thinks clearly and has friends in many places. But I hope I'm qualified to help you consider the spiritual aspects of your situation at home."

"If you're talking about Sarah obeying Abraham or of the husband being the head of the wife and the wife having reverence for her husband, I've already prayed about that."

Her voice began to waver with pent-up emotion. "I certainly will do what Clay wants, but don't I have a right to show him what he may not see because he's so emotionally involved over certain issues?"

The pastor smiled. "I don't remember seeing anything in Scripture that prohibits a wife from telling her husband what she thinks, as long as she supports him in what he eventually decides to do."

Shiloh returned his smile. "Thank you, Brother Sledger. That's what I needed to hear."

He nodded. "I pray that God guides you both."

Shiloh stood, feeling relieved. "I've been so concerned about my own problem that I forgot how much pressure you must be under from members of our church."

"There are pressures," he admitted, "but unlike Thomas Starr King, who speaks out for the North, and Dr. William Scott, who supports the Confederacy from the pulpit, I will not take sides."

"Like Clay," Shiloh mused.

"Not quite. God called me to minister to the whole body of

believers in our church, not to get involved in politics. I'll keep my opinions to myself and continue to preach tolerance, reconciliation, and understanding."

Shiloh hesitated before asking, "Do you think you can continue to do that, now that the war's started?"

"I expect to have some heavy burdens laid on me by members of our congregation. But if I took either side, that would split the church. So I will continue to be neutral, no matter what happens. My job is to be a shepherd to the people in my care, regardless of where they stand politically."

Shiloh walked toward the door. "I'll pray for you about that." She added silently, *But it won't be easy for you.*

───※───

Sitting in his office, Clay couldn't concentrate. He put on his hat and coat against the April chill and walked aimlessly down Market Street toward the bay. He didn't focus on any other pedestrians until he heard his name.

"Clay! I was hoping to run into you."

He roused himself from his preoccupation and recognized Cyrus Bixby.

"Good afternoon," Clay greeted his friend, extending his hand. "I was so deep in thought I didn't notice you."

"We're all doing a lot of thinking these days," the banker replied. "Let's step out of the way."

Clay didn't want to get into a political discussion with the strong pro-North man, but he had no choice but to follow Bixby.

Cyrus began, "Terrible news about war starting."

"Sure is," Clay agreed, casting about for a way to change the subject. He said the first thought that popped into his mind. "Any news about Theodore Judah getting funding for his railroad venture?"

Bixby studiously regarded Clay, realizing that he didn't want to discuss the war.

Silently berating himself for having been so obvious, Clay determined to follow through. "Not that you have any interest, Cyrus."

"Foolishness! That's what it is! The idea of trying to build a transcontinental railroad."

Clay stifled a satisfied smile. Foolishness, he remembered, was what Bixby had said years earlier when Clay sought a loan to build his struggling stagecoach line. He still believed he might have received the money had he not mentioned his plans to run a line to the Missouri River.

Clay couldn't resist the temptation to taunt the cautious banker. "I always rather liked Theodore Judah."

"'Crazy' Judah," Bixby said with a shake of his head.

Clay relaxed. "Not everyone agrees that he's crazy, Cyrus. Just this January a senator asked Congress to set aside a hundred million dollars for a Pacific railway."

Bixby snorted in derision. "It's a good thing Crittenden of Kentucky was there to point out that with the Union reeling like a drunken man, there was no sense in wasting money on a transcontinental railway."

"As I recall reading in the papers, he advocated first building up the Union, then building up a railroad."

"Yes, but Judah won't listen. In January he started showing a prospectus for his wild idea. But he couldn't get any backers."

"I might have backed him," Clay commented, "but I had other things on my mind. Years ago, I did invest in his short line. Shiloh and I attended a ball to celebrate its completion, from Sacramento to Folsom, in 1856. I wouldn't mind risking a little something on this transcontinental railway."

"As your banker, I'd advise against it."

"Just a thought. I read recently that last year railroads became the first billion-dollar industry in the country."

"That was back east where there are lots of towns close together."

"Even so, the idea appeals to me."

Bixby studied Clay thoughtfully. "Well, you certainly have enough to invest a sizable amount without getting hurt, even if you lose every penny of your investment." Lowering his voice to a confidential level, he added, "There are plans to organize the Central Pacific Railroad Company on the thirtieth of this month."

"Really? I thought Judah had gone back east to attend Lincoln's inauguration."

"He did. Leland Stanford went back with him. Stanford plans to return to run for governor in June, but Judah will stay in the East to work on a new prospectus."

"Stanford's already lost twice running for governor on the Republican ticket."

"That's true, but he's got a better chance this time because the Democrats have split into two factions. Besides, Stanford and James McClatchy now have their own newspaper, the *California Daily Times,* which is really a Republican campaign publication."

"Isn't he also backed by Mark Hopkins, Charles Crocker, and Collis Huntington?"

"Of course. Back in fifty-six, they took important roles in creating California's Republican Party."

Bixby added, "All four will probably sit on the board of directors for the railroad. But you know what's ironic? Judah got so discouraged in trying to get backers for his transcontinental railroad that he didn't offer it to them. Instead, he tried to get them interested in a wagon road over the Sierras to the Comstock Lode."

"So I heard." Clay glanced up and down Market Street at carriages and wagons moving steadily by in both directions. "I'll give some thought to being an investor with them."

"It's your money, but remember, I don't advise it."

"I understand. Nice talking to you, Cyrus."

As Clay walked away, Bixby called after him, "Wait! I want to talk about the war."

"Some other time," Clay answered over his shoulder. He hurried away, glad to have something to think about besides the decision he had to make about the war.

─────※❧※─────

Mara sat in Lyman Wallace's kitchen, pondering what to fix for dinner when someone knocked at the back door. *Samuel again!* she guessed as she went to answer the knock. *He certainly doesn't give up.*

A gray-haired black woman holding a small child by the hand stood on the back step.

"Yes?" Mara queried.

"You all please 'scuse me, Miss Mara," the older woman began, bobbing her head in a sort of bow. "Me'n my grandson here been workin' down Monterey way when we come on hard times." The words gushed out as though the woman were afraid she would be turned away before saying her piece. "I'se a widder woman, and my only son, he died sudden-like. Jethro here is his boy. Well, I heard from some folks downtown . . ."

"Come in, please," Mara interrupted, holding the door wide. She had heard similar stories many times. She had let it be known that she would never turn away anyone of color.

"Thanks kindly, Miss Mara," the woman replied without moving. "But if it's jist the same to you, me'n him will wait outside here."

"There's nobody home except me," Mara explained, still holding the door wide. "Come in."

Shaking her head, the woman explained, "We'uns won't feel right comfortable in such a fine house. But if you could spare us a bite . . ." She let her voice trail off.

"I'll be right back," Mara said.

She hurried back into the kitchen, quickly taking inventory of food she had left over and how much cash she had tucked in the sugar jar. She had reached into the cupboard when she heard a footstep behind her.

She turned her head toward the sound, expecting to see Lyman. Instead, Malvina walked into the room.

Malvina said icily, "I came to pick up some of my clothes, and I find you feeding your people again with my husband's food. Have you no shame?"

Mara met the other woman's disapproving stare with her own firm gaze. "I was reaching for my own money. But yes, I was also going to see what food I could offer someone in need." She added meaningfully, "I think that is what your 'white man's religion,' as you called it, would consider the proper thing to do."

"Don't you get uppity with me!"

Mara turned from the cupboard and took a couple of slow, deliberate steps toward Malvina. "You left this house of your own accord. Now I'm here, and I'm going to run it the way I think best. That includes helping that woman and her grandchild. That is, unless you think you can stop me."

Malvina involuntarily shrank back at the bold challenge. "You can't talk to me that way!"

"I just did." Mara's tone was calm but cool. "Now, if you'll excuse me, I've got something to do." She deliberately turned her back on Lyman's estranged wife.

"It's Shiloh's fault that you're so uppity!"

At that, Mara whirled, her dark eyes snapping, but Malvina's outburst continued.

"You grew up in her home thinking you were as good as any white person. But just wait! Now that we're at war, things will change. Clay's a southerner. Shiloh will turn her back on you like everyone else!"

Mara cried, "Don't you talk about Shiloh!"

Malvina swallowed hard and licked her lips. Her eyes held a mixture of fear and hate. "That sounds like a threat! Lyman will want to know about this!"

"Fine! Now, leave me alone. Don't you ever say anything against Shiloh again. Is that clear, Malvina?"

She deliberately used the woman's first name to show that they were on equal social footing. Then, without waiting for an answer, she returned to the cupboard. When she turned around again holding a gold double eagle, Malvina had gone. Mara waited until she heard the front door slam before returning to the woman who waited on the back step with her grandson.

～☙～

Two days later, Shiloh's father dropped by for a midmorning visit. As they spoke, Shiloh repeated what John Sledger had told her then added, "Papa, he said that you had discussed the possibility of civilians being arrested by the military during wartime."

"It's very possible. In my reading, I've found that it's quite common for governments to do wonderful things in the name of patriotism. Conversely, incredibly terrible things have also been done."

"Like the army arresting civilians?"

"That, among other things."

Shiloh held back her dread. "Such as?"

Her father shrugged. "Well, confiscating private property . . ."

"You don't mean that!"

"Unfortunately, I do. Everything you and Clay own could be in jeopardy."

Shiloh's eyes opened wide in disbelief.

Merritt continued, "That not only includes this beautiful house but all the land you two have in the central valley."

"Just because Clay might not agree with someone?"

"Not just someone, my darling daughter. Remember, the winner always writes the history. If your husband chooses to follow his native state, and the South loses, you could lose everything. But if you do, it will probably never make it into the history books."

"But that's so unfair! What about freedom of speech in this country?"

"It doesn't matter. Tyrants grab control by doing things in the name of patriotism, and if anyone complains, they're considered against the government."

Shiloh shook her head violently. "They might take all we've worked for all our lives? Even if *I* don't agree with Clay's stand?"

"The Congress of the United States could pass a law allowing confiscation of property under such patriotic-sounding phrases as 'suppressing insurrection.'"

"But California has community property laws. How could anyone take property that's half mine when I support the Union?"

"Ah, but you can't vote, my dear, so what power would you have against the state legislature if it proposed a law allowing seizure of property you and Clay own together?"

"I really can't believe such things could happen!"

"Under the cover of patriotic fervor, the state or federal government could require loyalty oaths of citizens and could even strip citizenship from anyone they consider enemies of the state."

Jumping up, Shiloh paced the carpeted floor, her mind spinning wildly. "They wouldn't dare, would they?"

"Depends on who controls the power structure. Right now, Democrats hold most of California's state offices, and some national ones. In the northern part of the state, the Union has strong support. Down south, toward Los Angeles, it's the other way around. But there's a state election coming up, and if that balance of power shifts from Democrat to Republican . . ."

"Lincoln is a Republican, isn't he?"

"He sure is."

Shiloh's thoughts tumbling out randomly. "What about the plan to form the State Home Guards? You said the other day they would be like the San Francisco Vigilantes."

"Not exactly. The plan is to organize them along the same lines as the Vigilantes."

"But that means they can take the law into their own hands!" Shiloh returned to her chair and sat for a moment in silent dismay. Then she rose quickly and leaned over to kiss Merritt on the cheek. "Thanks, Papa. I've heard enough to scare me half to death, but at least now I know what I must do to save us from danger."

Merritt rose and put his arm around her shoulders. "It won't be easy."

"I know," she said softly. With strength, she added, "But this is worth fighting for."

❧ CHAPTER 17 ❧

SHILOH RODE with Merritt in his coach down Market Street toward Clay's office. She barely noticed the beautiful early-May weather. Instead she sat deep in thought, mulling over the problems engulfing her husband and how she could help him resolve them.

Merritt's voice broke through her reverie. "Seems there's a flag flying from every post and window. Nothing like a war to bring out signs of patriotism."

A quick glance up and down the street confirmed his observation. "All Stars and Stripes," she noted. "Not a single Palmetto flag in sight."

"No, but look at the new flag hanging out of that window." Merritt pointed ahead and across the street. "That must be the new one the Confederacy has adopted."

Shiloh waited until a high freight wagon lumbered by so she could see the second-story window. "Sort of looks like ours," she observed, then flinched, realizing she had unconsciously identified with the Union. She sternly reminded herself to not make such a slip in front of Clay.

"It's attracting a crowd." Merritt eased the horse toward the curb. "Some of those drivers aren't watching where they're going."

A young man suddenly dashed in front of Merritt's carriage, dodged the teams in the street, and leaped upon the sidewalk in front of the flag. "You secesh traitor!" he yelled, shaking his fist at the man who had just hung the new flag.

Instead of defiantly shouting back, he started to sing, "Oh, I wish I was in the land of cotton . . ."

"Copperhead!" A second man on the street cried through cupped hands toward the singer.

Merritt pulled back on the reins and turned to watch. Traffic stopped in both directions as a crowd of men quickly gathered below the offending southern symbol.

"Papa, what's that song?" Shiloh asked.

"It's a northern minstrel tune called 'Dixie.'"

Shiloh listened to the male vocalist in the window raising his voice above the increasingly antagonistic cries of the people on the street. The lyrics filled the air. "Look away, look away, Dixieland . . ."

Shiloh exclaimed, "I don't care if it is a northern song, these men seem to think it's a southern tune. That man is going to cause a riot!"

Merritt clucked to the horse. "You may be right. Let's see if we can squeeze past these wagons and carriages before that happens."

Shiloh looked back while her father carefully freed the carriage. "They're starting to throw things at the window," she reported. "And someone is climbing up the wall to pull down the flag."

"I guess their passions have made them forget a man's right to free speech," Merritt replied. "Too bad in lots of way. It was good to hear that song again."

"Again? I've never heard of it before."

"I heard it in April of fifty-nine when I was on a business trip to New York. It's a bright and catchy tune. Spirited too."

Shiloh turned away from the scene spreading out of control behind her. "Yes, it is."

Clay's office building came into sight. Merritt offered to stay with the horse while Shiloh ran up to talk to Clay for a few minutes. She quickly climbed toward his second-story office then slowed as she neared the top of the stairs. She heard angry voices behind the closed door. One of them was Clay's.

Shiloh hesitated, wondering if she should enter. Clay rarely spoke so angrily. Concerned, Shiloh slowly opened the door and peered inside. A well-built man nearly as tall as Clay but much younger stood so that neither could see the door open.

Clay thrust his head forward so it was within inches of the other man's whiskered face and growled, "I'm tired of everyone pressuring me! I don't care if you're a member of the State Home Guards, the San Francisco Union Committee, or anything else."

The younger man did not back down, but neither did he try to stop the furious words pouring from Clay.

"And don't you dare compare yourself to the Vigilance Committee of fifty-six!" he thundered. "I was a member, and we did what citizens have a right to do when the law couldn't or wouldn't control people."

Shiloh stifled a gasp. She had suspected her husband had joined the Vigilantes. But Clay had never confirmed his involvement, and Shiloh hadn't wanted to ask.

Clay continued his angry denunciation. "This is a different situation! A man is guaranteed the right to think and speak for himself in this country. Before I was your age, I was already a soldier, defending what was right. I did it again in the Mexican War, and I've got the scars to prove it. I left my own blood on the battlefield."

Clay took a deep breath and plunged on, his voice rising with emotion. "So don't come in here sounding off to me about your committee being organized for . . . what was it called?"

The whiskered man started to speak, but Clay cut him off. "Oh, yes, for the 'detection and suppression of treasonable conspiracy against the Union.' I've earned the right to make up my own mind, to make an intelligent decision *when I'm ready to do it.*

"I will not stand for you or anybody else trying to force my back to the wall with your threats and intimidation. I want no part of you or your organization. Now, get out of my office and stay out!"

"You're going to regret this!"

Shiloh gasped as Clay's hands struck like a diamondback rattlesnake. He grabbed the other man by his lapels and shoved him violently toward the door.

Suddenly Clay stopped as though hit between the eyes. "Shiloh!" he exclaimed.

Shiloh stood silent, her eyes wide with surprise and fright.

Horrified that Shiloh had witnessed his outburst, Clay's wrath was so great that he could not stop himself.

He yanked the door open and wordlessly propelled the stranger through it. Then he whirled to face Shiloh, his face taut with rage, and demanded, "What are you doing here?"

Before she could answer, he commanded, "Go home! I don't want you anywhere near this office again! In fact, don't even come into town anymore. It's not safe."

He turned his back and stalked stiffly to his desk.

For a moment, Shiloh stood stunned that Clay had lashed out at her. Then she spun around and stumbled down the stairs.

She burst outside, barely able to see her father through the searing mist in her eyes.

Dropping the horse's feedbag, Merritt rushed to his daughter. "Shiloh! What happened?"

"I can't talk about it right now, Papa! Please just take me home!"

Mara could always tell when Lyman had gone out. It was the only time she heard the mansion creak and groan as it settled in the changing weather, its wooden joints straining at their handmade nails. Tonight, with a spring fog wrapping Rincon Hill in its silent grayness, she heard an unusual number of tiny scraping and squeaking noises.

She wasn't frightened as she hemmed a new apron, but she kept her tiny derringer handy from force of habit.

Restless, she put her sewing aside and wandered to the ornate mahogany door. Its upper half held frosted glass panes etched with delicate tea roses. Through the clear part of a rose, she could see the right column at the top of the front steps. Beneath the acanthus leaves of its Corinthian capital, the Palmetto flag flew defiantly.

Lyman Wallace had begun to display South Carolina's flag in early February. A few days ago, Mara had seen him unwrap two new flags.

He had explained, "This one is called the Bonnie Blue Flag." He held up the emblem with a single, white, five-pointed star in the center of a plain, light-blue field. "In 1810, when there was a Republic of West Florida for a short time, this was its flag."

"Where did you get it?"

"A friend of mine brought this one when he returned by steamer from the east. He says there's an Irish comedian named Harry McCarthy who sings a song called the *Bonnie Blue Flag*. It's very popular in the South."

Although Mara had no particular interest in flags, she had listened politely as Lyman picked up the second flag his friend had brought.

"This other flag," the lawyer explained, gently unfolding it, "is the new official flag of the Confederate States of America."

"Looks like the regular old American flag," Mara said truthfully.

"It is somewhat similar." Lyman spread his new prize out on the table so she could see all of it. It had two broad red strips at the top and bottom, the bottom one a bit longer, with a white stripe in the center. The corner held a blue square with seven white, five-pointed stars forming a circle. "These stars represent the original states that seceded. This flag is called the Stars and Bars."

"Like Stars and Stripes."

"Do not mention that in my presence again, Mara!" he had commanded.

Standing at the door, looking out at the Palmetto flag, Mara could still remember the passion in Lyman's explosive remark. He had ended the discussion by saying that he would replace the old Palmetto with the two new flags but he hadn't yet done so.

A sound made Mara turn around, her dark eyes flickering up the ornate, curved stairs. She stared. It had sounded like someone stepped on a creaky stair.

For a moment, she stood, assuring herself that no one was in the house. Before she returned to her sewing, she fingered her deadly little pistol. She picked up her thimble and fitted her finger into it then flinched as someone clumped heavily across the front porch and pounded on the door.

Palming the derringer, Mara moved quietly across the deep-carpeted floor. She could see a shadowy figure blocking out part of the door's frosted pane.

"Yes?" she called calmly through the door.

"It's Jefferson Locke."

A myriad of bad memories assaulted Mara's mind as she answered, "Lyman's not home."

"I didn't come to see him. I want to see you."

She tried to make her words final. "We have nothing to say to each other."

"Open this blasted door, or I'll break the glass and open it myself!"

Mara hesitated. The man didn't frighten her, especially with a gun in her hand. Still, she had no reason to talk to him. "You do," she replied calmly, "and I'll put a ball through your stubborn head."

For a long moment, Locke made no answer. Then he said quietly, "I believe you're capable of doing that, but I just want to talk. Now, will you let me in, or do you want me to stand out here so the whole neighborhood can hear what's on my mind?"

Without another word, Mara turned the long, heavy key in the lock and opened the door with her left hand. She saw with gratification that his eyes focused on the gun instead of her face.

He stepped inside and walked toward the heavy rocker she had indicated with a motion.

"Sit, speak your piece," she said coolly, "and be on your way."

The lawyer eased into the chair, his eyes still on the gun. "Careful with that thing."

"You're wasting my time," she warned, returning to the sofa but keeping the weapon in her hand.

With a sigh of resignation, Locke commented, "I don't suppose it would make any difference if you pulled the trigger. You've already taken everything I had."

"I paid hard cash for everything I bought from you," she reminded him. "You cannot blame me because you've over-extended your credit."

Her words obviously struck a sore spot. His anger flared, and he glared at her. "I *do* blame you. You once told me that someday you would buy and sell me. You remember that?"

"I remember." She laid the derringer in her lap and picked up her sewing. "So?"

"So don't sit there and try to pretend that you didn't plan to ruin me."

"You treated me worse than a dog." Her fingers flew, the needle flashing in and out of the apron's fabric. "You needed to learn never to treat anyone as you did me."

"So the price of my lesson was ruination?" His voice took on a rasping edge. "No, that's not the real reason. You set out to ruin me because you forgot your place."

"My place?"

"You're a nigra, pale enough to pass for white in some places, but inside, you're black as your heart."

"Careful," Mara warned. "You're starting to lose control."

He took a slow breath before continuing. "You'd like that, wouldn't you? Then you could claim I attacked you and you shot me in self-defense."

She ignored the remark. "For the last time, say what you've come to say, and get out."

"Very well." He leaned back, rocking gently. "I was doing just fine until you came along. I had plans, big plans. California would become a slave state. I would import nigras from around the world and sell them to planters in the territories between here and the Missouri River."

"I know all that. Get to the point."

"Politicians ruined that for me. They fought over territories that became states, and which of those would be free and which would be slave holding. Now they're fighting a war, and it's my last chance to do what I want."

"Stop rambling!"

He scowled at her. "Now's the time to withdraw California from the Union. Frankly, whether it becomes a separate nation or joins the Confederacy doesn't concern me. Either way, I can carry out my plan, but . . ." He left his sentence suspended in the air.

Mara waited in silence, trying to control her impatience to get the man out of her sight.

"I need money," Locke finished, his spirit draining with the admission. "I have people who will loan it to me if I have worthy collateral."

She questioned him with her eyes.

"Sell that waterfront lot back to me," he said, the words rushing out. "I'll need terms, but I'll pay you the purchase price with interest. You've got all you need without that lot. And I need a lot that can make some money. So how about it?"

"No." She said it simply, quietly, with finality.

For a long second, he stared at her. Then he almost choked on the words, "That's your final answer?"

She nodded and put down her sewing. "Good night."

He gripped both arms of the rocking chair and shoved himself upright. He stood teetering uncertainly on the balls of his feet, scowling at her.

Mara returned his gaze, her fingers lightly resting on her little gun.

Without another word, Locke left, slamming the door so hard behind him that the glass rattled.

Mara stared thoughtfully after him.

✦

Clay came home long after the children had gone to bed. Shiloh sat in the parlor alone, waiting.

She looked up but did not rise to greet him with her usual kiss. He stood quietly in front of her, and the tension between them increased.

Finally, he said contritely, "I'm sorry you had to witness my outburst this afternoon."

Angry that his shouting at another man was uppermost on Clay's mind, Shiloh demanded, "How could you order me out of there like that?"

Hanging his head, Clay admitted, "I was so angry at being threatened that when I saw you, I suddenly realized that you're in danger as well."

Shiloh waited, not quite sure how that accounted for Clay's cruel rebuff at the office.

He continued, "Everyone is so short-tempered. I don't want you or the children exposed to it."

"That doesn't excuse what you said to me!"

"I know, but I was so mad that when I saw you, I was still reacting to that anger. I just blew up without thinking."

"Did he really threaten you?"

"He certainly did." Then Clay added, "I didn't mean to frighten you, but when I saw you in the doorway, well . . ." He stopped, floundering.

Reaching out her hand, Shiloh rose to stand close to him. "Do you think you are in danger?"

Clay slid his arms around her waist. "Let's just say that we all need to be far more careful from now on."

"All of us?"

"I don't think anyone would bother you or the children. They want me, either to give money to their various causes, or force me to choose one way or the other. Once I choose which side to back, the danger is still not over. No matter which way I go, the other sides may seek revenge to make me sorry for my choice."

Releasing her, Clay turned and walked toward the window. Over his shoulder, he said, "It isn't just that other men are pushing me hard."

He turned to face her. "The truth is, part of why I treated you so rudely this afternoon is that I feel you pressuring me too."

"I don't want to go against you, but I have my own strong feelings."

She approached him, her voice taking on conviction.

"This terrible war started thousands of miles from here, but it's brought conflict into our home. In all our married life, we've never had any really strong differences of opinion."

"I know, and I wish I felt as strongly as you do about which side is right. I thought that when Lincoln took office, I would know for sure. So far, his calling up troops and other actions makes me think he's wrong."

"I don't." Shiloh reached out and took Clay's hands. "I see what he's doing as necessary to protect the Union. You see it as tyranny and usurping power, don't you?"

Clay shrugged but didn't answer.

She continued, "We disagree, but I'm very open and frank about my convictions while you keep your thoughts to yourself. I get frustrated because it all seems so logical to me."

"I never learned to argue, Shiloh. My father never wanted to hear any opinions from his kids. If we did say something, he considered it talking back, and he'd come down on us hard. I learned to keep my mouth shut, but he never changed my opinions."

"I'm not your father. You can talk to me."

"It's not that easy, but I'll try." He took her into his arms.

Shiloh leaned against him, feeling they had made some progress but sensing that he could not yet honestly share his feelings. And that, she knew, could be hazardous to them both.

~ع~

Mara served breakfast to Lyman but did not join him. She had also learned to take him a cup of hot tea and a bowl of sugar each evening as he retired. Until Malvina had moved out, it had been her job to serve the tea. Lyman had explained as he spooned two teaspoons of sugar into his tea that he always slept better after drinking the hot beverage. But he pointedly never invited her to join him in this ritual.

She understood that there were some things a man, especially one reared as a southern gentleman, might do and some things he would not permit. Mara knew that Lyman could claim her physically, but he would not eat with her. He had been reared to believe she should serve him.

Usually Lyman ate in silence, preoccupied with the day's plans. This morning he looked at Mara as she set water on the stove to boil for washing dishes and said, "That big black buck friend of yours told me something interesting last night."

Mara glanced at Lyman, wondering where he had met with Samuel.

"I hired him to clean my office; he was still there when I

stopped by to pick up some papers last evening. He showed me a little doll with a pin through it."

Mara blinked in surprise. So Samuel had kept the second doll she had made for him. "A doll with a pin?" she asked.

"Looked like one I found in my office some time ago. Malvina said she showed it to you, thinking it had something to do with some kind of magic you might know about."

"She showed it to me."

"She told me that you claimed you didn't know anything about such things."

"There are lots of things I don't know anything about."

"Well your friend does. He said that someone who receives a doll like that is going to die."

"Really?"

"What nonsense! But he sure believes it. He started telling me stories about people he had heard about who had gotten one. They had all died."

Mara casually asked Lyman, "You don't believe in the dolls, do you?"

"Of course not. But I kept thinking about what he said. I didn't like the way he kept talking about it. I'm going to let him go. And I don't want him hanging around you."

"He's my friend, Lyman."

"I don't care." He looked sharply at her. "There's something about him that bothers me. So stay away from him."

Mara slowly walked over to the table. "I'm no slave, Lyman." She spoke with controlled anger. "You don't own me. I pick my own friends."

"Be careful what you say!"

"Or what?" she challenged, defiantly placing her hands on her hips. "You'll throw me out again?"

He pensively studied her before answering. When he spoke again, it was with the cool, assured tone he used in court to make a powerful point. "No."

He paused to dramatize what he was about to say. "But I know he's a runaway slave."

Mara sucked in her breath in astonishment at what she sensed coming.

"He doesn't have those papers yet, Mara." Lyman's face showed no emotion, but he had a triumphant look in his eyes. He added softly, menacingly, "I would sure hate to see the slave catchers get him now."

He threw his napkin on the table and pushed his chair back. "I think I'll have breakfast downtown so you can be alone. You may want to think about what I said."

❧ CHAPTER 18 ❧

LYMAN SLEPT late on Sunday. Mara had just sat down to a breakfast of cornbread and bacon when Samuel knocked at the back door.

She opened the door, holding back her annoyance. "He's asleep," she announced in a whisper. "He doesn't want you coming around here any more. Please go away before he sees you."

But Samuel stood his ground. Something about him had changed. For the first time, he didn't remove his hat in her presence.

"He'll set the slave catchers on you!" she warned, glancing apprehensively behind her. "He threatened to do that last night."

"He can't scare me. I'm going to be a free man."

"But you're not yet! Please, go!"

Samuel hesitated a moment before shaking his head. "You wanted me to let you know when I was going to the islands to gather eggs. Mr. Briggs told me yesterday to get ready. We're going this week."

"Thank you. Now, please!"

Nodding, Samuel started to turn away, then stopped and lifted his eyes toward the second-story bedrooms. "What are you going to do when he dies?"

"He's not going to die. He doesn't believe in that doll."

"Maybe he doesn't, but I do. He's going to die."

As Samuel again started to turn away, Mara impulsively asked, "Where did you put the second doll?"

A slow smile spread across Samuel's face. "You'll find out when the time comes."

As he walked away, Mara realized that he had not respectfully removed his hat. He had also openly defied her by refusing to answer her question. She thrust those thoughts aside to begin to make preparations for going to the Farallons.

⁓꧁꧂⁓

Shiloh had always looked forward to the renewed sense of comfort she received each Lord's Day. But with each passing Sunday, she had become more apprehensive. While Clay tied the horse, the children dashed toward their friends. Shiloh waited to walk with Clay.

As they started toward the church, nine-year-old Philip's tearful call made her spin around. The boy ran toward them.

"Philip!" she exclaimed. "What's the matter?"

"Odell Radcliffe just called me a Copperhead! Ajay says I should punch his nose."

"That's enough, Philip!" Clay interrupted. Turning to Shiloh, he added, "You take care of Philip. I'll deal with Ajay."

Shiloh nodded, recalling how coolly Mrs. Radcliffe had acted toward her since news of South Carolina's secession.

"Listen, Philip," Shiloh said, kneeling in her long skirt before him. "You mustn't let name-calling upset you. We're all God's children, and that makes us family. We don't want to go into church angry. You must try to get along with everyone, including Odell."

Philip considered that for a moment. "Ajay and me fight sometimes, so why can't I punch Odell just once?"

"Because it's wrong, that's why." Shiloh straightened up and took her son's hand. "Now, let's go find Odell and be friends."

Philip hung back. "I don't want to! Ajay said being called a Copperhead is bad, almost like swearing."

Shiloh looked up in exasperation and was relieved to see Clay striding toward her.

"It's all right, Shiloh," he said. "The children have gone off to their classes. Philip, you'd better run along and join them. And stay out of trouble."

Watching the boy dash off, Shiloh asked wistfully, "Is it going to be like this for the rest of the war?"

"Probably, unless John can talk some sense into this congregation. Let's go hear what he has to say today."

A few minutes later, as Shiloh hung her bonnet and coat in the cloakroom, Mrs. Radcliffe eased up beside her.

"I'm sure you know, Shiloh," the former Michigan resident said softly, "that your husband can't sit on the fence much longer." She glanced around before adding in a barely audible tone, "He could be in jeopardy if he doesn't choose soon."

Shiloh recoiled at the threat. "Sister Radcliffe!"

"Oh, don't act so shocked! We all know you favor abolition, and it's your duty to get your husband to join you, even though he is southern born."

"Look," Shiloh began, but the other woman rushed on.

"I have heard some talk around. As a friend and a member of this church, I think you'd be wise to see that Clay joins us. Be sure he's on the right side."

Shiloh didn't reply but brushed by the other woman and hurried to sit with Clay. She didn't want to trouble him, so she tried to act natural. But she perceived a slight hesitancy from some longtime friends. She felt the barely discernible drawing back of warmth and fellowship.

Although they had come together for years to worship,

some members had slowly changed from week to week. Today Shiloh noticed a quick, almost furtive look in their eyes, especially those she knew had come from northern states, like Mrs. Radcliffe. In spite of Brother Sledger's sermons on reconciliation, brotherly love, and tolerance, there was an undercurrent of tension.

Shiloh unsuccessfully tried to wrap herself in the comforting lyrics of promise they sang. Even reaching out to hold Clay's hand did not help. Some unspoken threat stalked the worshipers.

John Sledger had never been late, but this morning he was nowhere in sight. That added to Shiloh's unrest. Just as she started to comment to Clay, the preacher entered from a back side door. As always, his massive chest and powerful arms strained the cloth in his coat.

Watching him stride in front of the choir to his usual high-backed chair near the pulpit, Shiloh thought he walked like a man unafraid. He had needed that fearlessness in the Gold Rush days when he was one of the first preachers in town.

Clay nudged her and leaned close to whisper, "Look at him. I wonder what's the matter?"

Shiloh looked closer and whispered back, "I've never seen him look so grim. Something must have happened."

In the middle of the hymn, he rose slowly. By now, Shiloh knew the whole congregation had noticed the strange look on his face. The singing trailed off as they watched him approached the pulpit.

He didn't say a word but stood for a moment before the open Bible. His blue eyes skimmed the congregation as though looking for someone. Into the silence, with everyone focused on him, he spoke.

His voice, whether in song or sermon, generally reverberated like thunder. But today his words were low, yet they held a power that clearly reached every ear.

"Brothers and sisters, you all know that I believe God called me to this church. He called me here to teach you His ways as best I know how. Ever since the first state seceded from the Union, I have refused to speak for or against either side. But that has not stopped members of this congregation from coming to me privately to urge that I take a stand."

Shiloh glanced at Clay, who watched Sledger intently.

"Last night," he said in a slightly louder voice, "a group of men came to my home with an ultimatum."

Shiloh heard startled murmurs and realized she had unconsciously contributed to the sound.

"They told me that if I did not stand here this morning and announce I had chosen a side, part of our church family would walk out, never to return."

A collective gasp swept the congregation. The pastor turned and lumbered rapidly back to the door through which he had entered moments before. "I regret with all my heart," he said over his shoulder, "that when I came over to unlock the church this morning . . ."

His voice trailed off while every neck craned to see what he was doing.

He opened the door and reached through it. Absolute silence gripped the congregation.

He pulled something toward him as he finished his sentence. "I found this!"

At first glance, Shiloh thought she saw a scarecrow: old clothes stuffed with something to represent a very large man.

Wordlessly, Sledger reached down to a rope dangling from the figure. Gripping the end of the rope, he dropped the figure, bringing small cries from the worshipers.

Sledger held the end of the rope high, so everyone could see the hangman's noose knotted about the figure's neck. Its stuffed pant legs swung in a deathly dance just above the floor.

While people stared in fascination, Sledger's mighty voice boomed across the sanctuary. "I have the dubious distinction of joining Dr. Scott in being hanged in effigy from my own church belfry."

Shiloh heard herself exclaim, "Oh, Lord, no!" Her words were drowned out by other worshipers' cries of surprise and dismay.

He paused dramatically, giving Shiloh and Clay an opportunity to exchange surprised glances and look around at other people. Some were clearly as shocked as they, but others sat stonefaced.

Clay leaned toward Shiloh and whispered, "Look at William Judd and Earl Quesenbery."

Shiloh shook her head in dismay. They had pressured Clay to join them in supporting the Confederacy.

Sledger's voice boomed across the pews, bringing all attention back to him. "You all know my southern roots."

Again, there were whispered exclamations as people anticipated his next words.

"But," the pastor continued, his voice rising with power, "I am God's man above all, and I will serve all of you, regardless of your political affiliation, as long as you want me."

He took a deep breath and added in a voice like a clap of thunder, "I pray that you good brothers and sisters will all understand. I will not take sides, and I will not be intimidated by anyone, not even the devil himself!"

Shiloh wanted to shout her approval, but there was a stirring behind her. She turned with Clay as Judd, Quesenberry, and other southern sympathizers with their wives noisily arose from their pews and pushed toward the aisles.

"Please!" Sledger pleaded. "Don't do this! Don't split our church! Don't walk out in anger!"

They kept walking toward the rear of the church and out the door. Sledger fell silent. Shiloh heard several women weep around her and became aware of men's voices in low conversation. She suddenly realized that people had begun staring at Clay.

Slowly, he noticed it too.

Shiloh whispered, "They wonder why you didn't walk out."

Clay didn't answer but lifted his hymnal and glanced down at the pages.

Sledger took his cue. "Brothers and sisters," he cried, his voice thick with emotion, "let us finish singing our hymn."

∾ CHAPTER 19 ∾

AFTER CHURCH, Merritt joined the family for the mid-day meal where he enjoyed laughing with his grandchildren. After they left the table, Shiloh and Clay recounted the morning's dramatic events.

Merritt leaned back in his chair and studied his son-in-law across the table. "Was that very difficult for you, Clay?"

"After the others walked out, I believe I was the only person of southern birth left. Everyone stared at me. I couldn't tell whether they were angry, suspicious, or pleased."

Shiloh explained, "We found out right after the service. Most of the Union supporters tried to congratulate Clay for making the right decision."

"But I hadn't made a decision," he said. "When I told them that, they backed off, not knowing what to think about me."

Merritt commented, "I'm sure you know that it's getting harder and harder for anyone with southern sympathies to get much of a welcome in San Francisco."

"I'm keenly aware of it," Clay replied. "The only Palmetto flag left in the city seems to be at Lyman Wallace's home. He keeps it flying in spite of having had rotten eggs thrown at it."

"I wish Mara would leave there," Shiloh said with a sigh. "With tensions so high, I'm afraid somebody might try to burn the place down or shoot into it. She could get hurt or killed."

187

Merritt asked, "Have you talked to her about leaving?"

"Not recently. When I try to talk to her, she gets upset. She thinks I'm trying to get her to move out on moral grounds."

"Aren't you?" Merritt asked.

"Partly, of course, but I'm also very concerned about her. She's like a sister to me. I don't want anything to happen to her."

Clay stood up. "Those kids are too quiet. I'd better go check on them."

When the door closed behind Clay, Merritt asked, "How's he holding up under all the pressure?"

"I'm concerned about him, especially since that awful day when you took me to his office."

Merritt hadn't pressed her for details of that day, but he had gone back downtown to ask questions. Eventually, he heard stories about Clay throwing Noah Oakley out of the office and why. However, Merritt knew that most stories were slanted by personal bias. He would prefer to hear Shiloh's account, yet he respected her privacy.

"You may as well know what happened, Papa," she said. Briefly she recounted what she had seen and heard in Clay's office.

She stopped short of telling him how Clay had reacted when he realized she had witnessed the scene. Shiloh could not bring herself to share such a personal incident, even with her father.

After a long silence, Merritt mused, "It's going to be harder and harder for either a neutral person or a southern sympathizer to live in this city. I'm sure Clay knows that, especially after this morning's incident at the church and Philip's almost getting into a fight because someone called him a Copperhead."

"That's so unfair! The children aren't responsible for what their father does or does not believe or do."

"Wartime and fairness don't go together. It seems to me that some adults are using their offspring to bring more pressure to bear on Clay through your children."

"I don't want them to suffer because of this. It hurts me, and I'm sure it hurts Clay too."

"The central valley and Southern California are largely against the Union."

Shiloh blinked, not understanding what that had to do with their discussion. "Yes, I've heard that," she replied.

"My editor friend gets copies of newspapers from all over the state. I like to read most of them so I know what's going on elsewhere. For example, did you know that down in the valley town of Visalia, Union soldiers were publicly jeered, and Jefferson Davis was cheered?"

Shiloh still wasn't sure where her father was going with such remarks. She shook her head and waited.

"Another valley newspaper," he continued, "called the *Tulare Post* changed its name to *Equal Rights Expositor* and printed stories that led readers to kill two men from a nearby military post. In retaliation, troops destroyed the newspaper plant."

"How awful! What happened to freedom of the press?"

"The real question is, what's going to happen to our other rights during this war, including the right of habeas corpus?"

Confused, Shiloh asked, "What's that?"

"A writ of habeas corpus requires that a person be brought before a judge or court for a hearing. It's a practice dating back to Anglo-Saxon common-law days, and it prevents the illegal jailing of a citizen. Without it, a person could be imprisoned without even knowing what he's accused of.

"My editor friend at the newspaper showed me a copy of the Constitution, but we disagree on what it means when it says . . . let's see if I can remember the wording or something close to it."

Merritt closed his eyes and frowned in thought. "Oh, yes. It says that the writ of habeas corpus shall not be suspended, unless in cases of rebellion or invasion when the public safety may require it."

Shiloh leaned forward in fear. "Rebellion? Like the war between the states?"

"That's what we were discussing. My friend wondered if, under that clause, men could be arrested for suspected treason, disloyalty, aiding rebels, or inciting or participating in a riot."

"What do you think, Papa?"

"The real question is what does President Lincoln think?"

Shiloh shook her head. "He wouldn't dare! Would he?"

"Power does strange things to people, Shiloh, especially wartime power. Do you understand what I'm saying?"

She slowly nodded. "I think so. You want us to move away from here. Right?"

"It's the only way I can see to protect your family."

"No, Papa!" She leaped up suddenly, causing her chair to almost fall over. "This is our home."

"I understand how you feel, Shiloh. But please, for everyone's safety, talk to Clay about it." He added softly, "Before it's too late."

At first, Shiloh didn't even want to mention her father's idea to Clay. She reasoned that he already had enough stress. Eventually common sense persuaded her to talk to her husband.

Shiloh walked into the parlor where Clay sat reading a newspaper. But before she could say anything to him, Mara came to the front door, asking Shiloh to join her for a short walk to talk. Shiloh let Clay know she would be back shortly and went outside with her friend.

"I'm glad you came by," Shiloh began. "We haven't had a good talk in some time."

"I know. We're both busy."

Shiloh resisted the temptation to bring up her concern for Mara's safety. Instead, she turned her attention to why Mara had come by.

"Is everything all right with you?" Shiloh asked.

"Nothing I can't handle."

Shiloh heard a hint of something new in Mara's voice. Usually, she spoke so emphatically that she left no doubt she could handle whatever came.

"Something different going on?" Shiloh guessed.

Mara had decided to tell Shiloh about Locke's visit and Jared's warnings. But now she wasn't so sure.

"Different?" she repeated. "Yes and no, I guess."

"That's a strange answer."

Nodding, Mara explained, "Lyman threatened to set slave catchers on Samuel if he came around again."

"I thought Samuel had bought his freedom."

"It's in the process, but it takes a long time."

"He strikes me as a good man, and he obviously cares for you. Not many men would wait all these years for a woman to change her mind."

Mara warned, "Don't start telling me what I should do."

"I only gave my opinion about Samuel," Shiloh protested.

The momentary flare of tensions caused them to walk in silence for a while.

Mara broke the silence with, "Jefferson Locke wants me to sell him back a lot I bought through Jared Huntley."

Shiloh's eyebrows shot up at mention of Jared's name. She had learned never to trust the man.

Choosing her words carefully, Shiloh commented, "I hope you're careful around Jared."

"I hadn't seen him much. He's been in Sacramento a lot."

"He should be right at home in the political arena there. I never knew a man who could look you in the eye and lie like he can. But even with his connections, his southern sympathies might get in the way."

"That won't be a problem for him. He'll switch loyalties as easily as you and I change clothes."

"That sounds logical." Suddenly, Shiloh looked hard at Mara. "He's the one who hit you, isn't he?"

Through angry, narrowed eyes, Mara said grimly, "He'll never do it again."

"He might if you give him a chance. Why do you even talk to him?"

"He says he can protect me from Locke."

"Locke? Did he threaten you?"

"Not exactly, but the fact he went to Jared after I refused to sell him the lot makes me wonder if he's planning something."

"I don't trust either of those two."

"You don't like any of the men I deal with, do you?"

"I just want what's best for you, and those two don't measure up. Neither does Lyman Wallace."

Mara stopped abruptly. "Don't start again!"

Shiloh knew she had taken a risk, but she had to try once again. "But it's so dangerous now. I've heard someone threw rotten eggs at the house because of that Palmetto flag. Next time, somebody may decide to shoot at the place."

"Someone already has." At Shiloh's startled expression, Mara hastily added, "Someone rode by in a carriage and fired musket balls. One of them hit the post where the flag is attached. The other broke an upstairs window."

"Please!" Shiloh gripped her friend's hands. "Move out before you get hurt."

"I can't do that; not yet, anyway."

"Why not?" Shiloh's words were louder than she intended.

"I need Lyman for some business ventures."

"Then pay him in cash, as you would any lawyer! But get away before something terrible happens!"

Suppressing a smile, Mara said, "Well, I do have another possibility."

"Take it! Take it!"

"Then you approve of my accepting Jared's request that I move in with him?"

"Don't tease me, Mara! You know what I mean."

The smile vanished. "Yes, I know." She spoke seriously.

"But I do have to meet with Jared one more time. I told him I'd think about what he said regarding Locke and me."

"Don't meet with him. Send a message instead."

"Nothing's going to happen. Jared knows better than to touch me again."

Shaking her head vigorously, Shiloh protested, "He's shrewd. If you turn him down again, he might find some devious way of dealing with you. Please stay away from him and Locke! Lyman too."

Irritated but touched by Shiloh's concern, Mara took a deep breath, then nodded. "Maybe you're right. I'll think about it while I'm out at the Farallon Islands."

"The Farallon Islands?"

"I'm interested in the seabird egg business. Your father gave me the name of Manton Briggs, who goes out to gather eggs each spring. Samuel's already going with him next week. I'll go see him and arrange to go as well."

"What if he turns you down?"

"He won't. I plan to take along some gold coins to show him I'm a potential investor in the business."

For the space of a few measured heartbeats, Shiloh considered what her friend had said. "All right, but as soon as you get back, let me know what you've decided."

"I will. What's going on with you?"

Taking a deep breath, Shiloh told her friend about her father's suggestion to move out of San Francisco.

⁓⧉⁓

In his office the next morning, Clay spent some time reading the usual stack of newspapers his clerk, Gustavus Maynard, collected for him.

The *Los Angeles Star,* although in the center of strongly anti-Union sentiment, urged readers to stay out of the conflict. Instead, the paper urged providing "shelter for all who may flee from the storm."

Pushing the *Star* aside, Clay picked up the *Marysville Express* from a small valley community north of Sacramento. Its editor seemed to have some strong connection to the Knights of the Golden Circle.

Not that they're much of a threat to the Union anymore, Clay mused. *Not since General Sumner moved so decisively after General Johnston's resignation.*

Putting the paper down, Clay reflected briefly on the conflicting stories he had heard about the Union's new supreme military commander in the West.

Clay reached for the *California Daily Times,* the Republican newspaper out of Sacramento. It had a short article about the progress of the Central Pacific Railroad Company and some of its directors.

Clay personally liked Judah, but he knew relatively little about the others. Clay made a mental note to ask his father-in-law whether he should invest more money in that company. Merritt had access to all kinds of information that Clay did not.

He glanced up at the sound of his clerk's voice.

"Just a minute, please. I'll see if Mr. Patton . . ."

"He'll see me! Now, stand aside."

Clay rose as his door burst open. His clerk exclaimed from behind the visitor, "Mr. Patton, I tried to . . ."

"It's all right, Gus," Clay interrupted. "Hello, Denby. Have a seat."

"Thanks." The stout man spoke around his habitual dead cigar stub. "Haven't seen you in quite a spell, Clay."

"I've been here."

"I know." Gladwin said, removing the cigar stub from his mouth.

Clay didn't appreciate his visitor's barging in on him. "What can I do for you, Gladwin?"

"You got it wrong. I came to do something for you."

"What would that be?"

Leaning forward, Gladwin said, "Now that you're a marked man . . ."

A frown tugged Clay's forehead into deep furrows. "A marked man?"

"After the southern sympathizers walked out of your church on Sunday, you're all alone in a mighty mean and nasty political situation."

"I've told you before, I don't wish to discuss my political choices."

"No need to use that cold tone with me, Clay. You are no longer going to be welcomed by the secesh people, and the Union men consider you suspect. That leaves you only one good alternative—me."

Clay slowly pushed his chair back and stood up. "You can be emperor of Pacifica if you can work it out, but I'm not going to help you. Now, if you'll excuse me, I've got some reading to do."

Gladwin's notorious temper showed in his gray eyes and the way he bit down on the cigar stub. "You didn't hear me out, Clay. I'm giving you a direction to go. If you turn me down, you've ruined all three opportunities. Let me explain . . ."

Clay strode around the desk and thrust his face close to Gladwin's. "You hear so much, you've probably heard what happened to the last man who came in here trying to tell me what to do and think."

Startled, Gladwin drew back.

Clay asked through clenched teeth, "Now will you leave on your own, or do you need my help?"

Backing toward the door, Gladwin blustered, "You'll be sorry about this!"

"I've heard that before," Clay reminded him in a calmer voice. He waited until Gladwin slammed the door then sank back in his chair.

What if he's right? he asked himself, shaking his head. *What's happening to me? That's twice I've lost my temper. At least Shiloh wasn't here to see it this time.* Clay stared thoughtfully toward the office door, aware that he was fast running out of options.

◈

In the early evening of the lengthening spring days, Mara pulled a shawl across her shoulders. She draped the right end so it hid the little derringer pressing comfortingly against her waist. If somebody had again started to follow her, she wanted to know who it was and why. She offered herself as bait, but whoever bit would get a nasty surprise.

She sauntered along Rincon Hill's fashionable residential district located on First Street between Harrison and Bryant. She passed homes of San Francisco's rich and famous people while resisting the temptation to see if someone was trailing her.

She saw no signs of that on her tour, which took her past other facilities that shared San Francisco's lowest hill. Fourteen years before, the hill had become a government reserve protected by a battery of 32-pounders. Half a dozen years later, on the eastern extremity, a marine hospital had been erected. A year ago, to the south, the first Catholic hospital on the Pacific Coast had been built.

Mara had begun her casual walk with every muscle tense, ready to respond if necessary. Turning around to head back to the Wallace mansion, she relaxed. There had been no evidence of anyone trailing her.

Rounding the corner of a high stone fence, she was startled to see Jared Huntley.

She stopped her sharp intake of breath and spoke calmly, "The next time I saw you, I expected it to be at the house."

Jared grinned knowingly. "And possibly upset Lyman? You know me better than that."

"I suppose I do." She glanced in all directions but could not see his carriage or driver. That bothered her. How had he gotten here without her noticing?

"You told me the other day that you would think about what we discussed," he said, coming directly to the point. "Have you decided?"

"About which? Running from Locke's vengeance, letting you protect me, or moving in with you?"

"Take your pick."

"What if I don't like any of those choices?"

With a shrug, Jared said, "I don't think you have any real alternatives. But in my opinion, the most dangerous thing you could do is underestimate Locke."

"Oh? Why is that?"

"He's got an interesting mind. For example, we know that he considers you responsible for his possible ruin. What if he decides to punish you indirectly? Suppose he thought the greatest pain he could inflict on you would be to strike at someone very important to you?"

Mara's face tightened. "Nothing had better happen to Shiloh or her family!"

"Don't tell me!" Jared held up his open palms in a defensive motion. "I'm just trying to protect you."

Biting back her sharp answer, Mara stalled. "I'm going to the Farallons to see how seabird eggs are gathered. When I get back, I'll have some answers."

She walked away with chills rippling down her back.

❧ CHAPTER 20 ❧

MARA HAD mixed feelings a couple of days later when she came to see Shiloh. Mara began with what she considered good news.

"I was really pleased that Manton Briggs gave in so easily to my request go to the Farallons. I guess my gold double eagles convinced him I was a potential investor in his business."

Shiloh suppressed a disappointed sigh. She considered the trip dangerous and unnecessary, but she knew that it was useless to argue when Mara had made up her mind. "When are you going?"

"Depends on the weather. Sometime this week."

"You be careful."

"How many times do I have to tell you that I can take care of myself?"

Shiloh thoughtfully regarded her friend before replying, "My, you're touchy this morning." When Mara did not respond, Shiloh asked, "What's bothering you?"

Mara hesitated before admitting, "A couple of nights ago, I thought somebody was following me again."

"I thought that had stopped!"

"It did, for quite awhile."

"Did you see anybody?"

"No, and I didn't hear any footsteps."

"Then how do you know it's happening again?"

"I can't explain it exactly. I just sort of felt as though someone were watching. I had a kind of tingling feeling at the nape of my neck."

Shiloh remembered other times over the years when her friend had seemed to sense things that eventually came about. Trying to calm her friend, Shiloh said, "It was probably just your imagination."

"I've thought of that, but last night, I set out to see if it would happen again. It didn't. I kept a close eye out; casually, of course. I didn't see or hear anyone."

"Sounds as if I'm right. You imagined the other."

"Just the same, I was startled when I walked around a corner and ran into Jared Huntley." At Shiloh's questioning look, Mara explained, "I don't know how he got there. He had obviously been waiting for me because he said he had come to warn me against Locke."

"You told me the other day that you would meet with Jared one more time. Are you counting this last encounter as the final one?"

Before Mara could answer, Clay burst through the front door, clutching a newspaper.

Shiloh glanced at his face and hurried toward him, "What is it?"

Clay paused, glancing at Mara. She rose quickly.

"I've got to be going," she said. "Shiloh, we'll finish our conversation later."

Nodding, Shiloh gave her friend a quick hug then closed the door after her. She turned to her husband.

"That new general wants to see me in his office this afternoon."

Shiloh's heart leaped to her throat. "What?"

"General Sumner sent word that . . ."

"But why?" Shiloh interrupted. "You didn't do anything."

"I know, but I thought of a possibility. Asbury Harpending came to my office earlier today. He's returned with letters of marque from the Confederacy, and he wants me to help finance the outfitting of a privateer."

"Privateer? You mean like a pirate ship?"

"When a country sanctions such a ship, it's called a privateer, not a pirate. But the purpose is much the same. Harpending wants to seize steamships carrying gold to the mint in Philadelphia then divert the bullion to the South."

"You turned him down, of course?"

"Certainly. But someone could have been watching and reported our meeting to the general."

"But the general has no way of knowing what you said, so you don't have anything to worry about." Shiloh tried to sound convincing, but dread tightened her chest. "Maybe it'll be like the time General Johnston called you in. It could be that this new general just wants to talk."

"That doesn't seem likely. There's more than meets the eye in all this. I mean, up to now, people have asked me for money or made veiled threats. I've turned them all down. But when the army starts getting involved . . ." Clay let his sentence trail off.

A tremor of fear shook Shiloh. She vividly recalled her discussions with John Sledger and her father about military arrests of civilians in wartime.

She was sure that Clay had the same thoughts, but neither of them voiced their concerns. Instead, Shiloh forced herself to urge, "Let me go with you! Please?"

"You know I can't do that. I've got to go alone."

"Then find Papa and ask him to come stay with the children and me until you return."

The moment the words burst from her, Shiloh regretted them. They revealed just how very frightened she felt. *Be strong!* she reminded herself. *He's got enough to think about without my concerns.*

She said quickly, "I know you'll be all right, but I would prefer to have Papa here until you're back."

"I'll find him," Clay replied. He was silent for a moment. "And maybe you should both pray for me."

~❧~

Mara had just fit the key into the back door to Lyman Wallace's house when Samuel came running up. She started to rebuke him for coming around after Lyman's warning, but the words died on her lips. Perspiration glistened on Samuel's curly black hair and slid down his dark cheeks.

"You got to hide me!" he puffed, whipping off his hat and glancing back the way he had come. "Slave catchers are chasing me!"

There was no doubt in Mara's mind that Samuel spoke the truth. Hurriedly unlocking the door, she instructed, "Hide in the bushes until I make sure Lyman's not here."

It took her only a couple of minutes to satisfy herself that the house was empty. She silently castigated Lyman for having put slave catchers on Samuel's trail.

But that's just like him, she fumed, heading toward the back door. *He's making sure that he won't ever have to worry about Samuel and me.*

Pausing, she mentally added, *Shiloh will be glad to know she's about to get her wish about Lyman Wallace.*

After glancing around to make sure nobody was watching, she called softly to Samuel. "Come on. Up the back stairs. You can stay in my old room. I'm not using it since Malvina moved out."

After assuring Samuel that she would return soon, Mara hurried back to the kitchen. Samuel could not stay long in the house. Mara probed her mind for ways to help him escape the city. She was tying her aprons strings when a loud banging on the back door startled her. She took her time answering, formulating what she would to say to the slave catchers.

Two rough-looking white men stood outside, their feet apart and braced as though they expected to be attacked. Each had a pistol stuck in his belt and gripped a short club. The men lowered these to their sides when Mara opened the door.

The burly man explained gruffly, "We're after a runaway slave. He escaped from his owner in South Carolina fifteen, maybe sixteen years ago."

Narrowing her eyes, Mara wondered why he seemed familiar. She noticed that both men stepped back slightly. She understood their unconscious act. This was obviously a rich white man's house. His servant or slave had to be treated with more respect than some blacks.

"We almost caught him back there," the shorter man added quickly, showing a mouthful of broken teeth. "He run this way. Big buck, six feet or so tall, well built, good muscles, maybe two hundred pounds. About thirty-five years old. You seen him?"

"Sorry," Mara replied calmly. "Mr. Lyman Wallace," she indicated the mansion with a motion of her head, "is from the South. He does not allow colored men around here."

The taller man laughed and nudged his companion. "I can

sure see why. Ain't she a looker? Don't see many high yeller gals around here."

Yeller gal! Mara mentally pounced on the term, recalling where she had seen this disreputable man before. In '49, when she had her outdoor bakery, he and three other slave catchers had tried to take Samuel and his friend, Joseph, into custody at gunpoint.

They cited the Federal Act of 1793 that allowed slaves who had escaped to another state to be returned to their owners. When Mara protested, the taller man had called her an "uppity yeller gal." Clay had intervened, pointing out that California was not yet a state, and the law did not apply. The catchers had not collected the three hundred dollars reward for each fugitive.

Mara smiled inside, recalling with pleasure how that interruption had caused her pie to burn. She had thrown the hot burned pie at the burly man's chest.

Glaring at the men, Mara said "The fact is, Mr. Wallace doesn't allow *any* men to hang around here, especially the likes of *you*." Her voice had taken on a sharp edge.

"Now see here . . ." the burly man blustered, jamming his finger close to her face. He broke off and yelped in pain as Mara instantly leaned forward and bit down hard.

She retreated inside, leaving him cursing as the shorter man laughed at him.

Over her shoulder, Mara delivered a haughty parting shot. "If you ever come around here again, Mr. Wallace will horsewhip you both within an inch of your lives!"

❦

Shiloh saw her father's lathered horse trotting up the hill. She hurried out to meet him so they could talk privately for a moment.

As she ran up to the buggy, Merritt said, "Clay told me what little he knew."

"Oh, Papa!" she exclaimed as he stepped to the ground, "What's going on?"

He held out his arms and enfolded her. "Don't be frightened. I'm sure it will be all right."

"But what possible reason could General Sumner have for calling Clay to come see him?"

Merritt didn't answer but held her silently until she pushed back in alarm. "What aren't you telling me?"

He reached into the buggy seat and picked up a thin newspaper. Shiloh recognized it as an eastern newspaper that had been delivered by Pony Express.

"Bad news?" she whispered.

Tucking the paper under his arm, he slipped his free hand around her shoulder. "Let's go inside where we can sit," he said gently.

In the parlor, Merritt handed the paper to Shiloh, saying, "Read this."

She glanced at the headline: "Lincoln Suspends Habeas Corpus," then asked with sudden apprehension, "What does this mean?"

"Remember we talked about habeas corpus the other day? Without it, a person could be imprisoned without ever being brought before a judge or even knowing what he's accused of."

"What's that got to do with Clay?"

"I hope nothing, but you need to understand what a momentous event it is to have that writ suspended by the president. Read the story. Then we can talk."

Skimming the page, Shiloh quickly grasped the significant facts.

In Maryland, General George Cadwalader, in command of Fort McHenry near Baltimore, had sent some soldiers to the home of John Merryman in the middle of the night. They had locked him up on charges of treason.

A writ of habeas corpus had been issued by Roger B. Taney,

chief justice of the U.S. Supreme Court. He ordered that Merryman be brought before him that very day in Baltimore.

Instead of obeying the justice's writ, Cadwalader sent a staff colonel who claimed that the general had been authorized by the president of the United States to suspend the writ of habeas corpus for public safety.

The chief justice then sent an opinion to Lincoln, citing habeas corpus requirements. Taney admonished Lincoln that the executive office can't violate the law.

Shiloh stared at the final words, then looked up at her father through suddenly blurred vision. "Does this mean the army is going to arrest Clay!"

"Not so fast! Not so fast!" Merritt took her hands and gently pulled her back down to the sofa beside him. "This happened back east. Besides, this isn't over yet."

"Could the president ignore a supreme court justice's order?"

"Lincoln could cite something that we found when we examined the Constitution. It is silent on whether Congress or the executive branch has the power to enforce a section dealing with rebellion."

As the terrible implications seeped into her mind, Shiloh observed, "So Lincoln could claim that the Confederacy is in rebellion and use the army...?"

"Exactly!" Merritt broke in. "He could arrest citizens without a trial, claiming that since the Constitution doesn't specifically forbid it, he can suspend habeas corpus. Besides, he's commander-in-chief of the armed forces, who's going to stop him?"

Shiloh could only stare in disbelief at her father.

He added, "Of course, from a political viewpoint, it wouldn't be wise for Lincoln to publicly do such things, so he would have an appropriate cabinet member do it."

Shiloh shook her head. "I just can't believe this!"

"Could this suspension of habeas corpus be why General Sumner called Clay into his office?"

"I doubt it. You can see from the newspaper that when a civilian was arrested by the military, soldiers went in the middle of the night. The man was not summoned as Clay was. Merryman was seized without warning. I'm quite sure that the general has another reason he wanted Clay to come to him."

"But what?" Shiloh jumped up, struggling to control her fear.

"I don't know. But…" he paused.

"What, Papa?"

He rose and put his arms around her. "Please Shiloh, for everyone's safety, talk to Clay about moving as soon as he comes back from seeing the general."

~ જ~

Clay arrived a few minutes before the appointed time of two o'clock, but half an hour had passed. At first, he brooded about the delay. Then he decided that it was deliberate. If he got impatient, his emotions might cause him to make a mistake.

He forced himself to relax and pass the time by trying to remember what he had heard about the oldest general in the U.S. Army. He was a friend of Lincoln's, strongly pro-Union, and a military leader given to impatience.

Clay had heard two especially intriguing stories about Sumner. One claimed that his thundering voice had earned him the nickname of Bull of the Woods, Bull Head, or just Bull. Another version appealed to Clay. It asserted that Sumner got his nickname after a musket ball supposedly bounced off his head in the war with Mexico.

A young soldier in dark-blue uniform came out of an inner office and approached Clay. "Please follow me, sir," he said.

Clay obeyed, silently praying that he walk away from Sumner in the same way he had left Johnston.

Sumner had a wide forehead with very gray hair that just brushed the tops of his ears. His full beard was white, emphasizing his prominent cheekbones and strong, direct gaze. He looked up from his desk and motioned for Clay to take a seat.

"I'll be brief," he announced in a voice that was a little lower than a roar. "I understand that you have been approached by parties representing all three divisionary groups currently at work in this state."

Clay slowly nodded but didn't speak.

"You have taken a firm stand against those representing the move for an independent nation," Sumner continued. "However, you have been ambivalent toward those seeking your support for the Union and the Confederacy."

Clay sat quietly, trying to guess where the general was going.

"I have heard of your astute business achievements with both the quicksilver mine and the stagecoach line. I congratulate you on being a self-made man."

Clay decided to keep still and listen.

"This war is going to cause great inconvenience to many people, Patton. A man's name and his reputation are synonymous. It's very difficult to clear one's name if it is ever sullied. Naturally, it is important that a man make wise choices." Sumner stood, causing Clay to also rise. "Thank you for coming in, Patton."

Moments later, Clay left the Presidio. He was grateful to be able to do so but he was also keenly aware of the clear meaning in the general's brief comments.

❧

Mara eagerly awaited for darkness and hoped that Lyman would retire early so she could slip out and help Samuel escape the slave catchers. She had hidden some food and clothing in a sack in the backyard. She had also thought of a way for Samuel to stay out of sight until she persuaded Lyman to call the search off. When she got back from the Farallon Islands, she would make Shiloh happy by leaving Lyman permanently.

Mara glanced out the parlor window and saw Lyman and

his estranged wife arrive in a hired carriage. Mara frowned, wondering if that meant they had reconciled or if she had just come to get something. Either way, it would delay her from talking to Lyman alone.

She was relieved when he said something to the driver, who nodded and wrapped the reins around the stock of the buggy whip.

The driver's going to wait, Mara realized with satisfaction, *so Malvina's probably not going to stay long.*

Mara was back in the kitchen before the front door opened.

Malvina cried, "It's not just *your* money you're giving to those Golden Circle friends of yours! Half of it's mine! That's the law in California."

"Don't tell me about the law!" Lyman growled. "And keep your voice down."

"Oh, so you don't want your fancy black woman to hear us quarreling? Well, I don't care if she does."

"You leave her out of this!"

Mara heard footsteps on the stairs and the voices faded somewhat, but Malvina's still sounded shrill and angry.

"Oh, you'd like that, wouldn't you? But will you like it when all this comes out in divorce court?"

Divorce? Mara's eyebrows shot up. She hadn't expected that.

❧ CHAPTER 21 ❧

CLAY HURRIED home to report on his meeting with General Sumner. But as Shiloh and Merritt congratulated Clay, his gaze fell on the newspaper headline.

He read aloud, "'Lincoln Suspends Habeas Corpus?'" Turning surprised eyes on his wife and father-in-law, Clay asked, "Is that true?"

Shiloh nodded, frightened by the change in her husband's face. "Papa got it from the Pony Express."

Clay's jaw muscles twitched as he turned to Merritt.

"I'm afraid it's true. I've read the article carefully. Do you know what it means?"

"Yes, and I know that it's wrong!" Clay answered emphatically. "Lincoln has no right to do that!"

Merritt replied, "The chief justice of the United States Supreme Court agrees with you, according to the story. But the president apparently will challenge him, and because he's commander-in-chief of the armed forces, I suspect he'll do what he wants."

Handing Clay the thin paper, Shiloh suggested, "You'd better read it for yourself."

Nodding, he sat down on the sofa and skimmed the text, his face darkening with anger. When he looked up, specks of fire glittered in his eyes.

"That's the way tyranny begins!" he cried, leaping up. "No one will dare use the right of free speech unless he's willing to risk being jailed without trial!"

Shiloh reached out to her husband. "Please! You're getting very upset!"

"I've got reason! So does every man in this country who dares to think or say or do anything that the power in Washington disagrees with!"

He turned and rapidly paced the length of the floor. Shiloh started toward him, but Merritt gently took her arm and held her back.

Clay stopped at the window and looked out, his long body stiff while his fists slowly opened and closed. Silence fell in the room.

Then Clay slowly turned to face the others.

Shiloh was relieved to see that the darkness had gone out of Clay's face.

In a calm voice, he announced, "The president has just made it easy for me to make my decision."

As soon as she heard Malvina storm from the house, Mara hurried to peer through the parlor window. The driver jumped down from his carriage and relieved Malvina of two carpet bags. When they were lifted aboard and his passenger seated, he drove down the hill.

Mara wasn't sure that now was a good time to talk to Lyman, but she had to know how he would react to her request. Whether Lyman agreed to help Samuel or not, Mara realized she had to get him out of her room before he was discovered.

She climbed the stairs and gently knocked on the closed bedroom door. "Lyman, it's Mara. I need to talk to you."

"Later." The word was muffled but understandable.

Pausing only long enough to strengthen her resolve, she replied, "It's important that we talk now."

There was a pause then an unhappy grumble. "All right. Come in, but make it fast. I'm in no mood for conversation."

She entered to find him moodily rocking in a large upholstered chair. She crossed the room to him. "I wish you hadn't set the slave catchers on Samuel's trail."

The rocking stopped. "Has he been here?" Lyman demanded.

"He didn't need to be," she replied evasively. "Two white men with clubs and guns came looking for him."

"I hope they've caught him by now."

When he began rocking again, Mara said firmly, "I want you to tell them to stop."

"You want?" Getting to his feet, Lyman glared at her. "Malvina wants! You want! What about my wants?"

Standing her ground, Mara said, "As you must know, your former partner is processing the documents so Samuel can buy his freedom."

"I don't care, and I don't want to hear about it!"

After taking a slow breath, Mara risked saying what she felt had to be done. "Very well. Then I'll be on my way." She turned.

"Where you going?"

"Back to my house, I guess." She opened the door.

"Wait! Wait!" Lyman called. He crossed the floor in his carpet slippers. "You don't have to act like that." He reached out to her, but she pulled back.

"I've told you before: There's nothing between me and Samuel but friendship."

Lyman smiled knowingly. "I've lived long enough to learn that a fine-looking man and a beautiful woman cannot remain just friends. Don't try to convince me differently."

Shrugging, she said, "Suit yourself. But regardless of what you choose to believe, I consider Samuel my friend. Right now, he's in trouble because you told the slave catchers that he's a fugitive. He's worked too long to buy his freedom for you to take it away when he's so close."

Lyman's eyes narrowed in warning. "Malvina is right. You are an uppity..."

"Don't say it!" Mara interrupted. "One of those slave catchers did, and he's fortunate that I didn't take the hide right off of him with my teeth and nails."

Her words were quiet but carried such force that Lyman cocked his head in admiration. "Maybe that's one of the reasons I find you so appealing." His gaze swept her from head to toe. "Among other reasons."

"Are you going to call them off?"

After a thoughtful pause, Lyman nodded. "If it will make you happy again."

"It's a start."

"All right, Mara. First thing tomorrow, I'll take care of it." He reached for her. "Now let's just enjoy being together for a while."

She let him pull her close, but her mind jumped to the next step in her plan. She had to get Samuel out of her room in darkness. He could hide at her house.

"Tomorrow might be too late. Those men are out looking for Samuel right now."

Drawing back, Lyman demanded, "You want me to put my shoes back on and deal with this now?"

"It's a thought."

"No! Now you've gone too far!" He returned to the rocker and dropped heavily into it.

"It's your choice." She reached for the door handle.

With a strangled groan, he hoisted himself to his feet. "I don't know what kind of spell you have over me, but it's beginning to scare me."

She smiled teasingly. "You'll be glad when you get back."

He sucked in his breath so sharply it whistled. His face lit up with anticipation, but she stepped through the door and into the hallway.

"I want some proof that you made them stop," she said firmly.

He threw up his hands. "How in the world am I going to do that?"

"You'll find a way." She gave him another teasing smile and closed the door between them.

❧

She gave Lyman a fifteen-minute start to be sure that he wouldn't return unexpectedly. Then she eased out the back door. Pausing to give her eyes time to adjust to the darkness, she retrieved the sack of food and clothing and took the pathway to the enclosed outside stairs.

As she placed one foot on the first step, she tensed, not sure if she had heard something in the blackness behind her. For a few seconds, she stood listening. She heard nothing more.

Not satisfied, she silently stepped back onto the path. She strained her eyes in the darkness but saw only the familiar dark bulk of shrubbery that grew against the side of the house.

Guess it was nothing, she told herself as she climbed the

enclosed stairs. Using her key, she opened the door and whispered, "It's Mara."

She got no answer.

"It's all right," she said in a hoarse whisper. "I'm alone. Everything's all right."

She heard only silence.

"Samuel, answer me!"

When she got no reply, she dropped the sack, suddenly afraid. Calling again, a little louder, she felt for the match holder mounted just inside and to the right of the door. Striking a flame, she reached up with her free hand to raise the glass chimney on the oil lamp.

Lifting the lamp high and shielding her eyes from the glare, she asked in a normal voice, "Are you here?"

When only silence answered her, she hastily searched her cozy dressing room and tall armoire.

She noticed his hat on the pillow but saw no other sign that Samuel had ever been in the room. Dismayed, Mara returned down the stairs to the kitchen. Fully alarmed, she lit a lantern and carried it with her left hand. In her right, she gripped her deadly derringer, then scurried back outside.

She couldn't find any readable tracks in the path by the stairway entrance. She raised the lantern high; its pale yellow-orange glow made familiar objects seem to leap to life.

Where did he go? Why did he leave? The questions whirled in her mind as she slowly moved the lantern in a futile effort to find some sign of what had happened to her friend.

Something glittered momentarily, no longer than the wink of a lightning bug, but it was enough to set Mara's blood racing. With deliberate casualness, she kept the lantern moving as though she had seen nothing.

Then, feeling goose bumps rippling down her arms, she returned to the house and blew out the lantern.

The single-shot derringer was not adequate protection against two slave catchers. She returned the little pistol to its hiding place in the kitchen. Leaving only the gaslight burning there, she made her way through the darkened house and felt her way along familiar steps to the second story. She entered the master bedroom and opened a drawer in Lyman's nightstand.

Gently she retrieved his heavy Remington army revolver and checked to see that it was fully loaded. Satisfied, she left the room as quietly as she had entered.

She draped a shawl over her right shoulder to hide the heavy revolver in her hand. Retrieving the lantern, she carried it through the house and out the front door.

Outside, she stood silently until her eyes adjusted to the darkness beyond the lantern's weak circle of light. Then she walked down the front steps, passing the Palmetto flag still defiantly flying from the post.

She went through the motion of lifting the light high while searching the front yard. Following the light as the darkness retreated before it, she walked the path around the house.

Mounting the back stairs, Mara quickly returned, carrying a package. She made sure that just enough light touched the package to make it visible to anyone watching, then purposefully headed toward the woodshed.

She set the lantern on the ground and opened the door, putting the interior of the shed in shadow. After silently dropping the sack, she melted into the darkness and slipped around the small structure.

When she reached the side of the woodshed facing the back of the big house, she waited, the heavy weapon making her arm ache. But she didn't have to wait long. In the pale lantern light, she made out the form of a man. He crouched low, a short club in his hand, running lightly on his toes toward the woodshed.

Mara waited to make sure he was alone. Satisfied, she let him sneak past the corner before she moved.

"Hold it!" She emphasized her command by pulling back the hammer so it clicked ominously.

The man stiffened in surprise, one foot off the ground, frozen before he could complete his next step.

"Don't shoot! Don't shoot!"

"Drop your club and the gun from your belt, then raise your hands."

As the man obeyed, Mara clucked disapprovingly. "You should know better than to carry a pistol with a shiny barrel. The lantern reflects off of it. Now, step over in the light where I can see you better. Slowly."

When he had complied, he turned slowly. Mara recognized the pockmarked face of the shorter of the two slave catchers.

She continued advancing toward him behind the menacing, long-barreled gun.

He protested through broken teeth, "Lady, this ain't what it looks like! I ain't no footpad, sneakin' . . ."

She broke in harshly. "Where's your tall friend?"

"He's back at the Barbary Coast. He didn't believe me when I said all we had to do was wait outside your place and then follow you to . . ."

"Stop babbling! Where is he?"

"I told you! He's back at . . ."

"Not him, the man you were chasing."

"That's why I was followin' you. I figgered you'd hid him out somewhere, and when I saw you with that package, I . . ." He stopped abruptly. "Don't you know where that runaway is, either?"

"I'll ask the questions!" Mara's tone was harsh, but the question that sprang to mind distressed her. *Where is Samuel?*

When the slave catcher spoke again, his voice suggested he had just thought of his own safety. "Look, I ain't seen that big buck . . . I swear I don't know where he is. I ain't seen him. So, you're gonna let me go now, ain't you?"

Mara asked mockingly, "What do you think? People will know I had to defend my honor when you sneaked up on me while I was getting wood for the stove."

"You wouldn't!" Terror caused his voice to squeak. "I never done you no harm! I wouldn't, neither!"

Mara forced a sad note into her words. "There's only one way I can be sure of that. Now, let me see where it would look best for them to find your . . ."

She turned slightly, giving him an opportunity to escape. Instantly, he took it, kicking the lantern over so the glass shattered and the flame went out. He ran around the far side of the building and disappeared into the night. Mara felt around in the darkness until she found the package she had prepared.

When the slave catcher's heavy footfalls faded into the distance, Mara's thoughts focused on Samuel. Loss engulfed her as she tucked the package under her arm. Carrying the heavy pistol, she headed toward the glow of the gaslight that fell through the kitchen window.

She asked herself questions that had no answers: *Why did Samuel leave my room? Where is he now?*

༺৩༻

The lamp burned late that night in Shiloh and Clay's bedchamber. Clay's terrible anger about the newspaper article had given way to brooding silence. For the last hour, he had sat in the hickory rocking chair he had bought for Shiloh when Ajay was a baby.

The chair's monotonous creaking raked Shiloh's taut nerves, adding to her frustration that she couldn't break through Clay's moodiness.

She slid out of the high bed, stretching to reach the floor and her carpet slippers. "Please, Clay," she said, pulling on her robe, "talk to me. I can't stand to see you like this."

He looked up. "What?" he asked absently.

"Talk to me," she pleaded, dropping to her knees before him. "Tell me what you're thinking."

For the first time in hours, he seemed to be aware of her.

"Thinking?" he repeated, lightly resting his fingers on her cheek. "I've thought of all kinds of things."

She bent her head slightly to increase the closeness of his touch. "Such as?"

Taking a deep breath, he explained, "Oh, I've thought about what I can do for the Confederacy, about how your father predicts that they can't win." Clay stopped as she looked at him with questioning, frightened eyes. "Why are you looking at me that way?"

"If they can't win, why join them?"

"Honor." He said the word softly, almost reverently. "It's a very important thing to a man, especially a southerner."

"But if it's a lost cause, what good will honor be when the war's over?" She shifted to a more comfortable position and rushed on.

"What about our children? What's it going to be like for them? We'd have to move to Southern California, but even then, when it's over, and if Papa's right, then what?"

"You really don't want me to do this, do you?"

She paused, feeling emotionally tormented. Then, very softly, she answered, "No. If I had a choice, I would prefer you not do this."

Clay's jaw muscles twitched, and his face puckered. He stood abruptly, pulling her to her feet. "Thank you," he whispered, and rushed across the room and out the door.

Stunned and uncertain, Shiloh stared after him until her eyes filled and she could no longer see the doorway.

⚜

Mara had not been on a ship since she and Shiloh had sailed into San Francisco Bay in 1849. Now she leaned against the mast of the sloop as it passed through the Golden Gate, heading for the seabird nesting sites on the Farallon Islands. She turned her face to the cool breezes and her thoughts to Samuel.

It disturbed her in a way she could not understand to know

that he had vanished without a trace. After Lyman had returned home the previous evening, Mara had surprised him by saying it didn't matter that he couldn't find either of the slave catchers.

Lyman had expected to be castigated for his failure; he showed his appreciation by being especially thoughtful to her. He even offered to drive her to the dock, but she had preferred to hire a rig, knowing that Samuel had planned to join the egg pickers on board this morning. She had not seen him among the twenty or so rough-looking men.

If those two slave catchers didn't get Samuel, she asked herself *again, what happened to him? Why didn't he wait in my room, as I asked?*

Her eyes swept the sea, as though there might be an answer there, then turned back to the egg pickers. They wore canvas boots with rope soles, trousers tied at the ankles, and shirts made of flour sacks worn upside down. The open ends were tied behind their necks so that the hard-shelled seabird eggs could be gently placed in the sacks.

Mara absently skimmed the assortment of hats and caps worn by different men. None of them was quite like Samuel's, she thought. Suddenly, she jerked with alarm.

His hat! He left it on my bed! If Lyman finds it . . . !"

"Mornin', Mara," a familiar voice said behind her.

She turned, her mind still spinning because of the forgotten hat. Then she stared, her mouth dropping open. "Samuel!"

He grinned at her; the sun glistened on his curly black hair. "I hope you didn't mind . . ."

"What are you doing here?" she interrupted, her tone mixed with unexpected gladness and sudden anger.

"I didn't want to risk getting you in trouble by staying in your room, so I came down to the ship and talked the captain into letting me sleep . . ."

"You what?" Her cry made every egg picker turn to stare, but she didn't care.

Samuel's astonishment at her reaction showed on his face as he explained. "The captain said if I'd do some work below decks, I could spend the night. I just now finished."

"You have been here since yesterday?" she broke in, turning furious eyes on him. "You left without a word, making me think something terrible had happened to you?"

A pleased light showed in Samuel's dark eyes, chasing away his surprise. "I didn't think you'd mind, and I didn't think you'd care."

Sputtering with rage and relief, Mara unsuccessfully tried to form a suitable reply. Instead, she shrieked, "Get out of my sight! And stay out!"

She whirled and made her way through the egg pickers and equipment to the farthest part of the bow she could reach. When Samuel tentatively approached her, she drove him off with an angry tirade that made the other egg pickers howl with laughter. Mara was still standing aloof and alone when they dropped anchor off the islands and lowered small boats over the side.

~~❧~~

It was nearly ten o'clock before Mara returned from the Farallons. She found Lyman waiting for her just inside the front door.

One glance at his stiff body and set jaw told Mara that he had found Samuel's hat.

He didn't greet her but said bluntly, "You shouldn't have lied to me." His tone was gentle, yet held a distinct hard core.

"I didn't lie to you, Lyman." She held up a sack. "I brought you one of those murre birds. I hope it'll cook . . ."

"Stop it!" he yelled, shaking the hat close to her face in the intensity of his rage. "You took that big buck for a lover while I was away! You brought him into my house. Then you have the nerve to stand there and tell me that you didn't? Do you think I'm blind?"

"It wasn't like that. I hid him from those slave catchers, but he never touched . . ."

"Get out!" He slapped at her hard with the hat, making her turn her face away from the stinging blows. "Out! Now!" he shouted.

She tried to stand her ground. "Listen to me . . ."

"Get out before I kill you!"

There was no reasoning with him, Mara realized. Without a word, she dropped the sack with the bird and left.

~❦~

Hours later, a figure stood motionless in the shadow of a tree trunk and faced the mansion where a light burned in a second-story window. He cast anxious glances at the sky, mindful that the full moon might momentarily break through the high fog. When his gaze shifted back, the light had gone out.

Tensing in anticipation, the shadowy figure continued to watch the building. A woman hurried out the front door, entered a buggy waiting at the curb, and drove away.

Carrying a sack and moving rapidly, the watcher crossed the street and drifted, silent as a shadow, to a side window. In a couple of minutes, he stood beside the high canopy bed on the second floor.

When the moon momentarily broke through the fog, he froze. Then the room plunged back into darkness. Seconds later, a heavy revolver fired, filling the room with explosive brilliance and deafening sound.

As the noise faded, the man reached into his sack and pulled out a dead black-and-white bird. He placed the limp animal on the chest of the still figure in the bed.

As silently as he had come, the invader retraced his steps. He stopped briefly before the Palmetto flag and saluted smartly.

It was done, and someone else would be blamed for the crime.

❧ CHAPTER 22 ❧

C LAY ESCAPED to his office early the next morning to consider his problems alone. After learning of Lincoln's suspension of basic civil rights, Clay seriously began to consider joining Asbury Harpending in outfitting a privateer.

Clay's contemplation was interrupted by his father-in-law's arrival. Clay wasn't surprised. He had rather expected that Merritt would try to convince him to change his mind.

Out of respect, Clay listened without comment as Merritt began, "You have every right to your opinion, but right now, you're very emotional. I would like to talk with you calmly and rationally. I agree that what Lincoln did is wrong, very wrong; but don't let that cloud your common sense."

When Clay did not respond, Merritt continued, "San Francisco is a Union town. If you support the Confederacy, you'll be branded a Copperhead. Your children will also suffer."

Clay broke his silence with a sharp reply. "Nobody has a right to bother my children because of what I believe!"

"Right has nothing to do with wartime emotions, Clay. Your children and Shiloh will face outrageous slurs. You'll all be shunned, even by people you've called friends for years."

"I don't need such friends!"

"Please hear me out, Clay." Merritt leaned across the desk to look directly into the younger man's eyes.

"I had no family most of my life, but now I've got a wonderful daughter, delightful grandchildren, and a fine son-in-law. I want to protect you all. I know that you also love your family, so I'm going to speak frankly: They have a right to be removed from the stigma that will be attached to your name if you persist in your present course."

Merritt leaned back before concluding, "Move them to Los Angeles or some other place that is pro-Confederacy, then follow your conscience. Don't put them through your war. And remember, whether you stay or go, your property will probably be confiscated. Now, I've said what I came to say. I pray that you do the right thing for everyone."

Clay sat in thoughtful silence as he envisioned his wife and children tormented. Through his frustration and anger, he realized he could not protect his family from San Francisco's high emotions.

In an effort to ease the tension, Merritt commented, "I heard that your friend Theodore Judah is finally getting some real interest in his transcontinental railroad project. Do you still have some money invested in that?"

With an effort, Clay shook off his dark thoughts to answer, "A few thousand. I'm thinking of putting quite a bit more into the company." He caught a momentarily look of disapproval on Merritt's face. "You don't think that's wise?"

"Since you asked, no. The railroad will be a big success after the war, especially if the Union wins. But there's an old saying, 'big fish eat little fish.' The time will come when Judah and others will be forced out, and only a few giants will remain."

Respect for his father-in-law's business acumen made Clay listen closely. "Such as?" he prompted.

"My guess would be Huntington, Stanford, Hopkins, and Crocker."

"I don't understand. There's enough prospective profit in a transcontinental railroad to make Judah and all the stockholders rich. So why force anyone out?"

"Greed, but most people won't remember that." Merritt stood. "Well, I've got to go. Thanks for listening to what I said about our family."

For several minutes after Merritt left, Clay sat brooding. Unable to reconcile the conflict raging within his soul, he decided to go out for a walk. As Clay stepped outside, he stopped, groaning inwardly as Noah Oakley and two other men, strangers to Clay, approached him.

Like Oakley, the strangers had strong builds. Clay guessed they were also part of the self-appointed Home Guard, intent upon detecting and suppressing treasonable conspiracy against the Union.

"A moment of your time, sir," Oakley greeted him.

"I'm busy," Clay replied bluntly. He tried to push by the trio, but they stepped in front of him. Clay's anger bubbled high, but he controlled it to warn, "I'm in no mood for this!"

"This is your last warning," Oakley replied.

"Or what?" Clay demanded in cold fury.

Oakley shrugged. "You're a former military man. You don't expect us to tell you our plans, do you?"

"Get out of my way!" The moment Clay said it, he knew how foolish it sounded. One man against three, all younger and stronger. Still, he was so angry that he braced himself to act.

They surprised him by stepping aside.

As Clay walked away, Oakley's voice followed him. "You have twenty-four hours to make the right choice."

※

Shiloh was delighted when Mara dropped in shortly after breakfast. They sat down in the front parlor.

Mara announced, "You'll be happy to know that one of your wishes has come true: I've moved back to my house."

Shiloh asked hopefully, "Does that mean . . . ?"

"Yes, Lyman and I are through," Mara broke in. Then she added, "Well, to be honest, he threw me out."

Shiloh listened attentively while Mara recounted how she had hidden Samuel and Lyman had found his hat.

A satisfied smile touched Shiloh's lips. "You seem to care more for Samuel than you let on."

"He's a friend, so of course I helped him. I persuaded him to stay on the Farallons with the lighthouse keepers until I can see Tucker, his lawyer, and try to expedite Samuel's freedom papers. The slave catchers won't find him on the islands."

"Sounds sensible," Shiloh commented. "Anyway, I'm glad that you and Lyman have ended that relationship."

"It wasn't a friendly parting," she said with a shrug, "but I'm through with him."

Shiloh hesitated before asking, "What about Jared?"

"I'm going to turn him down too."

"I'm so glad!" Shiloh joyously gripped Mara's hand.

"Mama! Mama!" Julia burst through the front door. "Ajay and Howell are fighting again!"

Both women followed the little girl outside to disentangle the fighting boys. Mara helped Shiloh clean Ajay up and quiet the other children. Then she announced she had to get going.

Shiloh scolded Ajay, "If you and Howell can't get along, I don't want you playing with him anymore."

"But Mama! He called me a Copperhead!"

The hopelessness of the situation vexed Shiloh, but she also could see that their relationships with many people would change because of the war. "Just the same," she said, "I don't like fighting, and . . ."

She broke off when she heard a knock at the front door. She hurried to answer it. A short, stocky uniformed police officer stood outside, his face grim.

"Yes?" Shiloh asked, trying to place his face. "Oh, Constable Logan!"

He had investigated the murder of her first husband. He still looked much the same, except that he had lost his hair.

"Morning, Mrs. Patton. Sorry to bother you." He looked beyond her to where Ajay stood watching. "Is Mara here?"

"No. Why? Is something wrong?"

Logan hesitated, his eyes on Ajay. "Uh . . . do you know where she is?"

Shiloh started to reply then paused, aware that something was wrong. Stepping outside and pulling the door shut behind her so Ajay couldn't hear, she parried, "Why are you looking for her?"

"It's police business, Mrs. Patton."

"You're frightening me!"

"I don't mean to, but . . ."

When he hesitated, Shiloh asked sharply, "What is it? Tell me, please!"

"Uh . . . did Mara seem upset the last time you saw her?"

"No, of course not. Constable Logan, I can't stand this! What's happened? Why are you asking these questions?"

Slowly taking a deep breath, he explained. "I want to talk to her about the last time she saw Lyman Wallace."

"Lyman Wallace?" Shiloh's hand flew to her mouth at the implication. "Did something happen to him?"

"He was killed last night."

"Killed?"

"Murdered in his bed."

"Oh, Lord, no!"

"Sorry, but it's true. Someone shot him to death."

Shiloh protested in astonishment, "Surely you don't think Mara had anything to do with that?"

"Something at the scene possibly points to her."

"What?"

"Sorry, I can't say."

"Whatever it was, Mara didn't do it! I've known her since we were little girls. She wouldn't kill anybody!"

"I didn't say she did, Mrs. Patton. But I've got to ask her some questions. Are you sure you don't know where she is?" When Shiloh shook her head in bewilderment, Logan added, "Sorry to bother you. Now, if you'll excuse me, I've got to find her."

Shiloh stood in shocked silence as Logan walked away. She told herself fiercely, *I know she said that Lyman threw her out, but* . . . Mara's words rushed back to Shiloh.

Mara had talked about taking Lyman's big pistol to drive off the slave catcher. And she had quarreled with Lyman last night after she returned from the Farallons.

No! Shiloh shook her head violently. *She didn't do it! She couldn't! But who did? And why?*

Shiloh ran back inside, knowing that she had to talk to Clay. She had to know more details about the murder. *Who found the body? When? What did Logan find at the scene to make him believe Mara was guilty? Where is she?*

Only then did Shiloh remember that Mara had planned to see Cornelius Tucker about expediting Samuel's freedom papers.

Shiloh made a quick decision. "Ajay," she said crisply, taking his arm. "I've got to leave on an emergency. You go find Lizzie and send her to me right away. Then go get your brother and sisters and wait in the kitchen."

Shiloh was almost to Tucker's office when she saw Mara leaving the building. Calling for her to wait, Shiloh rushed up and pulled her aside before lowering her voice, "Constable Logan is looking for you."

"For me? Why?"

"Lyman's dead."

Mara's eyes opened wide. "Dead?"

"Shot right in his own bed."

For a few seconds, Mara said nothing. Then she nodded. "So naturally, Logan suspects me?"

"He said he just wants to talk to you, but . . ."

"But what?"

"They found something at the scene that made him think . . . oh, no! He's wrong! I told him that! You wouldn't do such a terrible thing."

Calmly, Mara slipped her arm through Shiloh's and started walking along the sidewalk. "No, but somebody did. Let's turn down this side street where it's quieter. Then you go back to the beginning and tell me everything that Logan said. Every word."

The city's noise muted as the two women moved beside the solid walls of several businesses.

When Shiloh had repeated as many details as she could re-call, Mara asked, "What did you tell the constable?"

"Nothing. I didn't even think about you saying you were going to see Samuel's lawyer."

"Good," Mara replied approvingly. "But now what do I do?"

"Why, go to the station and wait for the constable, of course. I'll go with you, and we'll clear this up."

With a shake of her head, Mara dismissed the idea.

"I don't think so. Whoever killed Lyman apparently left something at the scene to implicate me."

"But you're innocent!"

"Proving that is another matter. I need time to think this through, to figure out who really killed him, and why."

Stopping abruptly, Shiloh clutched Mara's hands imploringly. "You're not thinking of running away?"

"No, just staying out of sight until I can make sense out of this."

"Logan will consider it running away! You'll be hunted as a fugitive! Please don't even think of it."

"You're the one who needs to think." Mara freed her hands and started walking again with Shiloh keeping pace. "Logan's already decided I did this."

"I could vouch for you . . ."

"Thank you, but you can't prove that when Lyman got angry and ordered me out of the house, I went—and that he was alive."

Shiloh started to protest but realized Mara was right. "Then I'll help you!" Shiloh exclaimed.

"You have a husband and four children. You can't run around and do what needs to be done."

"Then I'll get Clay and Papa to help. Together, we'll prove you didn't do it."

Mara smiled, but there was only a sadness to it. "With emotions as high as they are, some people might just be waiting for a chance to hang someone like me."

"Hang?" The word came out in a strangled sound. "They wouldn't!"

"I'm not so sure."

Shiloh wanted to protest, but her mind flooded with possible suspects, people who had reason to want revenge on Mara. Jefferson Locke's name first leaped to mind.

"I'm going to leave you here," Mara said abruptly, stopping again. "I don't want anyone to think that you conspired to help me. You can honestly say you don't know where I went."

"Wait! Wait! Please don't . . ." Shiloh's sentence hung in the air as Mara rapidly walked back the way they had come, rounded the corner, and disappeared.

⁓⸎⁓

Clay anxiously awaited Shiloh. He had come home after his encounter with Noah Oakley and his Home Guard companions. He thought about their warning. *Twenty-four hours before what?* he had wondered as he hailed a jitney driver to take him home. The driver had added to his concern by telling him about the murder.

"I just heard about Lyman," Clay said as Shiloh entered. "Are you all right?"

"Yes, just frightened. Let's go upstairs where we can talk."

"Your father's in the kitchen with the children."

Hesitating, Shiloh decided. "I'd like his thinking about this as well, if you don't mind."

"Of course not." Clay kissed Shiloh then took her hand and turned toward the kitchen. "I'll send the children out with Lizzie for a while."

Sitting at the table, Shiloh repeated her conversations with Logan and Mara. "She just walked away, and I don't know what to do," Shiloh concluded.

Clay had set aside his concern about the Home Guard warning. "If she didn't do it," he began, but his wife interrupted.

"Not *if!* Mara *didn't* do it; she couldn't have!"

Merritt spoke up quietly. "I believe Clay was trying to say that we should consider who really committed the murder."

Shiloh nodded. "I'm sorry, Clay. I'm just so concerned about Mara."

"It's all right." Clay took his wife's hand and held it on the table. "We really need more details. I'll go see Logan, but first, let's consider who might have wanted Lyman dead."

Clay got up to reach for a pad and pencil. It didn't take them long to compile a list. Clay read from the pad.

"Samuel was surely jealous of Lyman, but we know he was on the Farallons last night, so he couldn't have done it.

"Next," he continued, lightly running a pencil line through Samuel's name, "there's Jared Huntley."

Nodding, Shiloh agreed. "Both he and Lyman wanted to be appointed to the state supreme court, but there's only one opening. And he could be angry because he kept asking Mara to move in with him, but she refuses."

"So," Merritt mused, "Jared could remove a rival for both political office and a woman's companionship, but that would certainly have ended any chances he had of winning Mara."

"Jefferson Locke," Clay pronounced the name thoughtfully, consulting the list again.

"He's the most logical choice," Shiloh declared. "He has always disliked her. And now he blames her for his financial losses."

"Right," Clay agreed, "and Lyman fronted for Mara in buying property from Locke. He wouldn't have sold if he knew it was for Mara."

"Except," Shiloh explained, "I think Jared finally got that waterfront property for her when Lyman failed."

Merritt commented ruefully, "This isn't getting any clearer, is it?"

"Not so far," Shiloh agreed. She looked back to her husband. "Let's finish the list."

"Denby Gladwin. He's not very likely. He's always threatening people, but I don't think he's ever carried through with anything."

"His motive?" Merritt prompted.

"Political," Clay said. "Possible revenge on Lyman for switching away from supporting his independent nation in favor of the Confederacy."

"Doesn't sound like a strong enough motive to me," Merritt admitted.

When Shiloh nodded, Clay glanced down at his list. "The last one is Cornelius Tucker. He and Lyman had been partners for years until recently. But that doesn't seem a strong enough motive to commit murder."

"So where are we?" Shiloh inquired.

"We've only eliminated one person." Clay made a check mark beside Samuel's name. "He's the only one we know of who has an alibi. That leaves us with four possible suspects, unless either of you can think of anyone else."

When Shiloh and Merritt shook their heads, Clay continued, "That's about all we can do except tell Logan what we've discussed."

Shiloh protested, "We can't leave it there! At least, I can't! I've got help prove Mara's innocence!"

Taking her hand again, Clay explained gently, "You have no experience in murder. Besides, I'm sure Constable Logan would rather we leave the investigation to him."

Shiloh tilted her chin defiantly. "I'm going to do all I can to help Mara. That means following up on these people to discover who killed Lyman and pointed the blame toward Mara."

Both men tried to persuade Shiloh to let the constable do his job. Finally, Shiloh stood, aware that the discussion was not going anywhere.

"I'm going to offer my condolences to Malvina," she announced.

Clay thought about the deadline the Home Guard had set but decided not to add that concern to his wife's already overloaded shoulders. "I'll drive you," he said.

Pulling up in front of the Lyman mansion, Clay felt uneasy at the sight of several neighbors and friends, mostly women, standing on the front porch by the Palmetto flag.

Clay decided to wait in the carriage. Shiloh nodded to the women who had brought food to the bereaved and now stood talking in quiet groups.

Another older woman opened the door, introduced herself as Mrs. Ring, and invited Shiloh inside.

"Malvina's upstairs," Mrs. Ring announced, leading the way. Over her shoulder she asked, "Would you like some tea?"

"No, thank you. I'll only stay a few minutes."

On the second floor, they passed a closed door.

"It happened in there," the guide whispered, leading the way down the hall to an adjoining bedchamber.

Through the open door, Shiloh saw the new widow propped up with pillows in a high bed with a lacy white canopy. There was no lamp lit, and the shades were drawn.

"Another visitor, Malvina," the guide announced, then asked, "More tea?"

The widow did not look at Shiloh but replied, "This pot is cold." She motioned toward the nightstand. "And take that sugar bowl away. You know I never use it."

Mrs. Ring obeyed, saying she would bring hot tea, and left the room.

Shiloh shifted uncomfortably, waiting to be invited to sit down. When she realized that Malvina had not even really looked at her, she spoke. "I'm so sorry about your husband . . ." she began, but Malvina cut her off.

"Shiloh Patton?" she asked sharply.

"Yes, I heard about Lyman."

"I don't need your sympathy!"

The ferociousness of Malvina's words startled Shiloh.

"You're responsible for that black woman being so uppity!" Malvina's voice rose spitefully. "You shouldn't even associate with someone beneath your station in life, yet you treat her as an equal."

"Mara and I were little girls together."

"I don't care! You're responsible for her outrageous behavior!"

"I won't discuss . . ."

Malvina cut her off. "She never learned her place, and that's your fault! Thanks to you, she had the audacity to come right into my home and work her *vaudu* spell on my husband! Well, it worked! Lyman is dead, and she's responsible! I hope they hang her!"

"Mrs. Wallace, I . . ."

"You and your wealthy husband!" Malvina's tirade continued, her voice rising to a screech. "He influenced Lyman to give money to the Confederate cause."

"That's not true!"

"Don't tell me that! I know what's true! You and your husband have everything, while I have nothing. Between that woman and the Knights of the Golden Circle, I'll be left penniless with no one to take care of me. Now, take your false condolences and get out my sight!"

❈ CHAPTER 23 ❈

CLAY GUIDED the horse south toward their home while trying to console Shiloh.

"She was just upset over losing her husband," Clay said soothingly. "She's probably lashing out the same way at other people."

"No," Shiloh protested, "it was more than that. She was downright vicious toward me. I can understand how she feels about Mara. But Mara wouldn't have been there if Lyman hadn't insisted and Malvina allowed it."

"She is probably really angry with him but doesn't want to speak ill of the dead."

"That's still no reason for Malvina to say the nasty things she did to me!"

"I know it hurts. You tried to do the right thing, both in urging Mara to move out of that house and in going to offer sympathy to Malvina. She's the one with the problem. Try to overlook her and think about Mara. How can we help her?"

Shiloh forced Malvina out of her mind. "I don't even know where she is. Maybe at her house?"

"She'll surely know that they'll look for her there. That's why she won't come back to see you. Anyway, she can take care of herself."

"You sound just like her."

"Finding Mara is not as important as trying to figure out who killed Lyman." Clay absently flipped the reins along the horse's back before asking, "What do you suppose Malvina meant when she said something about *vaudu?*"

"She probably meant *voodoo*. It's some kind of superstition slaves of French-Haitian origin brought to Louisiana. We could ask Papa about it. He might know more."

They returned to their home to find Lizzie anxiously waiting by the front door. She opened it quickly, admonished the children to stay inside, and hurried down to the buggy.

Handing Clay a rock with a note tied around it, the maid blurted, her eyes wide with fright, "This done smashed through the front winder. Nearly hit Ajay too."

Clay quickly freed the note, aware that Lizzie could not read. Shiloh leaned close to silently read the crudely handwritten note over his shoulder.

"Your twenty-four hours are going fast. Next time, fire."

"Fire?" Alarmed, Shiloh raised her eyes to Clay's. "What twenty-four hours?"

Casting a warning glance at Lizzie, Clay said under his

breath. "I'll tell you inside." He raised his voice. "Thank you, Lizzie. Did you see who threw this?"

"No, but Ajay done said he seen a man on horseback ride by real fast jist 'afore the glass broke."

"It's nothing to be alarmed about," Clay said, trying to sound confident. He quickly stepped down from the buggy and reached up to help Shiloh. "You may return to your work, Lizzie," he said over his shoulder. "I'll talk to the children."

It took awhile to reassure them. Later Shiloh and Clay went upstairs so Clay could explain about his visit from Noah Oakley and the Home Guards.

As they reached the second floor, someone knocked at the front door.

With a groan, Shiloh whispered, "Now what?"

"Probably the constable. You wait here. I'll go."

Before he had taken more than a few steps down, the door below opened and Merritt stuck his head in.

"Anybody home?"

"Come in," Clay said, stopping with his hand on the banister. "We'd like to talk to you."

Shiloh called, "Come upstairs, Papa."

"I talked to my friend at the newspaper," he announced, climbing the stairs. "I've got some more information about last night."

"That's good," Shiloh replied, "but first, Clay, please show Papa the note."

Inside Clay and Shiloh's bed chamber, Merritt read the terse warning, then Clay explained about Noah Oakley's office visit with his two henchmen.

"So," Clay concluded, "that was about twelve hours ago. Time's half gone."

Shiloh demanded, "Why didn't you tell me before?"

"I had planned to. Then we heard about Lyman's murder. I didn't want to put any additional worries on you, so I decided to wait until a better time."

"Like when a rock came flying through our window?" Shiloh hadn't meant for her tone to sound so shrill. "What if it had been a firebrand? The children were here alone. What's going to happen when the time is up?"

"Easy! Easy!" Clay said, taking her in his arms. "I'll deal with Oakley today."

Shiloh looked up with concern. "Promise me you won't do anything rash."

Clay said grimly, "I can't promise that regarding anyone who threatens me or my family."

"Oh, please!" Shiloh whispered, "Let's just move away until this crazy madness is over."

"I'm not going to be run out of town," Clay said, his jaw tightening.

Shiloh tried again. "We've got the children to think about! If anything happened to you . . ." Her voice broke, making her fight for control.

"I'm not going to have my family living in fear!"

Clay's voice held such a note of finality that Shiloh stepped away from his embrace.

"Merritt," Clay said, his tone softening, "tell us what you found out about Lyman."

"It seems a neighbor noticed that the front door was open this morning. When nobody answered her knock, she got concerned and entered the house. She found the body and called the constable."

He paused before adding, "She also found a dead murre on Lyman's chest."

Shiloh blinked. "A dead murre?" Shiloh sucked in her breath, causing her husband and father to look sharply at her. She said, "Mara had been to the islands. That's what Logan meant when he said he found something at the scene that made him want to talk to Mara."

Clay shook his head. "It doesn't make sense."

"Yes, it does!" Shiloh replied. "Someone knew about the

birds and deliberately put one on the body so Mara would be blamed!"

"That's too obvious," Clay declared. "No killer would have left something behind that could be tied directly to him. Usually, anything left at a murder scene has been left behind accidentally."

"See?" Shiloh cried. "I told you Mara didn't do it."

"I believe you, Shiloh, but right now, the constable is looking for her. And running away the way she . . ."

"She didn't run away!" Shiloh exclaimed. "I told you what really happened."

"I know, but it still looks bad for her."

Merritt said, "There's something else."

Both Shiloh and Clay looked expectantly at him.

"The editor said the police report shows that a small doll was found under Lyman's bed. From the way it was described, I'm satisfied that it's a voodoo doll."

"Is that so?" Clay asked, adding quickly, "Shiloh and I were discussing that very subject awhile ago. When Shiloh went to offer condolences, Malvina was downright rude to her and said something about *vaudu*. Shiloh thinks she meant voodoo."

Shiloh asked, "What do you know about voodoo, Papa?"

"It's a belief system based on fear. I first heard about it years ago, when I was in the Sandwich Islands. There certain *kahunas*, or priests, could supposedly pray a person to death."

"Pray a person to death?" Shiloh repeated. "That's not the purpose of prayer."

"Of course not," her father agreed, "but the way it worked was simple: The *kahuna* let his intended victim know that he was marked for death. The target became so afraid and certain that the priest had the power to cause death, that the poor person died from fright."

Shaking his head, Clay commented, "I find that hard to believe."

"I know, but I saw it happen. And I've heard about others."

A frown slid across Shiloh's face. "I heard about Lyman

finding a voodoo doll sometime back, and somebody told him what it meant. But Lyman scoffed at the idea."

"Outwardly, maybe," her father replied. "But who knows what he secretly believed? It's like people who claim they aren't superstitious, yet they won't walk under a ladder or let a black cat cross in front of them."

Nodding, Clay added, "I saw men in the dragoons carry around several kinds of so-called lucky charms."

Still frowning, Shiloh asked, "But what if someone sent that doll to Lyman as part of a plan to kill him?"

Merritt turned thoughtful eyes on her. "One day when I was getting my hair cut, I commented on the barber's accent. He said he was a freedman who had been born in Haiti. He left because a *houngan* put a curse on him."

Shiloh and Clay knew that from Gold Rush days most barbers in California were descendants of slaves.

"I don't understand," Shiloh said. "Nothing happened to him. How do you explain that, Papa?"

"The barber told me that he went to a *houngan* here in San Francisco, and she took the curse off." Merritt paused, then added, "From his description, I knew he meant Mara."

"She's no *houngan!*" Shiloh cried indignantly.

"I didn't say she was," Merritt replied quietly, "but I've observed Mara. She's smart enough to let local Negroes think she is."

Clay observed, "They do show her a lot of respect."

"Unfortunately," Merritt mused, "both items found at the murder scene would seem to point toward Mara."

"Yes," Shiloh agreed, "but we don't even know where she is."

"Perhaps that's just as well," Merritt commented.

Shiloh turned puzzled eyes on her father. "How so?"

"Whoever killed Lyman obviously anticipated that Mara would be taken into custody and tried for murder."

Shiloh protested, "He wants to get her executed for a crime she didn't commit!"

"Exactly," Merritt agreed. "But if she remains free, then the murderer might get nervous and . . ."

Shiloh sucked in her breath. "You mean, he might go after her himself?"

"The thought occurred to me," Merritt replied.

Quietly, Shiloh asked, "She wouldn't be expecting that, would she?"

"She's smart," Clay said quickly, seeing new distress on his wife's face. "She'll be careful."

"Oh, I wish there was something we could do!" Shiloh's hands fluttered in agitation. "If only I could be with her. She's always been there for me when I needed her!"

Clay pulled Shiloh to him and held her tight. "Let's all try to think of something. Meanwhile, I'm going to find Noah Oakley and make sure he doesn't carry out his threat against us."

Shiloh started to protest, but a glance at his face kept her silent.

"Be careful," Merritt urged.

Clay nodded, kissed Shiloh, and left the house.

In his office, Clay opened the top right desk drawer and lifted out his 1848 pocket Colt in its holster. He hadn't carried it in years but had kept it oiled and polished so it was ready for use. He checked the loads then sat staring thoughtfully at the weapon. Should he carry it to face Oakley or not?

A familiar light tap sounded outside the door. Clay shoved the gun back into the drawer and closed it. "Come in, Gus."

The clerk stuck his head in. "Jefferson Locke insists on seeing you."

Puzzled, Clay nodded. "Send him in."

The former Tennessee lawyer and recent San Francisco land speculator looked terrible when he entered. The crooked teeth and rumpled black suit were the same, but his forehead showed deep furrows.

"Have a seat," Clay said, wondering if Locke was ill.

"I'll stand. What I've got to say won't take long."

"Suit yourself." Clay leaned back and peered at the man across the desk. His hair was untidy and more heavily streaked with gray than Clay remembered.

"I came to make you a proposition," Locke began in a voice that seemed a little unsteady.

"I'm listening."

"It's no secret that your wife's black friend and I hate each other, have for years."

Clay nodded but said nothing, wondering what Locke had in mind.

"I know the constable is looking for her so she can be charged with killing Lyman Wallace."

That didn't surprise Clay. By now, everyone in San Francisco knew that. "And?"

"She ruined me." Locke's voice turned bitter. "I got no use for her, but—she didn't do it."

That flat declaration made Clay lean forward in astonishment. Locke was the last person on earth Clay expected to defend Mara.

"How do you know that, Locke?"

"Because I know who did."

"Who?"

"I'll tell you after I lay out my terms and conditions." Locke licked his lips before continuing.

"You or your wife tell that black devil that if she'll sell that waterfront property back to me on my terms, I'll prove she didn't kill Lyman."

Slowly getting to his feet, Clay said, "We don't know where Mara is. But if you know she's innocent, you owe her . . ."

"I don't owe her anything! I only owe myself, and that's why I'm doing this!" Locke leaned forward and placed both palms on the desk. He glared at Clay. "She should give me that lot, free, for saving her worthless life! But I'll pay her for it. You tell her that!"

"I told you, I don't know where she is." Clay sat down

again. "Besides, even if I did, how do I know this isn't just some trick to get that lot back?"

Threatening color surged across Locke's face. "There was a time when I would have called you out for daring to say such a thing." His tone was flat, hard. "I would have demanded satisfaction on the field of honor. But . . ." he took a deep breath and straightened up. "I need that lot for collateral to save myself from bankruptcy. She needs what I know to save her life. That's a pretty fair exchange. You find her and tell her that."

As Locke turned toward the door, Clay stood again. "Even if I could find her, she'll doubt what you told me. She's going to want to know more, like how you know who killed Lyman."

For a long moment, Locke stood uncertainly, his hand on the doorknob. "Fair enough, I guess. I'll tell you this much: Last night I saw someone . . . uh . . . someone I had reason to talk to. I followed him, trying to catch up, when he started acting peculiar."

Clay raised questioning eyebrows.

Locke continued, "He started checking behind him. Fortunately, he didn't see me. Then he went on, and I followed, making sure to keep hidden. Finally he stopped across from Lyman Wallace's house. He stayed out of sight, and so did I."

Clay waited, afraid that if he said anything, Locke might refuse to say more.

Finally Locke went on. "There was a horse and buggy outside, in front of Lyman's, and a light on in the second story. Finally, it went out, and Mara came out, got into the buggy, and drove away." Locke stopped. "That's enough. You tell her that."

"Let me see if I have this straight," Clay said. "You followed somebody whose name you won't tell. You saw him wait outside Lyman's place and saw Mara drive away. Maybe I'm not very bright, but what does that prove?"

Locke half-closed his eyes before replying. "All right. I'll give you this you much more: After she drove away, I saw this man cross the street and enter the house. A little later, I heard a shot.

"The man then came back, stopped, and saluted that Palmetto flag that Lyman flies from the front porch pillar. I tried to follow him but lost him."

It sounded logical, making Clay slowly nod.

"So," Lyman finished, "that's how I know that Mara didn't kill Lyman. But if she doesn't come across with that lot, I'll never tell anyone else what I told you. If you tell the authorities, I'll deny it. It'll be your word against mine, and she'll hang. But I'd rather have my lot back than see that happen."

Opening the door, he added, "One more thing: I'm in a bit of a time bind. I want an answer from her by this time tomorrow. You understand that?"

Without waiting for a reply, he slammed the door and clumped noisily down the stairs.

⤙❧⤚

Shiloh looked up in surprise when Clay rushed into the parlor where she sat with John Sledger.

"Oh!" she exclaimed, jumping up and going to meet him. "I'm so glad you're back safely. How did it go with Oakley?"

"I didn't see him." Clay turned to other man. "How are you, John?"

He rose and shook hands. "Very well, thanks."

Shiloh explained excitedly, "Brother Sledger just brought some fascinating news about the murder."

"I've got some fascinating news myself," Clay replied, "but it can wait. What did you find out, John?"

"The doctor who was called to examine Lyman Wallace's body is an old friend. He had already told the constable, so what I told Shiloh will be common knowledge tomorrow."

"What did you tell her?" Clay asked impatiently.

Shiloh's excitement couldn't be contained. "Lyman was shot all right, but he was already dead when that happened!"

"What?" Clay exclaimed.

"It's true," Sledger explained. "The doctor said that his examination showed that death had occurred some time *before* he was shot. At this point, he's not sure what the real cause of death was, but he's quite sure it was murder, so he is going to perform an autopsy to find out."

Clay stared, unable to believe this second surprising bit of information in the past hour.

"The doctor explained how a body acts after death," Sledger said. "It's not a pleasant topic, but I am convinced that Lyman was dead before he was shot."

"Which means," Shiloh explained, "that two people wanted to murder Lyman. One succeeded, but the second one only thinks he did."

Clay's bewilderment made him sit down heavily beside Shiloh. "My head is swimming. John, are you suggesting that Constable Logan is going to have to look for *two* suspects?"

"He already is." The preacher shook his head. "What a strange turn of events. Really strange."

Shiloh sorted through her tangled and matted thoughts.

"Could that explain why there were two things left at the scene? I mean, the murre might have been left by one person, and the doll by the other. Each was meant to incriminate Mara. Whoever they were, Lyman's two murderers both wanted her to take the blame."

"There's another possibility," Clay said slowly, rolling the events around in his mind. "Why would somebody shoot a dead man?"

"We already know that," Shiloh replied. "He didn't know that Lyman was dead."

"Maybe," Clay agreed, "but what if it was only one person, and he was just making doubly sure? What if he did something he *thought* was going to cause Lyman's death, but later decided he had to make sure. He could have returned and fired the shot."

Shiloh and Sledger exchanged glances. "Of course that's a possibility, but I guess we won't know until this thing is solved," Sledger mused.

"When did the doctor say he would know the results of the autopsy?" Shiloh asked.

"Tomorrow sometime. Then I guess we'll know the real cause of death, but we still won't know if one or two people were involved."

"Either way," Shiloh said soberly, "Mara was supposed to be blamed. With this new information, is it possible that Mara might be cleared? But even so, she's not safe. The real killer or killers might go after her."

She read the agreement in both Clay and Sledger's faces. Mara could be in danger, but from whom?

Clay took a long, deep breath. "Jefferson Locke came by my office awhile ago and told me that he saw a man watching Lyman's house last night."

"What?" Shiloh exclaimed.

"He also claimed that he saw Mara leave and the killer enter. Locke heard the shot."

Shiloh questioned, "Can we trust Locke?"

"This time, I do," Clay said. "Locke is desperate. He needs that waterfront lot to save him from bankruptcy."

"Then we've got to find Mara," Shiloh said emphatically. "We've got to do it fast! But where can we even begin looking?"

When Clay didn't answer, she turned to him and saw that he had thought of something. She prompted, "What is it?"

"What if Locke was wrong?" he answered slowly. "What if the man he watched did see Locke? What's to keep him from going after Locke to make sure he doesn't tell anyone else what he told me?"

Shiloh caught her breath. "You mean, Locke's life could also be in danger?"

"It's possible."

Sledger volunteered, "I'll go find the constable and tell him everything we've discussed."

"Thank you," Shiloh said. "Clay and I will search for Mara." She added silently, *I hope we're not too late!*

~❧ CHAPTER 24 ❧~

S HILOH AND Clay vainly searched for Mara, fruitlessly calling at homes and businesses where Mara's Negro friends worked. In desperation, Shiloh persuaded Clay to let her talk to Locke, hoping he would tell her more than he had Clay.

Locke looked up from the untidy rolltop desk in his office. His bloodshot eyes made his face more haggard than it had been the day before. For the first time that Shiloh or Clay could remember, he had on an old pair of pants and a wrinkled shirt instead of his rumpled black suit.

Locke didn't greet them or even stand. Instead, he said bluntly, "You're wasting your time coming here. I'm not saying one more word than I did yesterday."

"I know that you and Mara have no love lost between you," Shiloh replied, "but she is very important to me. If you'll help us by giving us the name of the man . . ."

"No!" Locke slammed his palm down on the desk, sending papers flying. "You have my terms. When they're met, I'll give you the name."

"Please!" Shiloh held holding out her hands in supplication. "We think she may be in danger from whoever you saw at the Wallace home."

"She is not my concern."

"She should be," Shiloh shot back. "If anything happens to her, she won't be able to even consider selling that lot back to you."

Locke's eyes narrowed. Shiloh realized she had hit a sensitive spot. She added quickly, "In fact, you might be in jeopardy too. If that man saw you . . ."

"I thought about that after the fire last night."

Shiloh and Clay exclaimed together, "Fire?"

Locke ran an open palm along his forehead. "My house burned down. I lost everything." His eyes looked haunted. "I had to borrow the clothes I'm wearing."

"What started the fire?" Clay asked.

"I don't know. Neither do the firemen."

Shiloh asked with concern, "Do you think it was an accident?"

"Of course. What else could it be?"

"It might have been set on purpose," Clay reminded Locke.

"That's not going to make me change my mind!"

Shiloh flinched at the harshness in his voice, but she was desperate. "Whoever you followed has already shot one man. If he set your fire, he may try again."

"And," Clay added ominously, "you may not . . ."

Locke interrupted with a hoarse cry, "I will not be frightened into talking to you! Leave me alone."

In dejected silence, having run out of ideas for where to find Mara, they started home. Clay's thoughts drifted to the Home Guards' ultimatum. He was torn between wanting to help find Mara and the knowledge that he had better face Oakley before his deadline.

Shiloh and Clay arrived at home just as Merritt stepped down from a hired jitney.

"Any trace of Mara?" he asked, helping his daughter down from the buggy.

"Not a sign." Her voice carried mixed desperation and concern. "We tried to talk to Locke, but he wouldn't help us."

Merritt asked, "Did he tell you about the fire?"

"A little," Shiloh replied. "How did you know about that?"

"My newspaper friend told me about it. Someone deliberately set it," her father declared.

Shiloh glanced at Clay and saw him nod almost imperceptibly. It seemed almost certain that the man who had shot Lyman knew Locke had seen him. But, Shiloh wondered, was the fire a warning or an attempt on his life?

Clay interrupted her thoughts. "I hate to leave, but I've got some business that I must attend to right away."

"Before you go," Merritt said, "I learned something else that will interest you both. The autopsy has been completed."

"And?" Shiloh prompted.

"Lyman was poisoned."

Shiloh gasped. "How awful!"

Her father nodded. "Cyanide. The newspaper will carry the story in this afternoon's edition."

"Cyanide?" Shiloh shook her head. "I know it's a poison, but that's all I know about it."

"It can act very fast," Merritt explained. "Swallowing enough may lead to immediate unconsciousness. Death can follow in anywhere from one to fifteen minutes."

Clay asked, "How did Lyman get it in his system?"

"According to the doctor, it was probably mixed with something, but he doesn't know what. Cyanide has a characteristic bitter-almond smell, but not everyone can detect it. Fortunately, the doctor thought he noticed it when he was examining the gunshot wound. The autopsy confirmed it."

"Any chance Lyman committed suicide?" Clay asked.

"The doctor doesn't think so. Suicides don't want to suffer the convulsions that cyanide causes before death."

"So it was murder?" Shiloh knew the answer even before her father nodded.

"The question now," he mused, "is whether the same person who poisoned Lyman also fired the shot, or whether there were two people involved."

"And where is Mara?" Shiloh put in quickly. "She needs to know about this."

"You two go ahead in and talk things over." Clay bent and quickly kissed Shiloh. "I'll keep an eye open for her and be back as soon as possible."

"If you're looking for the Home Guards' office," Merritt volunteered, "try Montgomery Street near Jackson."

Nodding his thanks, Clay returned to the buggy and drove off. He remembered losing his temper and bodily removing Noah Oakley from his office. Now Clay hoped he wasn't doing a foolish thing by going unarmed to face the self-appointed guardians of the Union.

⁓⚬⁓

Mara stood in the silence of Jared Huntley's Black Point home and hoped that nobody had seen her slip in the day before. The huge house, closed up tight while Jared stayed in Sacramento, seemed like the perfect place for Mara to hide while she figured out who killed Lyman Wallace.

Peering through the shades, she remembered that Jared had told her with pride how each home here had privacy on several acres of land. She could only see the roof of one of the five other expensive houses on the finger of land that jutted out from San Francisco's north shore.

Offshore, Mara glimpsed a paddle wheeler churning its way along the bay's dark waters. But her thoughts were not on the beauty or quiet seclusion. Instead, Lyman's death occupied her mind.

Who had shot him and tried to fix the blame on her? Mara's dark eyes skimmed the list she had made of those who might be responsible.

Each had some sort of grievance against her, but who had enough to frame her for murder?

Locke is desperate, she thought. *He blames me for his financial problems. And he has hated me almost from the day we met.*

Carrying the list, Mara turned from the window. She walked slowly across the carpeted floor, her feet making only little whispers in the stillness. *Denby Gladwin? He's always threatening somebody, even Clay. But I never thought he'd want to harm me.*

Pausing before a window on the opposite side of the room, Mara barely noticed that the roses along the path had begun to show the promise of new life. When Jared had first brought her here in January, the bushes had seemed lifeless.

Cornelius Tucker? Mara glanced at the list again and shook her head. He had not approved of his former partner's relationship with her, but she'd had nothing to do with the break up of their law practice.

Besides, when she had seen Tucker the day before, he had been very cordial. He had assured her that he would do what he could to expedite Samuel's freedom papers. She had no reason to doubt him.

Samuel? Mara pondered the name with mixed emotions. Until recently, he had always treated her with respect.

I should never have made those dolls for him, she mutely told herself. *Now that Lyman's dead, Samuel will probably believe that silly little doll worked.*

Leaving the window, Mara wandered down the long hallway toward the bed chambers. *I wonder what he did with the second doll? It's not like him to refuse to tell me.* She thought of how angry she had been with him on the sloop heading for the Farallons. Still, she was glad she had convinced the lighthouse keepers to let him stay until she returned with his papers.

Shiloh is wrong about my feelings for Samuel. She's just so anxious to have me change the way I live.

Anyway, she thought, returning to her list, *even if I do make him a little jealous, he was on an island when Lyman died.*

Idly walking from one room to the next, Mara approached the room that Jared wanted her to share. His words rang in her memory: "You are the most beautiful, desirable woman I've ever known."

But she still remembered how crudely he had treated her a dozen years earlier. In his Black Point home, he had been less crude: "Come live with me. I'll give you whatever you want; more than any other man can give you."

With a toss of her dark hair, Mara sternly told herself, *Well that's not going to happen.*

She smiled, silently wondering, *What would he think if he walked in here now and saw me standing by his bed? Would he get the wrong impression?*

In her musings, she relaxed her fingers and the list of suspects slid to the floor beside Jared's marble-topped washstand. She bent to retrieve the paper. *Who else might have wanted me jailed for Lyman's murder?*

Before she could refocus on the list, something on the washstand caught her attention. Beside the rose-decorated ceramic pitcher, she saw a figure. She instinctively reached out and picked it up.

Startled, she exclaimed, "It's the second doll I made for Samuel!"

～≈～

The California Home Guards occupied one corner of a large office building on Montgomery Street near Jackson.

Taking a deep breath, Clay pushed the door open, still wondering if he was making a mistake to force a confrontation unarmed. But right now, Shiloh had enough troubles without the possibility of him getting involved with a weapons charge.

Noah Oakley and one of the men who had threatened Clay in his office shifted their attention away from a wall map of the city.

"I didn't want to wait until your deadline," Clay announced. He advanced slowly, placing each foot firmly to give him a solid brace in case they attacked him.

From years of driving stagecoach and dealing with all kinds of difficult men, Clay's discerning eyes glimpsed momentary fear or alarm in the two men's eyes. They stood, facing him, quickly regaining their composure.

Clay pushed his advantage. "Let's pretend your deadline has passed. What were you going to do then?"

He waited, standing still but solidly braced, ready to move

rapidly if necessary.

"Look, Patton," Oakley began, but Clay cut him off.

"*Mister* Patton to you, Oakley."

Oakley glanced at his companion, who had remained silent. "You know that no good soldier would tell his enemy what he's planning to do."

"Am I your enemy?" Clay parried, his voice quiet but hard, in command.

"You're the enemy of the Union," Oakley declared, putting a touch of authority in the words. "You're a Copperhead, a secesh . . ."

"Hold it right there!" Clay shifted his feet ever so slightly, his left shoulder thrusting forward a bit and his big hands curling into fists. "Who says so?"

"The Home Guards, that's who!"

"And who gave these guards authority to decide who's a Copperhead?" Clay's voice rose with controlled anger, but the power of his convictions was plain.

"What legal authority?" he asked loudly. "The state? The city? Or a bunch of men who haven't gone off to fight the real war back east but who hide behind patriotic-sounding words to intimidate anyone in San Francisco who dares to think for himself?"

Oakley's Adam's apple bobbed uncertainly before he said plaintively, "Our duty is right here, defending the home front."

"Your duty?" Clay snapped, his voice cracking like the whip he used with his horses. "Your duty is to stay out of my life. If you ever threaten me or frighten my wife or children again, I will personally come to you, Oakley! Do you understand me?"

When Oakley did not respond, Clay shouted, "Do you understand me?"

"Yes." The word was barely audible.

"Good!" Clay turned to the other Home Guard member. "Did you have any trouble understanding?"

He shook his head rapidly but didn't speak.

"Good. Tell your members that I may be only one man, but

I guarantee that this is one man you had better never cross again. Ever!"

For a long moment, Clay held both men with his eyes. Then, disdainfully, he turned his back and walked out. He didn't hear a movement behind him until the door closed after him.

"Whew!" he whispered, taking a deep breath. "Whew!"

❦

Shiloh sat in the parlor, her shoulders slumped, weary after the endless discussion with her father about where to look for Mara and who might have killed Lyman.

One killer or two? The questions beat at her like fists thudding inside her brain.

Merritt slowly rose from his seat. He bent and touched her shoulder.

"We're overlooking something," he remarked. "We've thought of all the logical places she might be. Maybe we should consider the opposite."

Shiloh looked up, surprised. "You mean places we think she wouldn't go?"

"Mara's a very shrewd woman. She knew not to return home, because the constable would surely look there. And she's staying away from you. Where is the most unlikely place she might go?"

Slowly shaking her head, Shiloh confessed. "I don't know. Maybe to some of the men she used to live with? No, that would hurt her pride."

"Where else, then?"

"Well, she could go to where Samuel lives, but I don't think she would risk incriminating him. Or . . ." she hesitated, then looked up with sudden hope in her eyes. "She told me that Jared Huntley had asked her to move in with him, but she said she was going to turn him down."

Shiloh stood up abruptly. "But he's in Sacramento, so his house on Black Point is empty. She's been there before with him. Maybe she knows where he keeps a spare key hidden."

Merritt said, "I can watch the children for a while. You and Clay need to check that place out."

Mara was puzzled over the doll she had found. *How did Samuel get it in here? Has Jared seen it? Does he understand its meaning?*

She stood scowling at the crude symbol of mystic powers. Was it possible that Samuel wanted her so much that he would want Jared dead, like Lyman?

The click of a key in a lock startled Mara. She darted into the hallway and glanced toward the back door as it swung open. *Jared! What's he doing here?*

He closed the door and turned around, stopping in surprise. "Mara! I didn't expect you!"

She walked toward him, feeling trapped. "I thought you were in Sacramento."

"I was, but I couldn't stop thinking about your promise to give me your decision about moving in with me when you got back from the Farallons." He smiled and hurried to meet her with outstretched arms. "Seeing you here makes me believe I already know your answer."

She deftly avoided his embrace. "Not so fast! Things aren't always what they appear."

A hint of a frown touched his brow. "Why else would you be here?"

"I guess you haven't heard." She took a couple of steps to stay out of his reach. There was no sense risking have him strike her again.

"Heard what?"

"Lyman Wallace was killed last night. Somebody entered his house and shot him in his bed."

Jared's lips pursed thoughtfully. "Are you a suspect? Have you come here to hide?"

"Whoever killed him planted some evidence that points directly to me."

"Remember I cautioned you about Jefferson Locke. I wouldn't be surprised if he was involved in this."

"I've spent hours going over who might want to blame me, including Locke."

"So you're here to sort things out."

"I realize it's possible that I might not get a fair trial."

"I can understand that. But don't you think your disappearance might be considered a sign of guilt?"

"I didn't feel I had a choice."

"Did you kill him?"

"Of course not! Why would you even wonder about that?"

"I was merely curious." Jared slowly approached her. "I can get you acquitted. You know that, don't you?"

"I hadn't thought of it."

"Well, take my word for it. I have the power and the connections to make lots of things happen. I always get what I want."

The phrase haunted Mara. The first time he said it to her, he had wanted her. At the time, she had answered that she also always got what she wanted.

Jared asked softly, "How about it? Do we have a deal?"

His crudeness revolted Mara, but she knew that she had to choose. If she turned him down, he would go to the police. Or would he?

She was jarred from her thoughts when he suddenly reached out and grabbed her hand.

"Where did you get this?"

Glancing down at the doll, she replied, "I found it on your washstand."

"Don't lie to me! I know what that is! And I know why you brought it here! You were not only going to turn me down, but you also want me dead!"

For a frightening moment, Mara thought he might hit her again. She protested, "That's ridiculous!"

As rapidly as his anger had erupted, it disappeared. "I guess it is." Releasing her hand, he smiled and apologized, "I'm sorry."

He took the doll from her and threw it casually into a corner. "Look," he said, "I'm going to check out a sloop for a friend of mine. Why don't you come along? We could cruise out toward the Farallons."

In spite of his smile, Mara sensed something wrong. *Could he know that Samuel is out there? No, Jared's been in Sacramento. He didn't even know about the murder.*

"How about it?" he asked, widening his smile.

"Well, it's not something I planned on doing again so soon."

"You don't need to plan! I'll do it for both of us. Besides, Logan won't look for you out there, but he might eventually come here."

Mara stalled, trying to think why she felt some alarm. "How long will we be gone?"

"Oh, just long enough to do what has to be done. What do you say?"

"Why couldn't we just sail up the coast? It must be beautiful this time of year."

"You don't want to go to the islands?"

There was something in his voice that frightened Mara. "It's not my choice. It's rocky and barren and very uninviting."

"Well, I haven't been, although I've heard a lot about it, especially about the seabirds. I'd like to see it. You could show it to me."

"I've never sailed north along the coast. If you'll head up that way, I'd enjoy coming along."

"If you insist. Very well. I'm agreeable. Go grab your shawl, and we'll be on our way."

"Right now?"

"There's no time to lose." Jared took her hand. "Come on. You can tell me your decision after we're under sail."

Mara momentarily hung back, but his tug was insistent. She yielded, but not without some misgivings.

⚜ CHAPTER 25 ⚜

BLACK POINT *is deceptively peaceful,* Shiloh thought nervously as she sat in the buggy. She forced her eyes away from Clay as he again knocked at Jared Huntley's stately frame home. The flapping of sails in a brisk breeze off the point caught her gaze, and she watched a two-masted fore-and-aft rigged schooner heading toward the Golden Gate.

At the sound of Clay's footsteps leaving the porch, Shiloh turned toward him. "No answer?"

"No, but she was here."

"She was? How do you know?"

"When we drove in," he said, nearing the buggy, "I saw two sets of fresh wheel tracks, which indicates that Jared drove in and then out."

"Can't be. He's in Sacramento."

"It's possible that Mara hired a jitney to come pick her up, but how could she summon one way out here?"

"Even if it was Jared, that doesn't mean Mara was with him."

"You're right. But I believe she was. See those two sets of footprints in the soft dirt?" Pointing to them, Clay explained, "They're also fresh, and one set is much smaller than the other. I'd bet that they're Mara's."

A sinking feeling swept over Shiloh. "But where did they go?"

"There's no way of telling. I've done my share of tracking and reading signs over the years, but nobody can follow a carriage track on a main road."

"I'm really getting concerned," Shiloh confessed as her husband put his weight on the step, causing the buggy to tip sharply toward him. "I have a very uneasy feeling about this."

She waited until Clay was seated before explaining. "I can understand her hiding out here while he's in Sacramento, but I can't believe she would go off with him."

"He's as rich as any of the other men she's consorted with, and Jared is more politically powerful than all of the others. Sounds like just the kind of a man she would want to replace Lyman."

Shiloh looked at Clay apprehensively.

He added, "You know it's true."

"There's more to it than that," Shiloh said.

"She told me she had planned to tell him to stay out of her life."

"They had a quarrel?"

"Worse than that. Remember when she had that bruise on her face? Well, she recently admitted to me that Jared struck her."

Clay didn't say anything, but Shiloh saw his jaw muscles tighten in anger.

"So," Shiloh concluded with a sigh, "I can't imagine why she would even get into a carriage with him."

"I don't mean to alarm you." Clucking to the horse, Clay added, "But maybe she didn't do it of her own free will."

Suddenly, Shiloh stiffened, causing Clay to ask anxiously, "What's the matter?"

"I just had an awful thought!" She closed her eyes as though to blot it out, but it was still there, sharply etched against a background of fear. "I've got to talk to Jefferson Locke again. Please, take me there right now."

"He's not going to be happy to see you."

"I don't care. Let's go!"

They rode in silence as Shiloh worked through her thoughts. Then she explained.

"I think Jared shot Lyman."

"What?"

"Don't you see? He was jealous because Mara returned to Lyman. Maybe he figured that if he removed his rival, Mara would move in with him."

"Jealousy can be a powerful motive," Clay admitted.

"We know that Jared has Mara, and he's probably expecting her to agree to move in with him. But she told me that she's going to turn him down. Oh, Clay! I'm afraid he'll hurt her!"

"But you don't know for sure that Jared shot Lyman," Clay reminded her.

"No, but I think Locke does. If he'll tell me, we'll know whether Mara's in as much danger as I think she is. Can't we go any faster?"

Clay pushed the horse hard. Foaming sweat formed on its heaving sides when they stopped in front of Locke's office.

"That was fast," Locke greeted them. "You found her and got my answer?"

"No, we didn't, but . . ." Shiloh began, but Locke interrupted. "What I said before stands." He turned his attention back to the papers on his desk. "You're wasting my time."

Offended by his rudeness and made bold by her concern for Mara, Shiloh bent down to bring her face even with Locke's. "Was Jared the man you followed to Lyman's house?"

She saw the flash of surprise in his eyes and knew she had guessed right.

"I told you before," Locke grumbled. "You get that woman to meet my terms, and I'll tell who it was."

"I saw the truth in your eyes," Shiloh declared, her resolve hardening. "We think Jared has taken Mara, but we don't know where."

"That's not my concern!"

"Yes, it is," Shiloh replied. "I'm terribly afraid that she's is in danger. If we can save her, I promise that I'll do everything in my power to get her to sell that property back to you. But you must tell me what you saw."

Locke shot a look at Clay, who said softly, "I think you'd better talk to her."

"Otherwise," Shiloh added calmly but emphatically, "I'm going to stay right here until you do!"

After hesitating a bit, Locke nodded and stood up. Shiloh straightened with him.

"I believe you would," he told her grudgingly. "Well, you probably know that I wouldn't sell that waterfront lot even though Lyman tried hard to get it. I was sure he really wanted it for that woman."

"Her name is Mara," Shiloh said pointedly.

Locke shrugged. "I wouldn't sell to him, but Jared Huntley offered to buy it. He tried hard. I didn't think about him wanting it for . . . uh . . . Mara."

"Yes?" Shiloh prompted impatiently.

"Jared not only offered more than I expected," Locke continued, "but he also promised that he would do a favor for me if I ever needed it in Sacramento. So I sold it to him. The next thing I knew, Mara owned it. Then, when another deal fell through, I needed prime real estate to back a loan, but she refused to sell the lot back."

Clay guessed, "So you've probably thought of ways to get even with Jared."

"Oh, I sure tried! But I didn't have anything on him that could hurt his career, so I began to follow him."

"Hoping he would lead you to something you could use against him?" Shiloh ventured.

"That's right. He wasn't in town very often, but whenever he was, I tried to keep track of where he went and what he did. The other night, I trailed him until he stopped and waited in the shadows across from Lyman's house. You know the rest."

After a slow breath, Shiloh thanked Locke then frowned as she thought of something else. "Are you sure you saw Mara drive away from the house?"

"Of course. She lived there, you know. She drove Lyman's wife right out of her own home."

"Did you see her face?" Shiloh persisted.

"How could I? It was dark, and I had to stay back so Jared wouldn't spot me." Locke shrugged. "But maybe he did anyway. The fire chief came around after you left. He said my place was deliberately set on fire."

"I'm sorry about that." Shiloh said. "Thanks very much for what you just told us. You've been a big help."

Clay helped Shiloh into the buggy and took his seat beside her. "You're sure a changed woman from when we first met," he said proudly. "In the past, you would never have done that."

"I had to do it to help clear Mara."

"Yes, I understand that," he said, picking up the reins, "but you're growing stronger in your own convictions too. I like that."

She smiled and gripped his free hand. "Thank you. But this thing isn't over yet, and I need my strength, and yours."

Clucking to the horse, Clay said, "Now we know for sure who shot Lyman. But I wonder if Jared knows he shot a dead man?"

Without waiting for an answer, Clay asked, "What made you ask Locke if he was sure he saw Mara drive off that night?"

"While I was talking to him, I suddenly thought of something. I don't think he saw Mara."

"You don't?"

"No, in fact, I'm quite sure it was someone else." Shiloh made an impatient gesture. "Let's not just sit here. Please take me uptown."

"Where are we going?"

"To find Constable Logan."

Logan invited Shiloh and Clay into his cramped office. The stench from the brass spittoons coupled with moldy smells from the ancient walls made Shiloh uncomfortable. She couldn't wait to get her visit over and return to the fresh ocean breezes outside.

"Glad you dropped in," Logan said, leaning back in a wooden chair that groaned as if in pain. "I saw your friend, Mara, awhile ago."

"You did? Where?" The excited words poured out of Shiloh as her anxiety eased.

"Standing on the deck of a schooner."

Shiloh cocked her head in surprise. "Where was she going?"

"I never got close enough to ask them. The vessel was already too far underway."

"Them?" Shiloh asked apprehensively.

"She was with Jared Huntley." Logan studied Shiloh. "Does that surprise you?"

"Yes and no." Fear drove Shiloh. "We thought they might be together, but I'm quite sure it's against her will. How can we find out where they were going?"

Logan chuckled. "Countless vessels go in and out of this harbor; how could anyone know where any particular one is bound, especially a small one?"

"Did you see the name of the boat? Maybe we could find out who the owner is. If we could ask . . ."

She stopped as Logan slowly shook his head.

"Your friend is probably just staying out of my reach because of the murder. She's a fugitive. If I'd had a boat, I'd have chased her on the water. But sooner or later, she'll end up in here." Logan jerked his head toward the long hallway behind them where two rows of cells faced each other.

"You don't understand, Constable," Clay said. "We're afraid Mara's life is in danger from Jared Huntly."

Logan's eyebrows arched in disbelief before he scoffed, "You're talking about one of the wealthiest and most powerful men in Sacramento. He wouldn't risk all that by murdering someone."

"He could make it look like an accident, like saying she fell overboard."

"I think you're unduly alarmed, Mrs. Patton. Your friend is just trying to keep out my reach."

"No," Shiloh protested, then added solemnly, "there's something you should know." She told him what Locke had said, then added with conviction, "I'm sure it wasn't Mara he saw leave Lyman's house just before he heard the shot."

Logan listened in silence then scratched his bald head. "That's hard to believe, but we'll follow it up, starting by interviewing . . ."

"Thank you!" Shiloh exclaimed, cutting in. "May we go with you?"

"This won't be a social call, Mrs. Patton."

"I know! I know. But I sort of remember something that might be helpful; I can't quite put my finger on it. If I could see her in person again and look around . . ."

"Mrs. Patton!" Logan's tone turned cool. "I've been conducting all kinds of investigations for years. I don't mean any disrespect, but I do not want or need any help from outside this office."

Shiloh drew back slightly, causing Clay to say hastily, "She's not trying to take over your job, Logan. But doesn't it make sense to use everything available to get to the bottom of this murder?"

With obvious reluctance, the constable nodded. "On one condition: Mrs. Patton, if you see or hear anything that makes you suspicious, you just sit there quietly until we leave. Then you tell me. Fair enough?"

"Anything to help prove Mara did not kill anybody."

Logan reached for his hat. "All right. Let's go."

❧ CHAPTER 26 ❧

SHILOH WATCHED Malvina leap out of bed, her eyes wide with terror as she grabbed Mrs. Ring. "Don't just stand there!" Malvina shrieked. "Get the doctor!"

Mrs. Ring shot an imploring look at Shiloh. "I don't understand . . ."

"It's all right," Shiloh replied quietly. "What's the matter, Mrs. Wallace?"

"You put it in the tea! I'm dying!" Malvina's face contorted in fear. "Do something!"

The door burst open, and the two men rushed in. Malvina turned imploringly to them. "I've been poisoned! Please! I need a doctor! Now!"

Logan turned questioning eyes on Shiloh. "What's going on here?"

Shiloh replied calmly, "Ask Mrs. Ring."

The neighbor didn't wait to be asked. "Shiloh put sugar in her tea and accidentally gave the wrong cup to Malvina, but I don't understand . . ."

"I do," the officer interrupted curtly. He took the sugar bowl from Shiloh's unresisting hands and sniffed the contents. "No bitter-almond smell," he said, glancing accusingly at Shiloh.

"No, it's just sugar," she admitted. She turned to Malvina. "You haven't been poisoned."

The panic left Malvina's face. For a second, relief flooded her features, but that was instantly replaced by fury. "You lied!" She leaped toward Shiloh with clawed hands. "You lied!"

Clay caught Malvina as Logan grabbed both her hands.

"I'd rather think I just proved that you killed your husband," Shiloh replied.

Malvina struggled wildly, but the officer held her firmly. "Clay," he said, "take your wife away until I get this sorted out. Mrs. Ring, please stay. I want to hear what went on here."

In the hallway, Clay demanded, "What in the world just happened?"

Shiloh looked triumphantly at him. "I proved that Mara didn't kill Lyman. Malvina did." Shiloh added contritely, "May God forgive me for tricking her, but it was the only way I could think of to show that she had poisoned Lyman."

~~~❦~~~

In the darkness below deck, Mara detected a change in the hull vibrations. The sloop was slowing. Next, she heard the two crewmen remove the forward hatch cover and drop the heavy anchor overboard. Its chain made a fearful racket, yet Jared slept in the bunk across from her, undisturbed by the noise.

Mara was grateful that he had accepted her suggestion that they not talk about her moving in yet. He had not even asked for a reason. Neither had he made any amorous advances when they retired to the two long bunks in the bulkhead.

But she knew why: He planned to kill her and Samuel. She was sure of that. She considered killing him in his sleep to save herself, but the thought was loathsome. Besides, she didn't have a weapon. Her derringer had been left behind, and her brief, stealthy search of the sloop's tiny galley showed nothing worthy of being considered a weapon.

He doesn't want any trouble with me until he's ready to act, she guessed. *He knows that I'm not going to move in with him, but unless I say something, he may delay hurting me. How long can I stall?*

A momentary flash of light told her they were near land. It came from the lighthouse on Tower Hill, the highest point on the Farallon Islands. She also heard seals barking on the shore.

How will he kill me? Mara wondered. *Will he make it look like an accidental drowning? No,* she reasoned, *he could have shoved me overboard in the night, out of sight of the crew. He's probably waiting until we land and he can get Samuel and me together.*

The Farallons were isolated, steep, barren pinnacles of an ancient mountain range that jutted upward from the ocean floor. Their jagged ridges and peaks were ideal for an "accidental" fall to the sea below, where great white sharks were known to prowl.

At least two egg pickers had fallen to their deaths in recent years. A simple push out of sight of others, and Mara and

Samuel would be dead. She knew that Jared could insist they had slipped.

If Mara and Samuel refused to climb, Jared would surely have another plan. He might force them into the sea to "accidentally" drown.

None of this is Samuel's fault, Mara thought ferociously. *He can't die because of me. There's got to be a way to save us both, but how?*

She listened to Jared's even breathing in the adjacent bunk. He was so sure of himself that he could sleep peacefully until time to act.

But Mara determined that Jared would not succeed. She was going to live. She decided she had to behave normally. She didn't want him to suspect that she had figured out his plan. She had to keep him off guard until she saw an opportunity to escape alive.

❧

Shiloh rose early for private prayer and Scripture reading in the familiar, snug comfort of the kitchen. The stove was still warm, and she quickly got the fire going and started coffee. She looked up at the sound of someone unlocking the back door.

Mara? she thought hopefully, then she saw her father.

"The news about Malvina and Jared is all over town this morning," he greeted her as she admitted him.

Shiloh motioned for her father to sit at the table while she finished making coffee. "What about Mara? Has she been cleared?"

"Logan had no choice after Malvina's confession." Smiling fondly, Merritt added softly, "I'm very proud of you. You not only cleared your friend's name but also helped catch Lyman's killer."

"There's still a problem. Jared is still on the loose somewhere, and Mara's with him."

"I know. I saw Logan earlier, and he told about seeing those two heading out to sea."

Dully, Shiloh declared, "I'm sure he's planning to kill her. He'll probably push her over the side of the boat and claim she fell."

Merritt reached across the table and took Shiloh's hand. "There's nothing any of us can do, except pray."

"I've done lots of that." Shiloh's voice almost broke on the words. "But I'd feel a whole lot better if we knew where to look for her. If we could do that, then maybe we could find her in time to . . ."

As she paused, Merritt asked, "What's the matter?"

"I just remembered, Mara told me that she had hidden Samuel from the slave catchers on the Farallon Islands. Maybe that's where Jared is taking Mara! Oh, Papa! I can't stand doing nothing! Can't we get a boat and go to the islands?"

"Hold on! It's a long trip out there. Even if we had a boat, by the time we got there . . ."

"But it's better than staying here and doing nothing," Shiloh interrupted. "We've got to try!"

"It would probably be a wild-goose chase."

"What would?" Clay asked, walking into the kitchen wearing his robe.

Excitedly, hopefully, Shiloh repeated her idea. She ended with an earnest plea, "Can't we at least try?"

Clay took her in his arms and held her close, but his eyes sought his father-in-law's. "What do you think?"

"As I told her, I think it's a wild-goose chase. But if something happens to Mara, and we didn't do everything we could think of, we would never forgive ourselves."

"You're right." Clay released Shiloh. "Merritt, do you know anyone who's got a fast boat we can rent on short notice?"

"Manton Briggs has a working sloop. I talked to him last night at the wharf. He was getting ready to sail out to the Farallons this morning."

"Of course!" Shiloh exclaimed. "The man who gathers sea-bird eggs! Mara told me about him. Let's go with him!"

Merritt protested, "He's probably already got a full load of egg pickers plus the crew; he may not have room for anyone else."

"Let's go ask!" Shiloh cried.

"Not so fast!" Clay caught her arm as she tried to dart past him. "If Jared is out there, it could be very dangerous. I'd rather you stay here with the children."

"But I've got to go! Lizzie can watch the children!"

Clay looked at Merritt, who suppressed a smile. "I think we just got ourselves a passenger."

~≈⊱~

Mara squinted into the sunshine as she walked toward Jared, who stood at the sloop's rope railing. The long hours of the morning had seemed interminable as she had been forced to stay below deck until she was summoned.

Before he could speak she asked, "Where are we?"

"Off the Farallons. Don't you recognize them?"

Mara turned dark, accusing eyes on him. With a touch of anger in her tone, she snapped, "You said we were going up the coast toward Oregon."

"Only a slight detour," he assured her cheerfully. "We'll go ashore and have a late lunch with the lighthouse keepers, then we'll head north. I hope you don't mind?"

"I mind," she replied briskly, then softened her tone, "but I guess it doesn't matter."

"Good! I didn't want to bother you last night, but we need to discuss how I can get you acquitted of the murder charges and talk about some other things."

Mara nodded, thinking, *He's enjoying this, like a cat playing with a mouse. He must want to get Samuel and me together. Well, once ashore, we'll have a better chance than out here on the water.*

Jared interrupted her thoughts. "Rowboat coming. They're sending someone out to take us ashore."

Mara turned toward shore, and her heart leaped into her throat. *It's Samuel!*

❦

Manton Briggs's sloop was so crowded with egg pickers and their gear that Shiloh barely had room to stand. The egg pickers were mostly rough-looking waterfront types. Shiloh, Clay, and Merritt had been able to get aboard because the vessel had a late start. There had been a problem with the tiller.

Shiloh had been invited to go below but preferred the open deck with the snap of canvas sails and the ocean breeze on her face. She stood between her husband and father near the single sail.

"Can't we go any faster?" she asked Clay.

"Briggs is going as fast as he can."

Shiloh nodded.

Merritt suggested, "Don't think about our speed. Try to keep your mind on other things."

"Good idea," Clay quickly agreed. "I still can't get over how you tricked Malvina with the sugar."

Shiloh smiled. "Guilty conscience. We knew her husband was poisoned with cyanide. I remembered that Malvina didn't take sugar in her tea but Lyman did.

"It finally all came together in my mind. Malvina was adamant about not using sugar when I dropped by to pay my condolences. She must have put the poison in the sugar bowl for Lyman.

"I tried to make her think I had found the sugar and had taken some for myself. Then I claimed I had accidentally switched my cup with hers. I hoped that would scare Malvina into confessing."

Merritt commented, "When she thought she was poisoned and blurted it out in front of witnesses, she couldn't take it back. Constable Logan said that she confessed in detail after that."

Clay shook his head. "I'm not sure I really understand her motive."

"There was more than one," Shiloh answered. "She hated Lyman for twice humiliating her by bringing Mara into her home. She was also angry that he gave so heavily to the Knights of the Golden Circle. Malvina became afraid that she would lose it all. In a divorce, she would only get half of what remained under community property laws. But if he died, she would inherit everything."

Clay nodded. "But risking a murder charge is worse than only getting half of an estate."

"Malvina didn't expect to get caught," Shiloh continued. "When she found the voodoo doll that somebody had left for Lyman, she saw a way to murder him and blame Mara."

Clay asked, "What does Mara know about voodoo?"

"I suspect she let it be known in the Negro community that she has special powers. Somehow, Malvina found out and made her plan to leave evidence pointing to Mara as the killer."

"She obviously didn't count on Jared shooting Lyman, not knowing he was already dead. For a while, Malvina must have thought her poisoning wasn't even going to be suspected."

"Murder will always come out," Merritt commented. "Now, with legal fees, she'll probably lose everything she inherited and still face a prison term."

Shiloh glanced ahead impatiently, then tensed and took a second look. "I think I see the islands!"

Both men faced forward before Clay reminded her, "Sometimes, when there's no fog, you can see them from San Francisco."

"I'm sure I see them," Shiloh said, shading her eyes against the glare of sun on water. "Oh, I hope we're not too late to help Mara!"

"We're still probably an hour or so away," Merritt said.

Shiloh fell silent, struck by memories of what she had said

to Mara about the divine law of sowing and reaping. Shiloh shook her head.

"Instead of fretting about something you can't control," Clay began, taking Shiloh's hand, "let me tell you what I've been thinking about."

Something in his tone made Shiloh nod. "All right, I'm listening."

Taking a deep breath, Clay began. "I have struggled mightily within my heart and mind about this. When I heard that Lincoln had suspended habeas corpus, I got very upset. I still think it's wrong, very wrong. It sets a bad precedent to take away a citizen's right to have a hearing before a judge."

Clay paused, frowning in concentration. "I wanted to strike back at that kind of action, which could be the start of tyranny. I was so upset I only saw one way to do that. Then . . ." he paused and turned to Merritt.

"I've thought long and hard about what you said when we were crossing the bay," Clay continued. "I mean, about the logical consequences and outcome of this war. But I also struggled with concerns about the safety and happiness of our family."

Clay took Shiloh's hand and added, "I was especially influenced by your strong opposition. But I really didn't see it clearly until I faced Noah Oakley and his Home Guard friend. I don't want my family in constant danger. And I don't want to have to move away for our safety. I realize there are more important things than my pride. Like our country. When I was a soldier, I was willing to give up my life because the nation is more important than the individual."

Shiloh's mouth dropped open as understanding hit her. "Oh, Clay! Are you saying . . . ?"

He nodded. "I've made my choice. I'm going to take the oath of allegiance to the Union."

Mara tried to swallow the lump of fear that formed in her throat at the sight of Samuel rowing alone toward the sloop. He manned the oars with his back toward the vessel. *He's too far away to recognize me,* she thought. In the same instant, she willed him to turn back. *Stop!* she silently screamed. *Go back! Go back!*

The bow of the little boat continued straight toward the sloop.

Jared's soft chuckle made Mara spin to face him. He had silently motioned to the two crewmen, who headed down the gangway below decks.

No witnesses! Mara thought. Her anger flared. "You knew Samuel was out here, didn't you?"

"People tell me things, even egg pickers."

"For a price," she snapped.

He shrugged. "It's nothing compared to what my share of the seabird egg business brings in."

"You told me you had never been here before."

"Did I?" he asked mockingly. "Well, it suited my purpose to say that at the time."

Slowly, Mara's flashing anger solidified into a controlled, hard fury. "I see. I think I also see a lot of other things." Her mind leaped back. "You were the one who made those footprints near the fence on my property."

"Very good." He applauded lightly.

"You also followed me when I thought you were in Sacramento."

"Every time I came to the city, I checked up on you. I must admit, you don't scare easily."

Samuel was close enough now for Mara to hear the oars splashing, but she didn't look back at him. Instead, she faced Jared, eager to have him tell more before his mood changed and he quit answering her.

"Why?" she asked while she tried to think of how to escape what she knew was coming fast.

"You know why!" Jared's tone hardened. "You drove me crazy with desire, starting with the first time I ever tried to get you to go to bed with me. I'm used to getting what I want, but you frustrated me."

His voice rose. "You gave yourself to other men and twice moved in with Lyman Wallace. You even let that big black buck out there have you, but not me. When I heard how you had hidden him here on the islands, away from the slave catchers, I finally realized you were going to turn me down again, in favor of him."

There was nothing to be gained by lying, so Mara nodded. "Yes, I was going to turn you down, but not in favor of Samuel. He's just a friend."

"Is he now?" The sarcasm was heavy in Jared's words. "You can lie to yourself, but not to me."

"I'm not . . ."

"Shut up!" Jared raised his hand as though to strike her, but stopped. "It took me a long time to realize you were never going to change." He added softly but with deadly meaning, "That's when I decided that if I couldn't have you, no one would. Ever."

"So you killed Lyman and tried to get me hanged for it?"

"It was a good idea, but it didn't work. So now we'll try something that I'm sure will work."

He took a couple of quick steps to a pile of rope and reached inside the coil. He stood up with a long-barreled revolver in his right hand. Pointing it over the rail, he called, "Hey, you, black boy!"

Mara watched Samuel twist his head around. He stopped the oars mid-stroke as he recognized Mara and saw the gun.

"Come alongside," Jared called, waggling the weapon's barrel. "Your passengers are waiting to board."

Mara ached for Samuel, but she was as powerless as he. The rowboat bumped against the sloop's hull.

"I'm so sorry, Samuel," she said under her breath as she took the seat Jared indicated with the gun.

Samuel didn't reply but watched their captor ease onto the seat beside Mara.

"Row for shore, black boy," Jared ordered.

Silently, Samuel reached for the oars.

"On second thought," Jared said with hint of smile, "take us around the side of the islands so we can see the seals and birds better."

Mara understood instantly. Jared wanted them out of sight of all possible witnesses—and any help.

~ CHAPTER 27 ~

A S THE MORNING wore on, Shiloh avoided looking toward the islands. Each time she had, they seemed no closer than before. The working sloop with its cargo of egg pickers was not made for speed, and that was the one urgent need if Mara's life was to be saved.

Merritt sensed his daughter's desperation and tried to divert her attention. "Shiloh," he said after a long silence, "there's something else we've forgotten."

Without interest, she asked, "Oh?"

"Clay will no longer be branded a Copperhead."

"Say, you're right!" Clay agreed. "When we get back and I take the oath, San Francisco should welcome me with open arms." He paused, then added thoughtfully, "Well, not everyone, I guess. Asbury Harpending and members of the Knights of the Golden Circle won't like it."

"They're a minority," Merritt reminded him. He shook his head. "I think General Johnston broke the back of that movement. It's just taken awhile for the Knights to realize they're through."

When Shiloh didn't say anything, both men turned to her with silent concern. She lifted her eyes to meet theirs.

"I'm so grateful about your choice," she admitted, her voice low. "But if anything happens to Mara . . ."

"She'll be just fine!" Clay interrupted, his voice confident and strong. "Focus on how to make sure she sells that lot to Locke. If she does that, then maybe those two will finally have peace between them."

"I gave Locke my word in order to save Mara's life. I'm sure that when I explain that to her, I can convince her to sell the lot back to him."

"There!" Clay interrupted, looking beyond her. "There they are! The Farallons!"

Shiloh whipped around, excitement gripping her as hope surged in her heart. "Yes! And there's the sloop!"

"Nobody's on deck," Clay said, squinting under the shade of his palm. "Not even the crewmen."

"They're probably ashore," Merritt guessed. "Look for a little rowboat."

"There!" Shiloh pointed. "I see it! Just going around that point of land!" She turned to her husband. "Please ask Mr. Briggs to follow them! Hurry!"

Clay leaped up and ran toward the stern where Manton Briggs stood beside the crewman at the wheel.

Merritt slipped an arm around his daughter's shoulder. "It's going to be all right. We're going to be in time."

"I hope so," Shiloh said hopefully, but she had a bad feeling as she watched the rowboat slide out of sight.

───※───

Mara sat stonily beside Jared on the rowboat's stern seat. Samuel was seated slightly forward of center, facing them while he rowed backward. He sent the bow through incoming waves that were increasing in size and speed. Perspiration poured off Samuel's forehead as he struggled to keep the boat from being swept sideways and overturned.

Jared seemed unconcerned while he kept the big revolver

pointed at Samuel's chest. "There will be a better view of both the birds and the seals just a little farther ahead," he said with no show of anxiety.

Mara showed no interest, but Jared seemed to delight in continuing his narration.

"There's a small colony of California sea lions on the rocky shore just past that big rock jutting out from the main land," he said. "Of course, there may be elephant seals mixed in with them. Sometimes they're so close together you can't see the ground."

"As we row next to that cliff," Jared continued, looking up, "you'll see hundreds of thousands of seabirds take wing in fright. They'll come right at us in a cloud. That's why the egg pickers climb inland and come down on the nests from above. Otherwise, the birds could knock them off their feet."

"All right!" Mara said sharply. "Enjoy your little game of mental torture with me, but put Samuel ashore."

"How very noble!" Jared's sneer made Mara flinch. "Say, black boy, did you know she cared that much about you?"

Samuel didn't answer, but the fury in his black eyes spoke for him.

Mara tried again. "He hasn't done anything to you, Jared. Let him go."

"You say he hasn't done anything, Mara?" Without waiting for an answer, Jared turned to Samuel. "Did you leave the voodoo doll at my place?"

For a long second, Samuel didn't answer. Then he nodded. "Yes."

"Why?" Jared demanded sharply.

Samuel fought the oars as another wave caught the boat broadside and tipped it sharply. When the wave passed, Samuel shrugged.

Jared said, "I'll tell you why. You thought that superstitious nonsense would scare me and I would end up the way you wanted me—dead."

Samuel responded, "You don't believe, but I do."

The words infuriated Jared. "You dirty black . . . ! I'll tell you who's going to die: You are! And she is."

"No," Samuel said, easing off on the oars. "Not her."

"I suppose you're going to stop me?" Jared challenged, thrusting the revolver forward.

"Stop it!" Mara cried. "If we don't get out of these waves, we're all going to die! Jared, can't you see that?"

For the first time, he seemed aware of the rolling waves. He glanced toward the rocky shore.

Mara's eyes followed his. Waves crashed twenty feet high, exploding into snowy foam and then showing pale tints of soft green in the falling spray. There was no sign of human habitation on shore, no witnesses.

Jared turned to face Mara with a smirk on his face. "First, I'm going to give you one more chance to choose. Go back with me and be faithful to me as long as you live, or I'll shoot Samuel and dump him overboard right now."

Mara glared at Jared. "I believe you would. Then you'll claim it was an accident."

"Why not?" Jared was obviously enjoying his power. He had never been able to control Mara before. "If his body washes ashore, it'll be too battered by the rocks to find a bullet hole."

"How do you know I won't say you killed him?" Mara demanded, stalling, desperately trying to think of some way out of an impossible situation.

"Simply because," Jared replied casually, "if you ever open your mouth, you will die too."

Mara looked at Samuel, knowing that Jared had no intention of letting either of them live. She waited until she glimpsed the next wave out of the corner of her eye. Quickly, she tried to divert Jared's attention toward Samuel.

She reached out to lightly touch his knees. "I'm sorry," she told him softly. "I'm so terribly . . ."

As the wave started to tip the boat, Mara suddenly twisted in her seat. With her right hand, she shoved hard against

Jared's shoulder and threw him off balance. At the same time, she struck at the gun with her left hand, knocking it so the barrel was deflected away from Samuel's chest.

"Help me, Samuel!" she cried, but the big man had already leaped forward.

He grappled with Jared while the boat, now free of any guidance, veered sharply as another wave caught it. It tipped sharply on its side.

Mara shrieked and used both hands to hang on to the edge of the boat, but the two struggling men fell overboard. The waves caught them, broke them apart, and swept them both toward the rocky shore.

"No!" Mara screamed, trying to stay aboard the tossing boat. "No!"

She had never rowed before but realized that the only way to save Samuel was to get him back aboard. She seized both wildly thrashing oars, dropped down where Samuel had sat, and pulled. The power of the water almost tore the oars from her grip, but she held on in desperation.

With a glad cry, she saw that the boat was being swept directly toward the two men fighting to keep their heads above water.

Jared raised his right hand high above his head and frantically waved as Mara bore down on him. At the same time, Samuel disappeared beneath the surface.

Screaming so hard her throat hurt, Mara thrust an oar blade toward Samuel as the boat slid past. He grabbed it so hard he almost pulled it out of the oarlocks. "Hang on!" Mara yelled above the sound of surf now dangerously close. "Hang on!"

It took all her strength to force the blade toward the boat. She finally pulled Samuel within reach and leaned out to help him roll over the side.

The boat started to tip crazily toward him. Mara grabbed frantically for the wooden seat and held on to keep from being thrown overboard. At the same time, she felt the boat start to

LEE RODDY

right itself. For a moment, she thought it had happened naturally, then she saw Samuel look behind her, his eyes widening
in warning.

He opened his mouth to yell but gagged on seawater.

Mara spun around to see Jared start to hoist himself out of
the water. He suddenly shot straight into the air so that his torso
was visible to the waist. He screamed and then was violently
jerked down below the surface.

Mara stared, not understanding.

"Move over!" Samuel panted. Then, with a mighty effort, he
struggled with the oars. Mara tumbled ingloriously into the
boat at his feet.

Without another word, Samuel concentrated on the oars,
fighting to keep the small craft from being smashed against
the rocks. A monster wave caught the boat and easily swept it
toward the shore.

"Hang on!" Samuel shouted. The boat struck an immense
rock, slid across it, then stopped.

Slowly, Samuel relaxed, letting the now-broken oars drop.
"We're safe here," he panted, trying to grin at her. "The crew
will come looking for us."

Nodding numbly, Mara turned toward where Jared had
disappeared. There was no sign of him. The waves rose and
fell ponderously. Mara saw a small patch of blood and
almost gagged.

Sobbing in fear and relief, Mara crawled toward Samuel and
into the arms he opened wide for her.

❦

Shiloh stood between her husband and father as they
searched off the foreboding Farallon Islands. She desperately
scanned the breaking waves and rocky shore but saw no sign of
Mara, Samuel, or Jared.

"Oh, Clay! Papa!" Shiloh whispered in anguish, "If we're
too late . . ."

"Don't say it!" Clay interrupted gently but firmly. He slid his arms around her. "We'll probably see them around the rock outcropping ahead."

"Have faith," Merritt urged quietly as the sailing vessel slowly rounded the desolate island cliffs.

"I'm trying." Shiloh tried to keep her voice from breaking. "I've prayed so hard! I've . . . look! Oh, my Lord, no!"

She saw the battered rowboat on the rocks. The waves had hurled it high on a flat boulder near the steep cliffs. Except for the gulls screaming overhead, there was no sign of life.

"They're gone!" Shiloh whispered in agony. "They must have fallen out when the boat crashed ashore."

"The boat's not wrecked," Clay pointed out. He cupped his hands together and shouted. "Mara! Samuel! Can you hear us?"

Only the sound of the crashing breakers and the gulls' cries replied. Shiloh began to shiver with fear. She gripped the thin rope railing so hard that her fingernails dug into her palms.

"Hello!" Clay shouted again. "Mara! Samuel! Answer me!"

Again, no response.

"We're too late." Shiloh breathed the words aloud before turning to collapse against Clay's chest.

He took a deep breath and held her tight.

Merritt let out a wild whoop. "No! They're alive! They're alive! See? Over there!"

Shiloh whipped around and followed her father's pointing finger. "Oh, thank God!"

Mara and Samuel had scrambled away from the boat and waves. They stood together on a rocky shelf, waving their hands above their heads.

Breaking free of Clay's arms, Shiloh joyously waved back. "Mara! Samuel! We'll get you off!"

It took awhile. Experienced egg pickers went ashore with ropes and worked their way down over the cliffs to reach the stranded couple.

Mara had held fast to Shiloh's hand since her rescue. Shiloh

277

turned and looked deep into Clay's eyes, knowing that as long as all of them were together, they could survive whatever the turmoil of war brought them.

Somehow, they would all build a better future.